# Just Remember I Love You

## DAN HAYES

# IN MEMORY

In loving memory of 1569.

The most beautiful girl in the world.

And in loving memory of memory of 1714.

Feeling strong.

# CONTENTS

## PROCEEDS

I have committed that 15% of the proceeds of this book goes to a young girl whose father passed away at the age of just 37. This young man was a friend of mine.

His daughter is seven and lives with her grandparents.

Buy the book and make a difference in a young girl's life.

Cheers,

Dan

# PROLOGUE

Sadly, my wife, Heather. or the H-Bomb, as she is lovingly nicknamed, passed away a few years ago.

It has been difficult.

I have a certain song I turn to when I feel sorry for myself.

"Mandolin Rain" by Bruce Hornsby and the Range is a song I have listened to over a thousand times.

Who am I kidding? It's more times than that. It's always on repeat—but who's really counting?

I'm not sure why I listen to it. It just works

for me.

It's about not knowing what you have until you lose it.

I think this is one of the most important life lessons that anybody can learn.

Sadly, I had to learn about loss.

Fuck.

For the first few weeks after Heather's death, I could hear her voice almost hourly.

I think I am mentally losing it.

Heather provides me with encouragement, feedback, suggestions, and, most certainly, well-deserved criticism.

I am far from perfect. Everything she tells me is sound, and most certainly accurate. I follow her advice without any exception.

The H-Bomb is still the H-Bomb. All-seeing and all-knowing.

After her death, life has been tough.

Lots of first firsts.

First sunrise. First sunset. First Thursday. First Friday. First time at our breakfast restaurant by myself.

These firsts are fucking horrible.

Heather isn't beside me.

I miss her horribly.

I am alone in this world.

It's challenging. I feel broken.

Fuck.

Heather often appears and helps me through the tough times with words of encouragement whenever I need it.

I often need this kind of support from her.

She never sugar-coats anything. She's blunt and honest. H-Bomb doesn't put up with my shit and my self-pity.

You will learn about the H-Bomb. The H-Bomb puts me in my place.

My conversations with Heather continue daily for six months after her death, usually early in the morning when I'm walking Tank, who is our beloved rescue dog.

For a little while in the beginning, Heather and I check in with each other to see how we're doing each day. I do most of the talking. Heather is a good listener.

When she speaks to me for the first couple years after her death, she reminds me of birthdays, wedding anniversaries, and major holiday events.

She also reminds me to eat more vegetables, to get more sleep, and to not worry about her.

She tells me that I am doing fine, all things considered.

I don't believe Her.

As required, she tells me that I need to suck it up. Those conversations are the hardest. It's hard to debate with somebody who isn't really there.

Sadly, as time marches on, I don't hear from her daily. Daily starts becoming weekly, then monthly, then quarterly.

Then I don't hear from her for months on end.

She always ends our conversations with, "Danny Boy, be safe!"

I miss her voice and her shit-eating grin.

I am somewhat concerned about my mental

health. I'm pretty sure that you shouldn't have conversations with people who are dead.

I have a gold-plated health plan from the company I work for.

About twelve months after Heather is gone, I decide I need to speak with somebody. I'm embarrassed, but I know I really have nothing to be embarrassed about

I'm supposed to be a tough guy. But I know I'm not.

Seeing a psychiatrist is like having a physical—there's nothing to worry about, and only good things can come out of it.

It's like a tune-up.

I spend three hours with a doctor. Given what has happened in my life over the last eighteen months, I'm told that I'm handling it well.

The doctor suggests that I should write about my experiences. I think that might help.

And thus, the story begins…

# 1 THE END OF THE BEGINNING

A picture of my wife in her police uniform is projected around the convention centre. That amazing smile showing lots of teeth, her dark hair, and her gleaming, green eyes that beam out to the 2,500-or-so people attending her police funeral. The majority of the people attending the funeral are police officers from around the world. Near the front of the room are friends and family.

There is a four-person police honour guard protecting Heather.

She is safe now.

The honour guards are members of her platoon. Collectively, their posture is stiff and sturdy. There's hardly a single line or wrinkle in their dress police uniforms. Members of the honour guard have been protecting her during the last three days of public viewing. Today, they are trying to look stoic but are having a hard time keeping their composure.

Heather's casket is covered with a Canadian flag.

Throughout the convention centre, there are hundreds of bouquets of Gerber daisies in a variety of bright colours. Gerber daisies were her favourite flowers. The flowers make the convention centre much brighter than it normally is, especially given what a shit day it is today.

The police bagpipes and drum core are finishing up a rendition of "Amazing Grace."

Fuck.

I hate this song.

I normally tear up when I hear it. Today, I am weeping openly.

My family, Heather's parents, and our friends, such as George, Brenda, Katie, and Brian, are here.

Several of my coworkers are here as well.

They're looking at me with that expression of pity. God, I hate that look. It's been a constant in my life over the last ten days.

I desperately want to be anywhere else, but here I am, and my name is being called by the Chief of Police.

"Auxiliary Officer Dan Hayes, Officer Ramos' husband, will give his eulogy."

I stand up and walk toward the steps to the podium. Chief Smith stops and salutes me, and I salute her back. She reaches her hand out to shake mine. She then gives me an impromptu hug and whispers in my ear, "You got this?"

"I got this," I respond.

"You got this" or "I got this" is what police officers say to each other as a form of encouragement when the going gets tough.

Chief Smith squeezes my hand and smiles at me. I know I'm about to lose it as tears start streaming down my face.

I'm wearing my auxiliary dress police uniform. Heather told me I look good in it. According to her, it brings out the blue in my eyes.

Sadly, I'm not feeling that today. The only thing I desperately want is to see her amazing, toothy grin and feel the warmth of her body beside mine.

I want to kiss her nose, as I have done a million times before.

I know that my wish will never come true.

Ever.

Fuck.

I feel sick. My stomach is turning in a million different directions.

I take a deep breath to calm myself.

I turn to face the crowd from the podium. This is the moment of truth.

*I can't do this. I don't want to do this*, I think.

Twenty-five hundred people are looking at me, and I look back at them. There are more people outside the convention centre watching me on large screens. I have been told the funeral service is being broadcast live on TV.

That look of pity that has become part of my every day is everywhere now.

Tears continue to stream down my face as I look at my family and friends. Sympathy tears are beginning to run down their faces.

People who don't know me are beginning to look uncomfortable. I feel the look of pity intensifying.

I take a deep breath and steady myself.

In my mind, I hear Heather's voice, *Danny Boy, you got this.*

*I got this, H-Bomb,* I think to myself.

H-Bomb was her nickname, and Danny Boy or Grandpa were her nicknames for me.

Everybody looks at me, and I look back for what seems like hours and take another deep breath.

Heather Ramos is or was—I am not sure how to refer to her now—the most beautiful woman I have ever seen. Her mom is Chinese/Filipino, and her father is Vietnamese/Filipino. She's extremely exotic looking, with perpetually tanned skin and oddly, green eyes. She's about five feet, two inches, and hundred and five pounds of energy and joy. She's also incredibly fit.

Was or is, how do I refer to her now? Tears well up again. *I got this*, I think. Or do I?

I smile back at the crowd, and most of my emotions get buried for a moment. I pick up the clicker that controls the computer in front of me and begin to advance the slide.

The next picture that appears is from five weeks ago, taken during our honeymoon. I had taken it during our first dinner at the resort we stayed in at the Grand Caymans. Heather has this shit-eating grin on her face and a glass of champagne in her hand.

She'd looked so beautiful in that moment.

I had to forever capture it with my phone because it was so special. The reason for the grin was explained to me immediately afterward.

"How do you like my cute little sundress, Danny Boy?" asked Heather, as she ran her tongue around her champagne glass.

"It's short and it shows off your hot body—what's not to like?" I'd replied.

"Dinner is three hours long, isn't it?" Heather asked.

"So I have been led to believe." It was a ten-course meal.

"Well, just to let you in on a little secret, I'm not wearing any panties. And, as you know, my HAB is looking particularly hot today," Heather teasingly informed me. HAB is our inside joke for "hairless Asian beaver." I'm not sure which one of us thought of this acronym. I think it was Heather, but when I hear it, I grin like a schoolboy.

Oh my God! Heather knew how to drive me crazy. The three-hour dinner had lasted for what seemed like six hours—I had a hard time waiting for dessert.

Of course, I don't tell the people attending the funeral this—but the photo is awesome. It's totally her, with that shit-eating grin.

*I got this,* I think again.

Finding my voice, I start, "I would like to thank everybody who is attending today."

My voice falters on the last two words as I try to begin my speech. I feel the tears welling up again. I take one deep breath in my belly which is followed by another.

Tears are now pouring down my face, and I am blinking rapidly.

My internal voice is screaming inside of me, *You got this! You got this!*

I look up and I see the police grief counselor getting out of his chair and slowly walking toward me. Time is moving slowly. I really don't want him fucking near me.

More tears. I don't know what to do. I gaze at the crowd, and all I see are people looking at me with pity.

Another deep breath. I grab a tissue from my pocket and wipe my tears away.

I take a step back and gather my thoughts.

I hear Heather's voice, *Daniel, please. You can do this. Be brave for me.*

I know it's only been a few seconds, but it feels like minutes.

I step forward.

I speak into the microphone firmly, "I got this."

The police grief counselor stops walking toward me. His name is Robert, and he is a very compassionate man. Sadly, we have met far too many times over the last two years. I couldn't do his job. How could one man deal with so many sad situations? Robert stands against the wall, waiting and hoping for me to get my shit together.

I take a deep breath and start the eulogy.

"Giving a eulogy is a heavy responsibility for those who knew the deceased. You try to capture who that person was because one of the last things everyone will remember is the eulogy. The majority of you didn't know Heather. I need to tell her story, who she was, what she did, and the people she loved.

"When I was asked to give the eulogy, I wasn't sure if I could. It's been a difficult ten days.

What do you say about a person whose life is taken far too soon?

"I know that a lot of the law enforcement people here today have traveled great distances to support Heather—her family and friends and her colleagues. I would love to meet all of you and thank you in person.

"Several nights ago, I sat in my backyard thinking of what to say. I heard Heather's voice, and she told me, 'Danny Boy, it's going to be a sad day. So, you need to brighten it. I know it will be difficult, but I know you can do it. You got this. I would like you to tell people about me and you and our crazy time together. I want you to tell our story and inspire them to make the world a better place.'

"To her family, friends, and colleagues—Heather wouldn't want you to be sad today. She had an amazing life because of you. I think we can all agree that she lived every moment of every day to the fullest and would want us to continue to do the same."

I take a deep breath and pause.

"I would like to specifically welcome three important guests today—Mr. and Mrs. Jones and their son, Steve. They lost their oldest son and brother Robert about three years ago. Robert was a colleague of Heather's and passed away while off duty.

"I know the past few years have been difficult for the Jones family, but I would like to share with you something positive that happened out of Robert's death. I hope it eases the pain you feel."

I pause. I look at the computer screen in front of me and see Heather's shit-eating grin, and I smile back at her.

*I got this*, I think.

I then start mine and Heather's story.

# 2 TWO WHITE GUYS WALK INTO A BAR

The words "Two White Guys Walk into a Bar" appear on the screens around the convention centre.

"I am going to tell you the story of how Heather and I met. It begins with two white guys walking into a bar."

I advance to the next slide. A picture of George and me appear.

George and I regularly meet in the afternoon for a pint at our local pub. We chat about sports, business, and generally anything and everything. Karla, the bartender, knows us well, as we are regulars there.

One afternoon, we stay a little longer than usual, and two gentlemen show up.

Two more photos appear on the screen—the smiling faces of Frank and Robert.

"Two Black Guys Walk into a Bar" appears on the screen, and I turn to the crowd, telling our story.

Frank is about six feet two inches, and appears to be quite fit. Robert, on the other hand, is a strapping six feet four inches, and could easily pass as a wide receiver in professional football.

We learn that Frank is Black and Native Canadian, and Robert is Jamaican Canadian. They referred to themselves as Toffee and Dark Chocolate, something which makes me laugh to this day.

These two gentlemen engage with George and I in some witty banter for about an hour, until we eventually get into sports trivia. George and Frank discuss the Chicago Cubs.

George suddenly declares, "Chicago is larger than the Greater Toronto Area."

"No way!" responded Frank.

"You've got a bet! I will bet the two of you shots from any bottle in this bar that Chicago is larger than Toronto," George declares. His bravado is amazingly misplaced. I know that the GTA is larger than Chicago.

Frank lights up, "You, my friend, are on. I don't want just any shot. I want the super hot bartender to stomp freshly bought grapes while naked. I want that as my shot."

George agrees, and they shake hands.

I whisper into George's ear, "George, Frank is a big boy, but Robert is huge. Let's not piss them off here."

I later learn that Robert was whispering into Frank's ear, "Don't be stupid about this. There are $250 shots here—that's a lot of money. They both look like scrappers."

Frank and George agree that I would search the internet on my phone for the correct answer. Sure enough, the first eight websites all state that the GTA is, in fact, larger than Chicago.

Frank basks in glory. George, while upset that he lost, takes it like a man.

"Gentlemen, well played! I'm a man who lives up to a wager. What will you have?"

Before Frank can suggest Johnny Walker Blue Label or some other high-end shot, Robert interjects, "We will take two Wild Turkey shots!"

Robert, being the gentleman that he is, chooses the least expensive shot in the bar.

After that, we start meeting Frank and Robert every Tuesday. We exchange contact information with them and start texting each other on a regular basis.

We later learned that they are both police officers. They are quite guarded with who gets to know what they do for a living. I'm not sure why this is such confidential information. George and I are rather laid back, and frankly don't care.

We continue to meet them every Tuesday for about eight months. One day, we receive a very sad text from Frank, which stops us dead in our tracks.

*George and Dan. Bad news. Robert is in a critical condition. He is not expected to make it. May be brain related. I found out last night. Just left the hospital.*

I respond in shock, *Holy shit! What happened?*

*Still figuring out.*

*Frank, I'm sorry to hear this. Let me know what time you will be there.*

The next day, we receive another devastating text from Frank.

*He's gone.*

George and I are both shocked. How did a young man like Robert pass away? Truthfully, life isn't fair. Bad shit happens to good people all the time.

Life events sometimes make us realize that we often take the wrong things too seriously and ignore the things that bring simple pleasure in our lives.

I attend Robert's memorial service.

Never have I seen Frank in his uniform

before, and I barely recognize him. He looks incredibly respectable in it.

Frank introduces me to his colleagues—everyone has their guard up. I'm the outsider, and I can't be trusted. There's a photoshoot of the platoon, and everybody places their cell phones on the table so they can have a copy of the photo. A wife of one of the guys takes all the photos—she's in law enforcement and is a trusted person. Nobody wants me to touch their phones. It's kind of sad. I have no axe to grind, yet I'm not to be trusted.

It's awkward. His colleagues don't know who I am. Frank is a gracious host, but the majority of Frank and Robert's work friends treat me with clear indifference or open distrust. I feel outcasted. We are here to celebrate a good man's life, and people are afraid to speak openly because they don't trust me. If there's one thing I've learned, it's that law enforcement people are extremely guarded. Perhaps it's instinctual. I consider myself a pretty harmless guy, so I can't understand the tension that my mere presence is generating in these people.

After all, we're all here to mourn the passing of a good man taken too soon.

I'm chatting with Frank when I see a cute blonde woman wearing civilian clothes approach us. She gives Frank a big hug and whispers something to him. Frank introduces us. I learn that her name is Linda. He then proceeds to tell her how I know Robert. She's Frank and Robert's sergeant. I find her quite charming. Linda actually finds the story of how George, Frank, Robert, and I met quite humorous. She's one of the few people who treats me well and remains unguarded.

The next day at the station, Frank is chatting with Linda, and he mentions that he was happy I showed up and that I could chat with people. Linda says that she thinks I'm a nice guy and asks if I'm single.

Frank regales her with my yellow fever, as he calls it. Yellow fever is, according to the internet, a term used to refer to a white man who loves Asian women.

Frank learns from Linda that a colleague

named Ramos has the salt and pepper disease. The salt and pepper disease is a term for younger women who like older white men with gray hair, which I have plenty of. And my blue eyes signify I am white.

Both Frank and Linda agree that we should meet, however, Ramos work partner named Smith is going to be a problem.

Smith is a  six foot four inch 230 pound cage fighter with six percent body fat. That's him. He actually is an amateur cage fighter, which means he likes to hurt people for fun. He's very protective of Heather, as I would painfully learn.

"Don't worry. My boy has the ability to deal with anybody. He can handle Smith," Frank quips.

# 3 INTRODUCTIONS

It is a pleasant Monday evening during early spring, I meet up with Frank and a group of buddies for a beer at our local pub. We're all in fine form as we crack our usual number of inappropriate jokes.

Frank gives me the once over. "You had to wear that ridiculous shirt tonight, didn't you?" he asks.

"Frank, at least I shop where they sell men's clothing!" I retort.

I hate wearing suits. The company I work for has a policy that men must wear suits and ties. I think it's the most absurd company rule in in the history of company rules. Being the rebel that I am,

I wear off the wall, funky shirts, and jeans designed by Robert Graham. They don't come cheap either—the shirts start at $200 US and may go up to $800 for a limited-edition model.

Tonight, I have a shirt on that essentially looks like a Vincent Van Gogh painting. It's loud and goes well with a nice pair of jeans and black dress shoes.

This shirt is funny, and men hate it. Women, on the other hand, love it. I've been stopped in the street hundreds of times by women who always want to know the story behind my shirts.

Tonight, for some reason, Frank keeps checking his watch every few minutes.

After watching him do this a few times, I ask him if he's got a better place to be than hanging out with us. I jokingly tell him that she better be hot if he's ignoring us.

"I invited one of the gang to join us for drinks, and she's late." Frank informs me, "She's your type." He has this huge grin on his face.

"You mean her penis is bigger than mine?" I

answer.

"Screw off, Dan. Can you stop joking for a minute? I'm serious. Ramos is hot. And she's Asian. I know how much you love Asian women," Frank states categorically.

Suddenly, Heather appears out of nowhere.

She has this unique ability to appear and disappear—it's like she is made of ninja dust. One blink of the eye and poof! She magically appears, disappearing in much the same manner.

Heather Ramos is the most beautiful woman I have ever met. She could be a model if she wanted to, she's that beautiful. Today, she's wearing jeans with a tight-fitting white t-shirt with pink sleeves that has "Who doesn't love a hot Asian girl?" printed on it.

I look at Frank and say in disbelief, "Are you kidding me, Frank?"

I turn my attention back to Heather. "I am so sorry if Frank has put you up to wearing that shirt. He can be such a dick sometimes," I say.

She responds back "Hi, I am Heather, and

you are? And by the way, Frank is not my fashion consultant. I decide what clothes I like to wear. And I like this shirt and, apparently, you do too!"

*What a wonderful way to make a first impression, Dan*, I think to myself.

"Hi, I'm Dan." I offer her my hand, and she shakes it firmly. And that's the first time I notice how small and delicate her hands are.

I glance at Frank, and he just smirks at me.

*What an asshole! He's setting me up because this girl is way too hot to have any interest in me,* I think. She looks like she's about twenty. I later learn that she's thirty-two, but regularly gets asked for ID everywhere.

I ask her what she would like to drink, and she requests a gin and tonic.

She gives me this amazing smile and thanks me for the drink. She and Frank then begin to banter about work.

Wow! She's small. Maybe five feet two inches, and about a hundred pounds. *I had thought that the police surely had a certain height standard,*

I think to myself—but I dare not say it out loud.

"So, what do you do for a living, Dan?" Heather suddenly asks.

"I'm a real estate appraiser. I specialize in valuing apartment buildings," I respond with confidence, because it's a question I've answered countless times.

Heather raises an eyebrow and says, "Interesting, I guess." She then rolls her eyes. Barely visible though is a mischievous smile. I don't miss it. She's teasing me.

"I'm essentially an accountant without the personality," I add.

George pipes up, "He's being modest. He flies around Canada valuing apartment buildings. He's a big deal."

George is always pumping my tires in an awesome buddy way. However, I know my place in the world. Heather's so out of my league that there's no way she would have any interest in me.

Heather looks at me and smiles, "Frank tells me you have thousands of awesome jokes. I want to hear at least one tonight to make up for that super interesting shirt you're wearing."

I stare into her beautiful green eyes. *She's actually smirking at me*, I think. *She doesn't think I have game.* It kind of angers me that she's challenging me.

It also pisses me off that Frank is trying to set me up with her. He knows that this girl is so hot she'll probably never be interested in me.

However, I do have some game. I always rise to the challenge. Attractive women don't scare me that much. I've negotiated numerous real estate transactions. Hell, I've even helped negotiate an international border crossing agreement once.

*I can do this*, I think to myself. I have to at least try.

For the next half-hour, I regale her with jokes. All my friends have likely heard these jokes at least several times.

Heather is doubling over with laughter—she hasn't heard any of them before.

I can't tell you the jokes because that would

be wrong. They're offside.

However, I can share with you the punch lines from the jokes I told Heather...

"When Pierre the French fighter pilot goes down, he goes down in flames."

"Big fart, no chief."

"If the 10th shot of tequila doesn't take the taste out of my mouth, I am not sure if the 11th one will."

"Curt and Rod."

"I am arriving, I am arriving."

"Up or down."

When I crack the best joke of all time, she's amazed. She's almost in tears from laughter, it's that funny. She's never heard the joke before, and the punchline is absolutely epic.

"Do you think I asked for a sixteen-inch pianist?"

After my impromptu comedic relief set, I look around. Both Frank and George are smiling. Heather is beaming. It's the first time I see her amazing goofy grin in all its glory.

It's a great moment.

"Oh my God, Dan. You are so funny. You're awesome. My face is going to hurt tomorrow from laughing so much. I haven't been this entertained in a long time," she says to me.

Heather then confidently asks me for my phone so she can add me to her contact information. She also does a little counter surveillance—she turns on the option on my phone that permits her phone to follow me wherever I go (I don't realize this until after we are married).

In the police world, dog walkers are considered a gem. They're amazingly predictable and usually follow a pretty strict routine, since dogs require walks on a regular schedule. If the police ever need to require information about something, they often wait to speak to the dog walkers.

Three days after I meet her, I see her on one of Tank's morning walks. This is no coincidence, I later learn. Tanky is walking off leash, exploring the countryside.

From a distance, I see this attractive woman

running toward me. She's wearing a sports bra and tight running shorts. As this woman gets closer, I think to myself, "Oh my God! This girl is so hot."

A few seconds later, I realize it's Heather. She has her signature radiant smile on her face, and she's covered in sweat. There's something so attractive about a woman who's covered in sweat after exercising.

"Hello, Danny Boy. What are you doing here? Are you stalking me?"

I love it when people call me Danny Boy. Most people get hugs when this happens. But this time, no hugs are exchanged, because I don't really know her that well.

"Tankfordian and I are out on our morning walk," I respond.

She's staring at me with her green eyes. "And who is Tankfordian, if I may ask?"

At that moment, Tank shows up for a few pets and some loving. Heather gets down and starts petting him. He responds by licking her face, turning in circles in front of her, and generally just being a menace to society.

Heather grins at me. I love her beautiful grin (to this day, it gives me goosebumps). "Oh my God! I love dogs, especially big goofy dogs like you, Tankfordian!" she says, as she pets and scratches his ears.

Tank knows a good thing when he sees it. He's all over Heather. Heather is speaking to him in doggy-friendly terms. "You're such a good boy!" "Can you shake a paw?" "Oh, you are so pretty, Tank."

Tank performs beyond expectations.

I had rescued Tank. When I first got him, he was a disaster. He had no manners and acted like a puppy even though he was fourteen months old. We had a rough first six months with lots of disagreements, but now, we're solid. He walks well off-leash. He only really jumps on me, and eventually Heather as he gets to know her better.

Heather is looking at me with her amazing grin.

"Okay, Danny Boy, this girl needs to finish

34

her run and get to work. Hope to see you soon. Be safe."

From that day on, we begin to regularly run into Heather on our morning walks.

It's a beautiful Sunday. I summon the courage and nervously invite Heather over for breakfast. Much to my surprise, she agrees.

Tank and I race home. I need to figure out what I'm going to make. I look in the fridge. I have bacon, orange juice, eggs, assorted veggies and fruits, and some artisanal bread.

Heather had told me she would be over by 7:30.

My plan starts to come together.

I happen to have a decent wine selection in the basement. I grab a bottle of champagne and toss it into the freezer. I hope Heather is a fan of mimosas.

I then proceed to chop up some onions and peppers, dice up some bacon, and then whisk together six eggs.

I decided that our breakfast will be mimosas,

fresh fruit, and western sandwiches.

Precisely at 7:30, there's a knock on the door. I open it, and there is Heather. She's dressed in yoga attire and looks absolutely breathtaking.

Tank is running circles around both of us.

"Oh, hello, Tanky! It's been a long time since I've seen you!" she says.

I welcome her into my house and offer her a seat at the breakfast table.

Heather looks at me and says, "It smells awesome in here! Frank tells me you're a good cook. What are you making us?"

I smile at her and bring out a platter of freshly cut orange and grapefruit slices, grapes, watermelon, pineapple, and some apple wedges. I place the platter in front of her. She has a look on her face that suggests she might be slightly impressed.

I offer her a cup of coffee, which she eagerly accepts.

While I'm in the kitchen getting the coffee ready, I start making the western sandwiches and getting the mimosas ready.

I bring her the coffee and set the champagne and orange juice out on the table along with two champagne glasses.

I open the champagne bottle, and the cork explodes with a big bang. I pour the orange juice and champagne into the glasses that I've already garnished with halves of strawberries.

Heather is all smiles, and they're all directed at me throughout the whole mimosa-making process. I give her a glass and propose a toast, "To breakfast and new friends."

We clink glasses, and Heather takes a sip, never taking her beautiful green eyes off me.

I look at her and jokingly declare, "Don't worry, I don't put out on the first date, and I don't expect you to either!"

We both burst out into laughter.

Breakfast goes smoothly. On the radio, the 70s station is playing cheesy songs in the background. Heather and I just get deeply lost in our conversation. We share lots of laughs and smiles, and this goes on for almost three hours. We're both very animated and are having a great time.

Heather suddenly looks at me with a serious look on her face. "What are you looking for, Danny Boy?" she asks firmly, never taking her eyes off me.

What an open-ended question. Is she talking about the winning lottery numbers or a relationship? I assume it's the latter.

"I am about to embark on a crime spree, and I'm looking for a partner," I respond back.

She bursts into laughter and says, "So am I, Danny Boy. So am I!"

Tanky is gently snoring underneath the breakfast table. He drowsily wags his tail in approval.

Heather looks at her watch. "Okay, Danny Boy. I have to head off now, but thank you so much for such a great breakfast! It was awesome! I could get used to being fed a good meal every Sunday morning."

"I make lunch for Frank every Sunday. If you want to stop by every Sunday morning, Tank and I have no problem with making you breakfast," I respond hopefully.

Heather beams at me, "Okay, Danny Boy. Next Sunday, I want breakfast at 7:30 again. But please, can Tanky not cook? He's far too cute to be working that hard!"

"Done!" I say, perhaps too eagerly.

We then have one of our many awkward moments. She leans in for a hug, and I offer a fist bump instead. So, I change my strategy and lean in for a hug, and she offers me a fist bump. *I'm such an idiot*, I think to myself. We ended up doing an awkward handshake. She offers me a smile, "I'm off, Danny Boy. Chat with you later this week. Take care!"

After she leaves, Tank and I have a post mortem on breakfast. Tanky points out that when a super hot girl, especially one you had just cooked breakfast for, wants a hug, you likely should reciprocate with a hug and not a stupid fist bump—

and most certainly not a handshake. Tanky is far too wise for such a young dog.

Sadly, I have to concur with Tank. I'm such an idiot. I'm sure I will never see Heather again.

We don't see or hear from her for a week.

Tank and I are out on our regular Sunday walk, and I'm feeling a little sorry for myself today. I really screwed up last Sunday with Heather. *What man shakes hands with an attractive girl when she clearly wants a hug*, I think to myself.

Almost at the same point as last week, we meet Heather again. She magically appears in her ninja-like manner, sporting her amazing goofy grin. Her green eyes are sparkling and full of life.

She looks at me and demands to know where Tank is. Tank appears and stands up on his hind legs. Heather grabs his front paws, and it almost looks like they're dancing.

The two of them are literally laughing at each other. Heather takes the lead as Tank dances with her for almost two minutes.

Heather is going into hysterics.

"Your dog has more game than you do, Danny Boy!" she exclaims.

*Great*, I think. *I'm already in the friend zone, and Tank might be potential dating material for Heather. This always happens to me.*

After the two of them stop dancing, Heather looks at me and asks, "So, Danny Boy, what are you making me this Sunday for breakfast?"

"What would you and Mr. Romeo like?" I ask as I point at Tank.

Heather just laughs. She's looking at me, her green eyes staring into my blue ones. "I want the world's best pancakes and some of your coffee, it was great!"

"Okay, Heather, that's easy to do. What time will you be over?" I ask again to confirm.

We've agreed on 7:30—this gives me just an hour to prepare. I'm so excited that I'm already thinking about how she likes her pancakes. Whipped cream and fruit on top? Butter or maple syrup? Chocolate chips or banana? Homemade pancakes are easy to make, but I can always complicate any recipe. I want it to be perfect for Heather.

Holy shit! There's only an hour to get everything prepared before her arrival. This woman already knows how to get her way with me. Tanky and I start to make our way back home.

Making the world's best homemade pancakes requires some skill. There are normal pancakes, and then there are Dan's famous pancakes.

I chop up some bacon, drop it into a frying pan, and toss in some water. I also toss in some maple syrup. While the bacon is cooking, I start my pancake batter. My secret ingredient is fresh lime juice and zest in the batter.

Heather arrives on time at 7:30.

She seems much more relaxed today than she did last weekend. She hops up and sits on the counter and smirks at me. "Coffee, please," she asks.

I pour out a cup of coffee and give it to her. I see her beaming over the top of the cup. "Danny

Boy, how did you learn how to cook?" she asks.

I smile back at her.

"I think it was on my parents' fifteenth wedding anniversary. So, I was about eleven, and I decided to make them dinner. I found a recipe for prime rib and Yorkshire pudding. My parents bought me the ingredients, and I followed the recipe. I'm pretty sure that I had never had prime rib and Yorkshire pudding up until then. I even made mashed potatoes and something for dessert—I can't remember what it was. The highlight of the night was my mom and dad telling me how good dinner was. They really didn't help me with anything," I respond back.

Heather looks at me. "So, let me get this straight. You are eleven years old when you follow a few recipes to make a gourmet dinner for your parents that most steakhouses have problems getting right. And this is your first real cooking experience?" she asks.

I nod my head affirmatively at her as I gently stir the pancake batter.

Heather bursts into laughter. "Danny Boy, all cards on the table. I have a hard time boiling water and not burning toast in the toaster," she admits to me.

I just grin at her.

"Heather, if you ever want a few cooking lessons, I can show you how to boil water!"

She grins back at me, "I'm sure there are a few strings attached to that!"

We both exchange grins. They weren't really grins—they're more like smirks. The first of many smirk moments in our relationship. I love it.

Heather loves my pancakes. She asks for seconds and thirds. I'm contemplating making more batter. This girl eats almost six pancakes. My pancakes are not small. I can only eat one and maybe a small portion of another one.

I have my first head-shaking moment with Heather. *This girl can pack the groceries away,* I think.

Between eating pancakes, she just smiles at me, and I grin back at her. She is so clearly enjoying the breakfast that it makes me happy. Happy bellies equal happy people!

Through her fifth pancake, Heather stops dead and looks at me with a sad face. "Danny Boy, I'm making a pig of myself. I'm sorry…"

I look at her and say, "No, you aren't. You are enjoying it! I love it when people enjoy my cooking, or, chefing—as I call it!"

"I didn't get to have a lot of Western food when I was growing up. My parents weren't born in Canada, but I was. I was always envious of kids at school when I was growing up. They got ham and cheese sandwiches and homemade cookies, while I got rice-based dishes with fish. I was so envious of the other kids."

I am exposed to Heather's first rant.

"Some kids would trade their lunches with one another. Homemade chocolate chip cookies for homemade peanut butter cookies. I could never trade with any of the other kids. None of the other kids wanted my food."

She continues, "When I was seven, these

45

cute little dolls came out. All the girls had them. They cost almost thirty dollars. My parents couldn't afford to buy me one at that time. So, my mom made me one. I went to school with it, and everybody teased me about my homemade doll. It was horrible. I cried myself to sleep for a long time."

I can tell by the look on her face that not having had the right doll when she was seven bothers her to this day. Kids can be so cruel at times. It's funny what still bothers us as adults.

*Wow*, I think to myself. *Heather had such a different experience growing up compared to mine.* I grew up in a privileged way. Not that my parents went out of their way to spoil me, but with the benefit of age and hindsight, I really didn't have a care in the world.

I look at my upbringing and Heather's here in Canada, and there is clearly a big difference. I like to think that I get the difference. But unless one has lived it, they most certainly can't understand the nuances of it.

It's humbling.

I decide to do something about it.

Heather has started joining the gang at the pub every Monday. Her company is most welcomed by us. Her female perspective usually calms down some of our more aggressive discussions.

Today, I walk to the pub with a gift bag containing a present for her. I picked up the gift this morning at the department store. The boys are all asking questions about what's in the bag. I explain that they're cookies for Heather. It's not, though. I can't explain the gift to the boys. I suspect I never would hear the end of it.

I hope Heather likes it. I'm a little concerned that it could be taken the wrong way.

The doll that Heather wanted as a child is still sold today. I picked one up and wrote the following in a card:

*I will always share my cookies with you, Heather!*

The card is signed by Tank and me. I put the doll and some homemade cookies into the gift bag and stuffed a ream of coloured paper into the top of the bag so that the contents of the bag won't be seen.

When Heather shows up, I get her a drink. We all engage in casual banter for a while. She keeps looking at the gift bag. She's always curious—it's most likely what makes her a great cop.

"What's with the bag?" she asks the gang.

Before I can answer, Frank jumps up and grabs the bag and says, "It's a gift to you from all of us. It contains cookies that Dan made for you. Judging by the weight of the bag, there must be a lot of them. Open it, Heather. I could use some of Dan's baked goods right now!"

Frank hands Heather the gift bag, and she accepts it.

Heather gives me an odd look. She knows it's more than just cookies.

"Frank, I know how good a cook Dan is. You have to be fucking kidding me to think that I would share his baked goods with you animals!

These are all mine, and you can't have any! I also know that Dan is the ringleader behind this and none of you guys were involved. Am I right?"

Frank, George and Brian all agree that it's a "Dan gone rogue" gift.

Heather guards the bag for the next hour. We all even up our respective tabs and head out. George and I are within walking distance of the pub, but the rest of the gang drive off.

The next day, Frank sees Heather at the station.

Frank smiles at Heather and says, "H-Bomb, I want some of Dan's baked goods! I introduced you guys—I need some commission!"

Heather looks at Frank with a stone-cold face. "Frank, either Dan pulled a big dick move on me yesterday or he's a sweetheart. Which one is it?"

Frank is taken back. "Heather, I am not sure what you're talking about. I can't imagine Dan being a dick to you, that's for sure," he tells her.

Heather beams at him. "I thought so. Dan doesn't strike me as a dick. Frank, he did something so thoughtful that it caused me a little heartache last night. I'm not used to having nice guys around."

I get a text from Frank. *Not sure what you gave her last night, but now she's like putty in your hands. She gets puppy dog eyes whenever your name is mentioned!*

Around 3:00, I receive a text from Heather.

*Danny Boy! Thank you for the doll! It brought out a lot of emotions when I opened the present yesterday. I realized I was carrying a lot of emotional baggage related to the doll. I feel so much better. You are a good friend! I want you to teach me how to boil water on Sunday! See you then.*

# 4 YOU ARE FAT!

After a few Sunday breakfasts, Heather breaks to me the unpleasant news, which I already am aware of.

"Daniel, you're overweight and have high blood pressure. I can tell by looking at your red face. You need to lose some of your flubba flubba. I can tell you were in shape at one time. Let me train you."

Being a middle-aged man, metabolism slows down. Work interferes with working out, and shit happens. I get it. I also understand why it happens, and I'm not proud of it.

For some reason, I don't take her comments

personally. I don't make excuses. She's right. I own the situation.

And then it begins.

I am schooled.

I am made to understand that I am weak and need to pull up my socks. It's humbling.

Heather tells me that my diet is good when I have my own home-cooked meals, but I need to stop having four-hour client lunches. Also, I need to cut down on my beer consumption—she thinks I should drink only vodka and water.

Four days a week, we go to the park near my house at 6:00 am. She puts me through boot camp. I'm told what to do, and corrections are made about my form. The heaviest weight I pick up is a fifteen pound medicine ball.

The fifteen pound medicine ball is thrown, violently shaken, used in push-ups, sit-ups, and to run with, and it generally makes my one hour with Heather a living hell. I also spend a great amount of time sprinting, often sprinting with the ball held out in front of me.

One day, after our workouts, as I am stretching, Heather comes walking behind me. She suddenly slaps my ass and tells me, "Danny Boy, your ass is looking fine!"

I grin. I've lost twenty pounds in the span of one month.

After the first month of exercise, we begin the wounded man drills. These drills are from the military. One person is deemed injured and, so, the other person has to carry them to the other side of the soccer field.

I toss Heather over my shoulder and sprint across the soccer field. I'm breathing hard, but I'm not out of breath.

Heather looks at me and says, "Okay, Danny Boy, it's time for me to carry your old, fat ass across the soccer field. Get ready!"

"Whoa, girl! it's one thing for me to pick up slightly more than half my body weight. It's entirely different for you to pick up a hundred and eighty percent of your body weight. I don't want you to hurt yourself," I tell her.

Heather grabs the collar of my shirt, balls it up with her fist, and brings my face down level with hers. Our noses are about two inches apart.

"Excuse me? Did you just tell me I can't carry you because I am a small girl, Daniel? You think I am weak!?"

Shit. I'm such an idiot. I stand there as she looks me dead in my blank face. It doesn't take long for Heather to break awkward silences.

"If you think I'm weak and can't carry somebody your size, you are mistaken. Very badly mistaken, Daniel."

I remain speechless.

I am thrown over her shoulder, and she sprints across the soccer field. Heather's sprint is far faster than mine.

We do this twenty times each. I'm amazed at how strong she is. During the wounded man drills, she doesn't say anything but just glares at me.

We finish up, and I offer her a bottle of ice-cold water. Heather accepts it, but she looks angry. She then begins her speech.

"Daniel, I can do anything a man can. Don't you forget that. I can do it in a cute sundress *and* look hot while I am doing it," she says as she puts me in my place.

As I get to know her better, there is no doubt in my mind that she can do everything better than most men can. There is most certainly no doubt in my mind that she can do it in a cute sundress and look way hotter than any man.

After eight weeks of training with Heather, I'm informed that we're on the final training week. I'm down almost thirty pounds.

I miss my beer, carbs, and beef.

I look great though, so I really shouldn't be complaining.

It's early October, and the mornings are cool.

Heather informs me that I have four tough workouts ahead of me. If I can survive them, I will get a gold star, and there are special awards attached to a gold star.

I grin. *Gold stars sound like a lot of fun*, I

think to myself.

We meet in the park at 6:00 am. It's dark. Sunrise is at least an hour away.

"Daniel, get in the creek and give me fifty push-ups," I'm told.

I walk into the creek and drop down and do fifty push-ups. The water is cold. As the water isn't that deep, I am only partially soaked.

After I'm done, I stand up and see Heather smirking at me.

"Good boy, Daniel. Give me fifty sit-ups in the creek."

*Fuck! The water is cold*, I think to myself.

I do the sit-ups.

I'm now shivering. I never get cold. I am now cold.

Heather orders me to the soccer field, where I run wind sprints along the full length of the field.

I begin to warm up from the wind sprints. I'm then commanded to do burpees, jumping jacks, and a variety of different exercises. I just focus on her commands and do the exercises she asks.

I am ordered back to the creek and told to lie in the cold water for ten minutes. Heather just glares at me as I lie in the creek.

"Daniel, I think you can become stronger. I can see that you're definitely improving, but you can do even better."

Ten minutes in the cold water feels like ten years. I feel like an ice cube.

Heather orders me out of the water and tells me to sprint to my house. Both of us sprint to my house, and I let us in. I'm shaking because of the cold.

I'm dripping wet, standing in the front hallway of my house. I race upstairs, strip off my clothing, and jump into the shower.

I'm in the middle of a hot shower, trying desperately to warm up, when Heather walks into the washroom and casually sits on the stool beside the tub. She stares at me through the shower curtain.

"Danny Boy, you did great today! I'm so proud of you! You're after it, aren't you? I have to go now! See you tomorrow bright and early!"

After she leaves, I spend a few more minutes in the shower. I'm exhausted. It's about 7:45 am, and I need a nap. I crawl into bed, and Tank curls up beside me.

I'm asleep for about thirty minutes when my phone starts beeping from incoming texts. It's Frank.

*Come on, man, she's eating this shit up. She wants all of us to do it, but none of us want the abuse. You're the only person she's persuaded to get into the water. You're making us look bad at the station. So, stop it,* I am told.

I respond back. *Frank, I have three more days of this shit. You introduced me to her. You should have warned me!*

Dead silence from Frank. In fact, he doesn't have the courtesy to text me until the end of my four days in hell.

Day two starts. I'm back in the water and running sprints up and down the soccer field. I'm hanging upside down from the children's playground equipment doing sit-ups.

Heather has saved the best for last. I'm ordered back into the creek. I'm completely submerged. She then orders me to run to the sandbox in the playground and roll around in the sand. The sand sticks to my wet skin, and it makes me uncomfortable and irritating. This is pretty much how I feel about this whole bootcamp thing, but Heather's energy and enthusiasm is so contagious.

I'm then ordered to run wind sprints up and down the soccer field. The sand is chafing every part of my body.

After the sprints are done, I am exhausted. Every inch of my body is shaking.

I'm then ordered back into the water, for eleven minutes this time. At least the sand will be washed off of me when I get out. The water doesn't feel as cold as it did yesterday. After my eleven-minute cool down in the stream, we slowly jog back to my house.

Heather grins at me and says, "Danny Boy, you're making this look too easy! Tomorrow, I have something special planned for you!"

*That doesn't sound promising*, I think to myself.

I have little cuts and bruises all over my body from the physicality of the workouts.

I have to go into the office today for a staff meeting. My colleagues stare at me. I've lost a ton of weight in a short period of time. On top of that, I'm always bruised and have scrapes all over my body, including my face.

The second in command of our group pulls me aside. "Hey, Dan, is everything okay? You look really skinny and, um… appear to be beat up all the time."

*How do I explain what I'm doing*, I think to myself. The explanation would be far too long and abstract, and it's likely that nobody would believe it.

I just respond, "All good, Angela."

It's Day three. It doesn't start well. Heather starts me off by having me laying in the water for five minutes. After that, she gets me to roll around in the sand for two minutes.

We then go for a half marathon. It's twenty-one kilometers. The sand is chaffing in areas of my body that should most definitely not be chaffed. Everything hurts. None of the pain I feel is going to stop me from running. However, it irritates me to no end.

I haven't run this distance in years. Our running pace is fairly slow. We finish the run in about two hours.

I'm exhausted—but Heather, on the other hand, looks refreshed.

We're standing on my front porch when she suddenly grabs my hand, gets up close, and stares up at me. I can feel the heat from her body.

Heather is silent for a minute and just stares at me.

"Danny Boy, you killed it today! I am so proud of you. Go have a hot shower and have something to eat. I'm off to the station. Be safe!" and then she slaps my ass.

I can barely hide my big goofy grin as I watch her walk away from me.

Just as she leaves, I feel an odd tug in my heart. I'm beginning to really like this girl. Her personality, attitude, and motivation really resonate with me.

I stagger upstairs and take a shower. I lie down on my bed and sleep until noon.

When I wake up, I see the following text from Heather.

*Danny Boy—you killed it today. I'm very impressed with your running and stamina. Tomorrow will be a cakewalk compared to today. I'm bragging to Frank and the boys about what a good sport you are. Keep it up!* 🙂

It's my first happy face combined with an ass slap from Heather. I think this could be the start of something! I'm thrilled.

Day four begins. It's raining, and the autumn rain is cold. Heather tells me we're just going for a short five kilometer run. Nothing too tough.

Our run is progressing well. Heather is asking me questions about my job and family. It actually is a very pleasant run. All my cuts and scrapes ache, but not too bad. We're twenty minutes into our run when we see something incredibly disturbing on the side of the paved trail we're on.

We see two bodies.

They aren't moving.

I walk toward the bodies to check if they're breathing at all. I extend my fingers down to check for pulses on their necks.

"Dan, don't touch them! I am calling the police!" Heather yells at me from behind.

The colour drains from Heather's concerned-looking face, she looks as pale as ever. She exhales deeply and tells me that the emergency services will be arriving shortly.

"Daniel, did you make contact with the girl's skin?"

"Yes, I did. What's wrong?"

Heather takes a few steps back.

"Dan, do you feel drowsy or sick right now?"

I feel exhausted and somewhat sick from the

exercise.

"Heather, I feel good. What's up?" I ask her.

Heather explains how she thinks that the couple we just found were overdosing on a drug that can be absorbed through the skin.

She's worried that I may have some of it on my fingers. Apparently, this drug is so powerful, emergency responders actually carry a drug on them now that can counter its effects.

The police, paramedics, and fire department show up almost at the same time. They put on special masks and gloves and start inspecting the bodies.

Heather informs a firefighter that I touched one of the bodies. I'm led away and told to sit down on the bumper of the ambulance. For the next ten minutes, I'm questioned about how I feel. My blood pressure is taken. I explain that I feel fine. Then, the questioning about my bruises, little cuts and scrapes begins. They want to know why I look like I've been in a fight.

I don't even know how to begin to tell the

story. I point to Heather and simply state, "She's training me."

The paramedic looks at me and says, "Ramos is training you? Nobody is that crazy, my friend. She's begged everyone and anyone to train with her. I think the longest anybody has lasted is about three days. How long have you been training with her?"

I answer back, "Almost nine weeks."

The paramedic gets up, walks over to a cop and relays what I've told him. They both stare at me for a few minutes. I suspect they don't believe what I said about having been training with Heather for almost nine weeks.

"Ramos, come here for a moment!" the cop yells over at Heather.

Heather walks over to them. The paramedic, the cop, and Heather huddle in a conversation. Both the cop and the paramedic start glancing over at me. Heather then looks over at me and grins.

The paramedic and the cop are now staring at me with a look of astonishment on their faces.

Heather and the paramedic walk over to me, and I am informed that I am cleared to finish the run. Only three more kilometers to cover.

Luckily, we finish the run without any further incidents.

We get back to my house. I'm really exhausted.

Heather grabs my hand and looks into my eyes, "Grandpa, you killed it this week. I am so proud of you!"

Between my exhaustion and the virtue of me being a stupid male, I don't fully understand the implications of her next comment.

Heather tells me that I have earned my gold star, and she would like to introduce me to her family and friends.

Most of what she is saying is lost on me. I'm exhausted. I need a shower and my bed.

Before she leaves, she grins at me and tells me, "Danny Boy, your old grandpa ass did amazing! I didn't think you could do it! Tonight, drinks are on me at the pub."

Sadly, I don't make it to the pub. Around 2:00 in the afternoon, I feel like I need a nap, and I already slept through most of the day. I'm woken up by Tank around midnight. He needs to go outside to pee.

As I'm waiting for Tank to finish, I look at my phone—there's an odd text from Heather.

*You didn't make it to the pub today. I'm assuming you're asleep and safe. Daniel, you better be safe. I don't like it when people are unsafe. After you read this text, please text me back that you are safe.*

It's kind of an odd text message, I think. I suspect this is somehow related to her job. I can't imagine some of the things she has seen or dealt with. Be safe, I think, is a good thing to say.

I text Heather back. *All safe. Sorry, I fell asleep around two and just woke up. Be safe!*

She immediately texts me back a happy face.

# 5 I MEET THE H-BOMB

Every couple has that meet-the-parent moment. Heather's parents are gracious hosts. They welcome me into their home and are glad that Heather is dating somebody.

Meeting Chris Smith, Heather's police partner, for the first time was… alarming. Chris is always angry—he's a monster of a man. With six percent body fat, standing at six feet four inches tall, his hobby is cage fighting. As in, two people walk into a fenced cage anticipating the glory of beating the shit out of each other. The best way to describe Chris would be how he thinks of himself as an apex predator. He sits at the top of the food chain and looks down and surveys his domain.

Funny enough, Chris is married to one of the sweetest women I have ever met. Her name is Grace, and she is a tiny Filipino woman. When she is around, Chris becomes a different person, somewhat puppy-like and gentle.

Chris and Grace invite Heather and I over to dinner.

Grace answers the door and gives Heather a big hug. Then she turns to me and says in her sing-song Filipino accent, "Oh, I know why Heather likes you—the salt and pepper hair!" She promptly gives me a hug. She's tiny, maybe five feet tall.

Chris saunters to the door and immediately looks angry when he sees me, kind of like the I-disturbed-his-Saturday-afternoon-by-shitting-on-his-favourite-chair angry. Heather and Grace both immediately turn to him as they both say at the same time, "Chris, play nice."

Chris grunts something along the lines of, "I always play nice."

The girls head into the house, and Chris

stands in the doorway, blocking my way in.

I extend my hand and say, "Hi, Chris, it's a pleasure to meet you. Heather has told me so many nice things about you."

Chris smirks at me and extends his hand. His hand is at least twice the size of my hand. I feel like a small child shaking hands with an adult.

His hand envelops mine, and he starts squeezing. He looks me in the eye and says to me in a slow measured voice. "If you ever hurt Heather physically or emotionally or break her heart, I will fuck you up."

I find the term "fuck you up" very interesting. It sounds worse than a beating, like I might not be able to walk again for a very long time.

He continues to squeeze with excessive force, literally crushing my hand.

I have this unique ability to ignore pain. For some reason, my high pain tolerance enables me to shut off my pain receptors and function normally.

I hate bullies. And this guy, very clearly, is a

big bully. I look back and smile at him, which only causes him to squeeze harder.

I look him directly in the eye and continue to smile at him. He increases the pressure on my hand. My hand is slowly being crushed, but I just smile at him. And then it happens. There is a loud crack, and my hand officially breaks.

We both know my hand is broken.

I smile at him and whisper into his ear, "You just broke my hand. You're lucky I don't want to embarrass you in front of your family. Chris, there is only one king of the jungle, and I am it."

I then stick my tongue into his ear. He immediately releases my hand and jumps back and screams out, "That's so fucking gross!"

I don't know how I come up with this stuff, but this particular one is on my personal highlight reel.

For the sake of keeping the peace during the remainder of the evening, I keep a chair distance between him and me. My hand is swollen, and it looks absolutely disgusting. Chris is an animal. We treat each other like we're fighters in a ring. We keep circling, never engaging.

Chris glares at me during the entire evening. Every once in awhile, I blow him a kiss when nobody is watching. If I'm king of the jungle, he has to know who the alpha male is. I see it pisses him off, which pleases me.

During dinner, Heather notices my hand. "What's wrong with your hand? It looks swollen." Grace perks up and starts glaring at Chris. He's done this before. Now, both Heather and Grace are glaring at Chris.

I lie. "I was at the gym today hitting the heavy bag and heard a pop. I haven't thought about it until you just mentioned it."

Chris and I exchange looks. It would be so easy to rat him out and watch Grace and Heather rip him apart. But I don't. An alpha male wouldn't do that. The girls are looking at my hand. Grace, who is a nurse, is convinced that my hand is broken.

I smile and try to reassure everybody.

"Dan, you need to get to a hospital to have

this checked."

Grace calls ahead to the hospital so we get priority. Look at me making new friends and getting frequent flyer miles already.

I'm just glad we're leaving early and I don't have to be near Chris anymore. Since I'm the one who always drives, I instinctively jump into my truck in the driver's seat, and Heather jumps into the passenger seat. We then run into a small problem. In the dark, I somehow have to put the keys in the ignition with my left hand since my right hand is essentially useless. After fumbling for about thirty seconds, Heather states the obvious, "This isn't working, I'll drive."

We then proceed to switch spots. Heather takes five whole minutes to get the mirrors, seats, and the air conditioning ready for her to drive. What takes her the longest time is finding her favorite radio station. She finally settles on a 90s hip hop station. As she reverses my truck, she looks at me with her beautiful toothy grin and says, "I love trucks!"

I just shake my head. God help me.

Grace has worked her magic. Upon my arrival at the hospital, I go directly to the green room. Upon entrance to the green room, I get to see an emergency room nurse within twenty minutes. The nurse looks at my hand and informs me that I need x-rays. Having had x-rays one too many times before, I know that the one guarantee in life is that the x-ray facilities are physically as far as possible from the emergency room.

X-rays take about an hour. The ER doctor walks up to where I'm sitting on a bed. Heather is sitting beside me playing on her phone.

"Tell me again how you broke your hand?" the doctor asks.

"I broke it hitting a heavy bag at the gym," I lie.

The doctor shakes his head, "Strange. What you're describing is an impact injury, but It looks like your hand was crushed."

Heather looks up from her phone, "I'm sorry, doctor. Can you please repeat that?"

"It looks like his hand was crushed in a vice and not an impact injury. Two very distinct injuries."

Most people remember the first time they meet somebody. Early this morning, I met the H-Bomb for the first time.

Heather grabs my broken hand, gives it a little turn and proceeds to give me what I would describe as an evil smile.

"Daniel, how did you hurt your hand?" she asks in a very sweet, innocent voice.

I smile back, "I'm pretty sure I broke it at the gym."

"Daniel, if you are lying to me, I will find out, and it might alter your relatively healthy state."

"Pretty sure I hurt it at the gym." I stick to my lie as she slowly squeezes my broken hand. I'm in agony. Her hands are so small—I can't believe this hurts more than what Chris did to me earlier in the evening.

The doctor looks at us and shakes his head. He instructs us to sit in the waiting room while I wait for my turn in the orthopedic unit. I'm escorted to the cast room to get prepped for a cast. Patients are given a choice of colours for their casts– pink, blue, white, or black. The cast technician asks me what colour I would like.

Heather pipes up, "I think he would look good in pink." The cast technician looks at me, and I shrug my shoulders. *Whatever*, I think, *it's just a cast*. My shirts are far more colourful than my pink cast.

It's two am by the time we leave the hospital. I live two minutes away from the hospital and the division where Heather works. Her place is at least fifteen minutes away. Roll call is at seven am.

"Hey, thanks for being here with me today. If you want, you can crash at my place. At least you will get a few hours sleep." I tell her.

"I'm not going to sleep with you, Grandpa. I doubt your heart can even handle a little hottie like me," she says as she smiles at me and shakes her ass in my general direction.

"I'm fully aware of that. Can you stop busting my balls? I'm tired," I respond.

We get to my house, and she forces me to take the pain medication, along with a variety of vitamins, aspirin, and other stuff she finds in my cupboards. She then gives me a can of beer to wash the medication cocktail down.

I'm pretty sure I'm not supposed to mix all that stuff together. She calls it "Po-Po candy." I do as I am told. There's no sense arguing with her.

I'm beginning to feel drowsy. I ask her what she wants to wear as PJs. She looks at me with a look that I later describe to people as "Heather is dealing with a man of below average intelligence." And it's usually directed at me.

"You're such an idiot. Do you know how hot I am? And you want me to wear PJs? Are you sure you like women?"

I feel really drowsy. I don't know how to respond. I'm exhausted, so I lay down in bed. She asks me how bad the pain is, but I'm too numb and tired to respond. I wake up ten hours later.

When I wake up, Heather isn't there. Neither is Tank. I normally wake up at 4:30 am. It's now early afternoon. I'm by myself. The house is quiet. My phone is beside me. There are a few text messages from Heather.

*I walked Tank this morning and took him to doggy day camp. I'll pick him up and bring him back home when I'm off work.*

*I really like driving your truck, so I took it to work. It's mine now.*

*You snore. So, stop it.*

*I would like pork chops and bean salad for dinner, please.*

As I look at my phone, I'm confused. This seems to be a dramatic acceleration in our relationship.

I try to go back to sleep, but my phone starts buzzing. I look at it. It's an odd text from Frank.

*WTF have you done?*

I respond back, *Chris broke my hand last night.*

*No, you fucking idiot, you lied to the H-*

78

*Bomb. She's a God-damn walking-talking lie detecting machine. We are all so fucked.*

*Why are you in trouble?*

*Because now I know about the lie. You don't lie to the H-Bomb. You know why she's partnered with Smith, don't you? He's the only one big enough to slow her down when she goes off. He can't stop her either... only slow her down.*

Now that I think about it, I don't even know why they call her the H-Bomb. I pose the question to Frank, and his response isn't really encouraging.

*She's known as the H-Bomb because everything is fucking tranquil right up to the point she explodes. And then shit gets vaporized.*

Interesting word choice: "vaporized."

Frank texts me back, *Remember the story I told you about the female officer who destroyed the biker? That was the H-Bomb.*

The biker story went like this. 911 gets a call about a domestic abuse situation. Chris and Heather responded. The guy is on the front lawn—he stands about six foot three and weighs over three hundred

79

pounds. Heather is nearest to him, and he tries to take a swing at her.

Heather has been training in various martial arts since she was five. She blocks his punch with her elbow. Think how hard your elbow is—try lightly punching it. Fingers are made up of a lot of small bones. So, they don't stand a chance during a high-speed impact with an elbow.

His hand shatters. Heather then kicks her boot into the biker's knee and blows it out. Ligaments are snapped, everything let's go, and he falls to the ground. She isn't done yet. While she's attempting to put handcuffs on him, he continues to struggle. Chris now has control of the biker's badly broken hand, and the handcuffs are on the right wrist but not the left. The biker is lying on his stomach and continues to struggle. Chris and Heather are screaming at him, "Stop resisting! Stop resisting!" because they can't cuff his other hand.

Frank described in greater detail what happened next. "So, Chris looks at H-Bomb and she gets this look on her face, best described as demonic. She drops down on one knee, grabs his wrist with both hands and starts bending the guy's elbow backward, with her other knee as a pivot point. She then falls backward. She breaks the guys arm clean through at two spots, above and below the elbow. It was nasty."

In less than two minutes, she breaks the guy's right hand, blows out his knee and breaks his left arm in two different places. That's my H-Bomb.

# 6 OUR FIRST FIGHT

A few weeks after my hand is broken, Heather invites me to a private function at the police association building to celebrate something. Nobody knows what we are celebrating, but we are celebrating it. We take a cab there. Heather, as always, looks stunning. She's wearing a low-cut dress that doesn't leave a lot to the imagination.

Frank has brought his wife Amanda. She's an attractive, tall blond who is a real estate agent.

Amanda and I talk shop for a bit. At some point during our conversation, she wants to know how long Heather and I have been married. I burst out laughing and inform her that we are just friends.

I don't say this, but we haven't even slept together.

"Really? I'm shocked!" she says. "I think she really likes you. Watch. Every few minutes, she looks over at you."

Perfect timing indeed. Right at that moment, Heather looks over at me, and I give her a big grin. She smiles back in return and walks over to where Amanda and I are standing.

"I am so sorry if he is bothering you. We don't let him out too often because he's so old, right, Grandpa?" Heather jokingly tells Amanda.

Heather is drinking cosmos tonight. She's on her third. She looks slightly buzzed—rosy cheeks and a bit of a perma-grin going on.

The music stops, and the DJ announces, "Frank and the H-Bomb are up next."

I look at Heather, and she smiles back at me and mouths the words, "Karaoke, be right back!"

Frank and Heather get on the stage, and they both grab a microphone.

There are a lot of people cheering them on— lots of whistles and catcalls can be heard.

I don't know what to think. Based on my observation, I suspect they sing karaoke quite a bit. But this being my first outing with them, I don't know what to expect.

The music starts, and it's an oldie—"I Got You Babe" by Sonny and Cher. They both kill it. People are up dancing. I am shocked at how good they sound. They're amazing!

They then break into, "You're the One That I Want" by John Travolta and Oliva Newton John.

My jaw drops. I had no idea that the both of them could sing as well as they do. They could be professional singers. On the other hand, my artistic skills are so limited that I have a hard time drawing a straight line with a ruler.

As the song ends, Heather jumps off the stage and walks over to me.

She grabs my left hand, as my right hand is still in a cast. "Let's go over and say hi to Chris and Grace, Danny Boy."

We walk over to where Grace and Chris are standing. Grace gives me a big hug, and in her sweet, warm, sing-song voice says, "Hello, friend!"

Chris just glares at me, "Nice pink cast." I glare back at him.

"Nice shirt. Do they sell men's clothing where you bought it?" I respond.

Grace intervenes, "Boys, play nice, or we'll have to send you to bed without dinner!"

It's an extremely awkward conversation. Chris and I don't acknowledge each other's existence, but we both speak nicely to the women. At one point, both Grace and Heather are looking at Chris when I blow him a kiss. He stops mid-sentence and just glares at me.

Heather looks at the both of us. "The two of you will have to learn to get along, or I doubt either one of you will be getting laid tonight." I perk up. The possibility of getting laid excites me. It's been a while.

Chris continues scowling at me for the next hour. It just pisses me off to no end. I blow him another kiss. Shit! It doesn't go unnoticed this time. Damn it.

H-Bomb suddenly appears, "Daniel, did you just blow Christopher a kiss?"

"I did," I respond.

Frank sees what's going on, so he comes over and says, "Who wants a shot? I'm buying." He's trying to stop a rapidly escalating situation before it gets out of control. Unfortunately, it's already out of control. I just don't know it yet.

Heather isn't buying it. She knows something's going on.

H-Bomb is now on a tear. A vein on her forehead is beginning to appear and pulsate.

"Christopher, why is Daniel blowing kisses at you? Does it have something to do with his broken hand? Please tell me you didn't break his hand in one of your displays of macho bullshit."

Grace also gives Chris the evil eye—I'm enjoying this.

Frank, on the other hand, looks extremely worried.

Chris, being the stupid man he is, decides to double down with this gem of a statement, "He didn't beg for me to stop like all of the other guys you bring around. He even stuck his tongue in my ear and said he was the king of the jungle, and that I was lucky my family was around because he didn't want to embarrass me."

Heather narrows her eyes. She grabs one of his fingers, starts twisting it, and states in a deeply menacing tone, "I will deal with you tomorrow, Christopher, after I've had time to think about what you've said and done."

I enjoy this very much. Chris is so going to get it. This might be the best night of my life.

Heather then marches over to Frank, "Did you know about this, Franklin?"

"Yes, Heather, I did. I was afraid something like this would happen. I told both of them that you would find out, because you always do." Frank looks at his shoes.

I look at Chris. Grace is speaking to him in Tagalog—he's also looking at his shoes.

These two tiny Asian women literally chewing out these two large men—I wish I could get a picture of this. I almost laugh out loud. This is so much fun.

Heather then starts on Frank, "Franklin, I thought you were my friend. Why wouldn't you tell me? I am extremely disappointed in you. Promise me you will never withhold something from me again. I need to know that you are my friend, and friends don't have secrets."

Frank continues staring at his shoes, and he responds, "Yes, Heather, I will."

Heather then stomps over to me, and I realize that she has saved the best for last. I am going to bear the brunt of the H-Bomb. I'm so fucked. I'm going to be vaporized.

"Daniel, I don't even know where to begin. You're just like all the other men I've dated. You all lie to me. Well, let me tell you something, I was going to have sex with you tonight. I likely would have made your eyes roll into the back of your head. I'm that good. But, bravo, you're never going to experience my magical abilities."

Long pause.

"Ever."

A crowd of people have gathered now. They all know who the H-Bomb is. They all know I'm in serious trouble, given her speech.

"Daniel, do you have anything you want to say to me?"

I can't make eye contact with her. I start looking at my shoes. "I'm sorry," I respond.

As most people in the world are righthanded, police officers are always taught to grab a person's right hand and twist it behind their back for the come-along maneuver, as it is called.

Heather grabs my right hand, and her small hands wrap around my cast as she twists my arm behind my back.

She announces in a loud voice, "Daniel, you are my guest here, and you are no longer welcome." She gives my arm a bit more of a twist, and the familiar burning sensation of my hand breaking runs up my arm. She frog-walks me outside and slams the door shut. The door is locked, and I can't go back in.

With my left hand, I reach for my phone to call for a cab and head home.

The next day, I go to the hospital. Sure enough, my hand has been re-broken. It's the same doctor and cast guy. They both shake their heads and ask, "What happened?"

I mumble to both, "I slipped and fell."

"No problem. The cast this time will be bigger and stronger to prevent this from happening again. What colour cast would you like?"

I respond, "White, please."

The next day, I text Heather, *I shouldn't have lied to you about my hand. I'm sorry.*

Her response is firm and appears five seconds after I send my text, *Don't contact me again, ever.*

Well, that's that. *Good job, Danny Boy. You fucked that up pretty well,* I think.

I get a text from Frank the next day, *Don't contact her. She's on the warpath.*

A week goes by. I don't hear from Frank, which is odd. I text him and get no response.

Another week goes by, and I get a message from Heather, *Daniel, we should speak in person.*

I text her back, *Okay. When and where?*

*I'm sitting outside of your house right now.*

I walk outside, and there she is. She actually drove over in a cruiser. It's the first time I see her in uniform, and her hair is up in a neat bun. She looks stunning. She also has a gun—Frank has already informed me that she is impressively accurate with it.

"Daniel, I may have been too hard on you. Christopher explained what he did to you. It wasn't fair to you that I let it happen. He's notorious for that. I'm sorry I didn't stop him. Grace also likes you, and she's also very sorry. She has made it clear to Christopher that his behaviour was unacceptable, and he is not to do that to anybody ever again. But, Daniel, I need to know that you will always tell the truth to me if we are in a relationship."

I respond, "Yes, I will, Heather!" I reach out to give her a big hug, and she does the same.

She sees my new monster cast and asks,

"What happened to the smaller pink cast? I thought it contrasted nicely with your blue eyes."

Should I lie to her about her re-injuring my hand? No, not after what she just said.

"Um, when you bent my hand behind my back, it broke again."

Her eyes narrow, "Daniel, are you saying I broke your hand?"

I look down at my shoes, "Yes, Heather, you did."

Then, there's just silence. I quickly look up to see her stomping off to her cruiser, and she drives off.

An hour later, I get a text from Frank. *WTH! Couldn't you just lie to her about how you broke your hand again? She's moping around the office now. Well played, dummy.*

Around 8:00 pm, there's a knock on my front door. I go downstairs, and Heather is there. She has a bottle of my favorite scotch and takeout food. We eat our food, and she pours me one scotch after another.

"Danny Boy, I'm sorry for breaking your hand. I hope you aren't mad."

"A pretty girl, a bottle of scotch, and good food. We're all good," I respond.

"Okay," she whispers. She stands up, takes my scotch out of my hand, and puts it down on the coffee table. She bends over and kisses me on the lips. It's our first kiss! And it's fantastic. I have a stupid grin on my face afterward.

"Maybe if you behave yourself next time, I'll use tongue," she says. "I have to go now, but why don't we go to the pub later this week for dinner?"

## 7 FIRST NIGHT TOGETHER

It's always exciting for every new couple to spend their first night together. Hopefully, both parties enjoy themselves and it's memorable.

That's not what this chapter is about though—it's about the next day.

Heather has to be at the station by 7:00 am. It's about 5:30 am when I wake up. I hear the rain pounding against the window. *It's going to be one of those long rainy days where we might not even get to see the rainbow*, I think to myself.

I look over at Heather. She's sound asleep. I really haven't moved yet, but I guess I have woken her up. I hear her mumble, "Good morning, Danny

Boy. Thank you for last night!"

"Good morning, gorgeous. What can I make you for breakfast? It's 5:30, and you need to be at the station at seven," I tell her. I am still beaming from last night.

"Mmm… French toast would be amazing!" she says in a sleepy murmur.

"Okay, you stay here, and I'll make you French toast. I'll bring breakfast to you when it's ready. You can have breakfast in bed as long as you promise not to get crumbs everywhere!" I laugh at her.

As my friends can attest, I love cooking. So, when a pretty, naked girl asks for French toast, I'm going to make the best damn French toast there can be.

I pull out all the stops and prepare my special French toast. First, it's crusted in oatmeal. After that, I put in cream cheese, lime zest, fresh mint, and blueberries between two slices. Then, finally, I bake it in the oven. I have always figured that if you can give a woman one more positive reason to come back for a visit, she most likely will.

I also make a pot of coffee.

Heather yells down at me, "Oh my God! That smells so good. I'm coming down."

While I'm setting the table, I feel her arms wrap around me. Her body is still warm from the bed.

"Morning. It smells so amazing down here," she says.

I kiss her on the nose for the first time.

"Welcome to Chez Dan's. We specialize in serving fantastic meals to pretty girls."

"I am sure you do, Danny Boy. I guess I should hurry up before the next pretty girl appears for breakfast," she says, giggling.

Heather sits down at my dining room table while I put the French toast on her plate and head back to the kitchen to get her a cup of coffee. When I get back, which is only about thirty seconds later, she's already halfway through her portion. "Oh my God! This is so good. I've never had anything like this before—the cream cheese, the blueberries… Oh my God!" she groans out.

God, that girl can eat. For such a small person, she sure can pack away the food.

"I am glad you're enjoying it—I made it especially for you," I say, feeling proud of myself.

While I eat my French toast, she sips her coffee and simply stares at me. It feels like those beautiful green eyes are staring into my soul. It's a little unnerving. I have no idea what this beautiful woman is thinking.

I don't say anything. She stares at me the whole time, watching me eat my French toast. I wonder what she's thinking about, but I remain silent.

She breaks the silence with a fart. We both go into hysterics—perfect timing on her part. We both laugh so hard that tears are pouring down our faces.

"Off you go for a shower, you farter. Let me clean up the dishes and make your lunch, Ramos." I say, still laughing at her impromptu way of ending the silence at the breakfast table.

The rain is still pouring.

When Heather informed me the day before that she was spending the night, I had gone into planning mode. I wanted to feed her three great meals. Dinner last night, breakfast this morning, and her lunch for work today.

I fill a thermos with coffee so she doesn't have to go out and get wet. Using the prime rib that I cooked last night, I make a roast beef sandwich for her lunch, stacking the roast beef thick between two slices of rye bread. One piece of bread has cream cheese on it and the other slice has spicy horseradish and green relish. I put the sandwich in a plastic container so that it doesn't get crushed. I then make a quick salad with lots of different veggies to add colour in another plastic container. An apple and banana get put in a third plastic container. The fourth container contains my favourite homemade salad dressing. The fifth container contains homemade cookies I had made the day before.

I attempt to put the thermos and the five

plastic containers in a grocery bag, but it just doesn't fit. I grab my small backpack and put everything into it. Everything fits, but just barely. The backpack has some weight to it. Oh, well.

I decide I want to write her a note, thanking her for last night. I grab a pen and a sticky note and write down, "Thank you for last night!"

That doesn't sound right. I'm beginning to panic a bit. I really want her to come back—we had a lot of fun last night.

I have a brainstorm—why not write the title of one of those cheesy songs from the 70s I like so much? Which one, though? Since it's raining outside, I select "Laughter in the Rain" by Neil Sedaka.

I write the title down on the sticky note as neatly as I can, but it doesn't turn out great:

Laughter in the Rain by Neil Sedaka – Search for it!

I then add a smiley face, my name, and a paw print from Tank.

I put the sticky note on one of the plastic

containers and close the backpack.

Heather comes downstairs, and she looks stunning. There's something about her look, like she's incredibly happy. She bursts into her shit-eating grin, which always makes me laugh.

"I can't stop grinning. Frank will know exactly what happened. He's going to tease me horrifically today," she says.

"Well, the backpack full of food is also very likely a dead give-away, and you driving my truck to work will probably seal the deal," I say as I hand the backpack to Heather.

"What the hell is in this?" she asks.

"Well, you expended a lot of calories last night. I can't have you fainting at work, can I?" I smirk at her.

Heather just laughs at me. She grabs my hand and gives me a big kiss on the lips.

"I'll talk to you later, Grandpa!" She smiles and slaps my ass and then walks out of the house.

The station she works at is within walking distance from my house. Heather pulls into the station driving my truck. As she gets out of the truck, Frank pulls up beside her in his car.

It's pouring rain and they both run into the front entrance.

"Ramos, did you get a new truck, or are you driving Dan's truck? What? Why are you grinning so much? Did you guys…?"

"Franky, we did. For an old guy, he has lots of stamina! He only used his safe word twice."

"Well, that would explain your super smirky face! What's in the backpack, Ramos?"

"My lunch, Franky. Dan made it for me. He's worried that I expended too many calories last night, and he doesn't want me to faint on the job."

"Roger that, Ramos! Catch you later."

Thirty seconds later, my phone buzzes. It's a text from Frank.

*I have no idea what you did to her last night, but I haven't seen her smile like that before.*

I don't bother to respond. Sometimes, silence is golden.

Heather is in the women's locker room, and

her sergeant sees her. "Ramos, why are you grinning so much?" she asks.

"Well, Sarge, this girl got laid last night!"

Her sergeant high-fives her and says, "Good for you!"

Their lockers are beside each other, and Heather can't fit my backpack into it. Heather starts unpacking the backpack, and she sees the sticky note.

She mutters to herself, "What the fuck does he mean by this?"

"What's wrong, Ramos?" her sergeant asks.

"He wrote something on a sticky note. I have no idea what this crazy whitey has written. Is it a poem, maybe?"

Her sergeant looks at the sticky note. "Ramos, look it up! I think it might be a song."

Heather finds the song online. A few additional female officers gather around, and they listen to the song. It's totally cheesy.

Without exception, they all think it's sweet that I took the time and energy to recommend it on a sticky note.

One of her fellow female officers says, "I don't know, Ramos. You may have found yourself a keeper there. He cooks, and he's romantic. Sounds like the real deal."

## 8 MUSKRAT LOVE

"Smith, I need a code black run on Dan. Here's the information. Please don't fuck this up." Heather looks at Chris with her most H-Bomb face.

"Ramos, I don't like him. I don't trust him."

"But you're not the one dating him. I am."

A "code black" is a celebrated event within law enforcement. It signifies that a member believes that they have found their Mr. or Ms. Right. It's a last-minute background check on the potential boyfriend or girlfriend. It's illegal for the police to do a background check on any person without a probable cause. Probable cause can be a traffic stop. You can't just randomly look somebody up because you're curious.

A code black is run like this. The requesting officer tells their partner that they need a code black and provides them with the following information: name of the person, address, vehicle type, license plate number, and a date, which is three days from when you ask for the code black. This information is typed and printed out on any random printer outside of the station. It never has handwriting on it, as that can be traced back to a person.

The partner then passes the paper to an officer in the division. The game of hot potato then begins—the paper is passed around to many different officers. Nobody knows who it's for—therefore, everybody has plausible deniability. The last officer who gets the paper pulls over the person in question, runs the background check, and prints it off, leaving it in a folder labeled "Code Black" in an area of the station that is hidden away from all cameras and direct views. The requesting officer gets it twenty-four hours after the date given on their request paper. Pretty simple, really.

One morning, as I'm backing out of my driveway, I get stopped by a police officer. I live on a quiet residential street, and it's around 6:30 in the morning. The officer slowly approaches me and says, "Sir, can I see your driver's license, registration and proof of insurance?"

I pull the requested items out of my glovebox and ask the officer, "What appears to be the problem, officer?"

"Your headlights aren't on," he states, "I'll be right back."

*That's odd*, I think. *It's daylight outside, and this dude is wearing sunglasses!*

About five minutes later, the officer is back. He gives me everything back and says, "Sorry sir, I didn't realize what time it was. Have a nice day." He promptly returns to his cruiser and drives off.

As I later learn Smith somehow gets a copy of my code black. It pisses him off so much that he grabs Frank and rants to him about it.

"This is fucking unbelievable! This guy is way too clean, he's a fucking unicorn. Look at his record. One interaction with the police in forty-four fucking years. What sort of fucking idiot would admit to having had a light beer six hours before at a fucking ride stop?"

Frank, by this point, apparently had had enough of Smith. "Shut the fuck up, Smith. Dan is a buddy of mine. He's a good guy. You're just upset because you think of Ramos as your little sister. Just let it go, man. Don't you see how happy she is? We haven't had a lot of H-Bomb explosions going off lately. Don't fuck this up for the both of them."

As Smith stomps off, he looks at Frank, "If you hadn't introduced them, this wouldn't be fucking happening. It's your goddamn fault they met in the first place."

An hour later, Heather approaches Frank. She looks pissed.

Frank always has lines for the ladies, so he breaks out, "What's up, buttercup?" He hopes Smith hasn't done something stupid.

"I code-blacked Dan. He came back pristine. I'm not used to having a nice guy in my life. Do you know that when he packs me my meals, there's always a sticky note with lyrics from some random, cheesy 70s song. Whenever I'm on my break, I find the song online and listen to it. It always makes me laugh. This is what I got today."

Written in my horrible handwriting is "Muskrat Love." And below that, I'd written "Love, Dan and Tank," with a little paw mark—Tank's signature.

"It's great you code-blacked Dan. I'm glad he is clean. I had no doubt. So, what's the problem?"

"Well, when I listened to the song, I cried because it's so sweet. It's about muskrats, and they're in love and get married," Heather blurts out.

And then it happens. The H-Bomb appears. "Franklin, I never cry. Daniel made me cry, and no man has ever made me cry about muskrats being in love before. This is all through a stupid sticky note, too! I hate him. If he was here right now, I would hurt him. I would armbar him. I would choke him out." Heather appears to be going on one of her epic rants.

Frank being Frank is desperately trying not to laugh. He spits out, "Ramos, is it that time of the month? Go take some drugs and calm down. Fucking muskrats, I hate them!"

Heather stomps off, yelling at Frank, "It's not that time of the month, asshole!"

I get a text from Frank a little later, *WTF, dude? Muskrats in love? I saw H-Bomb at work today, and out of nowhere, she tells me she's crying over some song you showed her. Dude, no more muskrats in love, or the homicide squad will be attending your house soon.*

*How worried should I be?* I ask.

*Very*, is his response.

*What have I done?* I think to myself.

Two hours later, there's a knock on my door. H-Bomb is standing there, and she's pissed. I've never seen her this angry. She has a vein in her forehead that pops out when she's angry. It's further out than I've ever seen before.

"Daniel, you made me cry today over a

stupid fucking song about stupid fucking muskrats in love with words that were written on a stupid fucking sticky note. I don't cry over anything... ever." Heather grabs me with both hands by the collar of my shirt and brings my face down to her level. We are now eye to eye.

*Oh, fuck, did I fuck up really bad? Mental note to myself: no more mentioning of muskrats in love on sticky notes if we are still dating.*

She looks at me and says, "Do you know how pissed I am at you, Daniel? Pissed isn't a strong enough word. I'm super fucking pissed, and you want to know why, Daniel? You are forcing me to say something that I have never said to a man before." She just glares at me.

I'm terrified and have no idea what to say. I stammer out, "I won't bring up muskrats again."

She continues to glare at me and quietly says, "You fucking idiot, it's not about fucking muskrats." She doesn't say anything for a little while and just stares into my blue eyes. She finally says, "I love you, Daniel John Hayes."

And that's that.

That's the first-time Heather tells me she loves me.

Heather then drags me upstairs to my bedroom and ravages me for about two hours. It's fantastic.

The next day at the office, one of my colleagues, VJ, walks up to me and says, "Well, Mr. Smirky Pants, what's that stupid grin all about?"

"Yesterday, Heather told me she loved me for the first time, VJ!"

"That's amazing, Dan."

VJ is a rock. She's always willing to help when things get crazy at work.

"Should we be planning a wedding yet?" she teases.

I laugh out loud, "Not quite yet. Baby steps, VJ, baby steps."

# 9 CUTE ASIAN HOOKER

It's Thursday, and Heather and I are scheduled to meet at the local pub around 5:30 pm. She's been here with me a couple times before.

My schedule is much more flexible than hers. I get to the pub about half an hour before we're scheduled to meet. As usual, I chat with the regulars about current events and business—it's a constant in my life.

Heather shows up wearing her workout gear. Yoga pants, a tight t-shirt, and her amazing grin. She looks stunning. She says hello to a few people she knows and saunters over to me. She kisses me and, for some reason, gives me a slip of her tongue.

It does not go unnoticed by the regulars.

She whispers into my ear, "Just trying to make you look good in front of your pub friends, Grandpa."

I notice for the first time that a lot of the regulars are looking at her. It's a weird feeling to see other men lusting after your girlfriend.

We sit down, and she orders her go-to drink—a gin and tonic.

"Hey, we need to go shopping this weekend," Heather smirks at me.

"Okay, for what?" I ask.

"Chris and I have been seconded to the vice squad, and we're going to bust Johns. We need to buy me a few hookerish outfits."

"Hookerish outfits" is a term I find interesting and mildly exciting. Lots of fun possibilities, I suspect.

"By the way, I finally got paid on that big portfolio I appraised. Why don't we make a long weekend out of it and go to Niagara Falls?"

Heather claps her hands and has a big goofy

grin on her face. "Oh, Danny Boy! We are going to have fun!"

On Saturday, we drive to an outlet mall on the way to Niagara. We wander around the mall for an hour looking for suitable hooker attire. I didn't realize it was going to be such a difficult task. We're in a store that sells clubbing wear. I'm going through a rack of dresses, and I pull out a short white, leather dress

"How do you like this one?" I ask.

"Danny Boy, I am looking for something that screams sex-addict-Asian-hooker, not cute-Asian-hooker," she quips.

I put the dress back on the rack and start searching again as I mutter, "Sex addict Asian hooker, not cute Asian hooker."

"I hear you muttering, Grandpa," Heather yells over at me.

The sales lady gives us an odd look.

We continue shopping this way for a few hours as we walk around the mall. I select some outfits, and I am told it's not "hooker-ish enough" each time.

As we walk around, I start seeing the same couple over and over again. They appear to be following us. The woman is tall, likely close to six feet. The guy is about my height, which is materially short of six feet. He's watching us like a hawk. They make an odd couple. When I stare back at them, they both look away and pretend to be shopping around, only a short distance from us. As if they couldn't be any more obvious, the guy picks up a book and starts reading it upside down.

I grab Heather's hand and whisper in her ear, "That couple at my six. They're paying far too much attention to us. It feels like they're following us. The dude is reading a book upside down."

The one thing you learn when dating a police officer is that they're never off duty even when they're off duty. You never know who you might run into when you're out doing your daily errands. Bad guys shop too.

Heather glances at them and whispers back, "Yes, something isn't right. Follow me."

She grabs my hand, puts her head on my shoulder, and makes googly eyes at me, as I call them. We then execute what is called a counter surveillance drill. How it works is that you either walk or drive into a dead end to see if they follow you down a dead-end road. If they follow you down, it is likely that you're being followed. It's amazing what you learn when you're dating a police officer.

So, off we go and find a dead end. Sure enough, they're behind us. I am getting ready for a fight—nobody is going to hurt my little H-Bomb. She likely doesn't need my help, but I'm ready.

We walk right back at them like we took a wrong turn. Heather lets go of my hands and says to me, "Get ready."

The man points at me and, in an authoritative voice, barks, "Police. You, come to me, and don't look at your female friend."

I walk toward him. I know this will all be sorted shortly. Heather will show her badge or something and we we'll be on our way.

I smile at the guy, even though he looks extremely unhappy. "What are you two doing here?" he asks.

I respond back by lifting up the shopping bags I've been carrying for the last few hours. "Just a little shopping with my friend over there." I turn to look at Heather.

He grabs me by the shirt. "I told you not to look at her. What were you shopping for?"

I'm caught flat-footed. I am a rule follower. To always tell the truth is my motto—it's too hard to remember the lies.

"My friend and I are shopping for hooker outfits for her work."

With the benefit of hindsight, I should have lied to the man.

The cop looks at me in amazement but not in a positive way.

"Un-fucking believable! You know I'm a police officer, don't you, fucktard? I take great pride in putting human traffickers in jail for a long time."

I think to myself, now would be a great time for Heather to identify herself as a police officer.

The cop just stares at me, steam is literally coming out of his ears.

I finally hear that awesome laugh of Heather's. The female police officer yells over, "She's with us. She's going undercover next week, and they're buying a few costumes for her!"

The male officer looks at me, "You were actually telling the truth. Un-fucking believable. Don't do that, dummy!"

That's an interesting thought—don't tell the truth to a police officer.

I look at him and smile, "Honesty is always the best policy."

Our shopping comes to an end. We have sufficient hooker outfits to last her for two weeks.

We then drive the remaining distance to Niagara Falls. I've reserved a suite on the 51st floor of the casino, overlooking the falls. The view from our room is amazing. The falls look spectacular from this standpoint.

In the corner of the bedroom is a hot tub. We order a bottle of champagne, soak in the hot tub for an hour, and watch the world go by. We hardly speak. We're simply just enjoying each other's company.

It's now 7:00 pm. We have dinner planned at the steak house in the casino. Heather jumps in the shower first to get ready. After she's done showering, I take a shower. I'm feeling slightly buzzed from the heat of the hot tub and the cold champagne.

Heather has asked me to wear my new suit, without a tie. She tells me that with my salt-and-pepper hair and my suit, I kind of look like a famous movie actor.

Heather has decided to be evil tonight. She's sporting one of her new dresses—it fits her like a glove. It has cut outs in the back, sides, and front. Standing in front of the full-length mirror, she admires herself. She flashes me her amazing grin.

"Grandpa, this dress is far too revealing, and I am way too hot for an old guy like you. Perhaps I should make sure the paramedics are standing by for you in case you need CPR."

I take a step back to admire the view. The amount of side boob and cleavage she's showing is impressive, even by her standards. I'm not sure how the dress is actually staying together, given all of the cut outs.

She completes her outfit with a pashmina shawl that essentially hides the majority of the exposed skin.

We take the elevator to the ground floor and are escorted to our reserved table.

I like to think that the people who were staring at us as we walked through the restaurant consider us a fairly attractive couple. Although, deep down, I know it's all her.

The waiter approaches us and offers an apology right away, "Hi, my name is David. I'm terribly sorry, but our air conditioning isn't working right now, and the restaurant is very warm. We have been told it should be up and running within the hour, but I just wanted to let you know it might be hot in here for a little while. We are deeply sorry for the inconvenience."

I look at Heather. She nods her head, indicating that she's okay with it.

"David, thank you for being honest. I think we're okay with that. You likely didn't break the air conditioning, so no worries," I tell him.

He then takes our drink orders.

It is warm. I take off my jacket and hang it on one of the empty chairs at our table.

Heather usually has a fairly cool body temperature, whereas my body temperature runs extremely hot. Oftentimes when we go to bed at night, Heather first snuggles up to me, somehow getting by Tanky who sleeps and plays defense between the two of us most of the time.

Her feet are always cold. She wraps them around my legs for warmth and snuggles up against my body. This is my favourite time of the day. I can smell her shampoo and feel her warmth, and it's comforting. This lasts usually for about five minutes, and then the H-Bomb appears.

"Daniel, you are way too hot for snuggling. Stop being so hot," I am informed on a nightly basis.

I explain to her that I'm just warm all the time, and she retreats to her side of the bed.

It's so warm inside the restaurant that Heather removes her shawl. After we finish our appetizers, she heads off to the washroom, forgetting that her dress is quite revealing. As I watch her walk past every table, every single person literally stops whatever they are doing and stares at her.

A funny thing happens. As she walks past the bar, a few men stop her and starts buying her drinks. I'm killing myself laughing. At one point, she has at least five cosmos lined up in front of her.

Heather also looks much younger than her age.

After she comes back from the washroom, two frat boys show up at our table. They want to know if they can take my daughter out to the nightclub tonight. I burst out laughing.

Heather explains to them that she is older than they think she is. While she is very flattered, her going to the club with them isn't in the cards tonight. They look bitterly disappointed and retreat to the bar.

We have an enjoyable dinner with lots of laughs and exchange googly eyes with each other for the next two hours. I still get shivers when I think of her googly eyes. I'm sure people looked at us and wondered what the forty-year-old man was doing with a twenty-year-old girl.

We essentially ignore the outside world, and, as always, our dinners are all about our little world at the table and ourselves. We're killing ourselves laughing and having so much fun. After eating most of the dinner, I excuse myself to go to the washroom. I even put my suit jacket back on, that's how classy I am.

I go to the washroom and look in the mirror. My stupid shit-eating grin makes me laugh. I am buzzed and I have red cheeks. I shake my head at my reflection in the mirror. I think to myself,

*You're such a lucky idiot to be dating Heather.*

In the mirror, I see a blur—a larger man jumps at me.

And then it happens.

Somebody starts choking me with their hands wrapped around my neck.

It's not just any choke—this choke is the kind of choke that could be life-ending, or at least life-changing.

I've trained for this for years. Never had I thought it would actually happen though.

Here's the thing about choking with hands— fingers are very small levers. To defeat a small lever, you need a larger lever. So, I execute a textbook Israeli defense to a choke. It involves a few elbows to the jaw and a groin strike with the back of my hand—extremely effective and, most importantly, easy to complete under situations of stress and fear. My attacker is now incapacitated on the floor.

I recognize him. He's one of the frat boys who wanted Heather, "my daughter," to go clubbing with him.

*Why does this shit happen to me?* I wonder.

I grab hold of a waiter outside of the men's washroom and explain what has happened. Security is summoned.

Shockingly, the security is aware of this individual and aren't surprised by what happened. The young man is taken away, and nothing more is said to me.

I return to our table, and Heather now has four more drinks lined up in front of her.

I smirk at her—she knows what's happened. The bruising on my neck is somewhat apparent and the waiter had let her know what happened and that I was okay.

We finish our dinner and then proceed to the casino.

Heather is walking slightly in front of me while I am carrying her shawl. People are staring at her. I'm sure people think I'm her bodyguard. This is funny.

We get to one of the casino bars and order

drinks. Before they arrive, Heather stares into my eyes and asks me for a favour.

"Dan, I need to do a little role playing before I join the vice squad. I need you to walk up to me and proposition me for sex. If I don't have my game face on from the get go, we aren't going to be successful."

"Roger that, H-Bomb," I tell her.

I grab my drink and walk fifty feet away. I think to myself, how hard can it be to proposition a "hooker" for sex—especially when we're dating?

I walk up to Heather and smile and wink at her. "Hey, how are you doing?" I ask.

H-Bomb appears, "Are you fucking kidding me? 'Hey, how are you doing' and a wink is not smooth at all. Try again!"

I retreat and gather my thoughts.

*I got this. I have game*, I think.

I approach Heather again.

"Hey girl, do you like stuff?" I ask.

She bursts into laughter, "You are clueless, aren't you, Danny Boy!"

Heather begins to text on her phone. My phone buzzes in about twenty seconds, indicating that I have a text. I see the following message.

*Franklin, Dan and I are trying to role play at the casino so that I am ready for the vice squad next week. He has no game. He clearly has never spoken to a prostitute before. Can you help him?*

Frank responds back, *You're the one dating him—not my issue. But I guess I can help him out. Again, not my issue.*

Heather is four feet away from me. I stare at my phone. *Are they kidding me?* I think.

I text them both back. *Is there anybody here glad that I don't know how to order sex from a prostitute?*

Heather responds back, *Good point, Danny Boy. I'm glad you don't!*

Frank, being the gentlemen he is, gives me a few pointers. My first line to Heather is what follows. I say it confidently with conviction.

"Hey, Buttercup, I'm looking to party tonight. You have any interest in a three-hotdog chocolate fondue?"

I honestly have no idea what it means.

Heather bursts out laughing, "Oh my God! Only Frank would break that out first!"

A few of Frank's lines:

"Hey, Baby, how do you feel about a cauliflower surprise?"

"Oh, Baby, you look like you know your way around a hot salami party."

My favourite, though, is this:

"Hey, Honey, have you ever had your boat docked by a sailor who knows his stuff?"

# 10 A TOUGH SHIFT

Tonight is Heather's third week with the vice squad. It's been pretty uneventful up until now. Tonight, things change.

My cell phone rings at 2:00 am, it's an unknown number. I assume it's Heather and answer with my standard, "Hello, Gorgeous!"

It's Smith. "Hello, Ugly," he responds.

I find it odd that Smith is calling me. We aren't particularly close, given everything that has happened.

"Ramos has been hurt, and we're at Eastern Hospital. She's fine. She wants you to pick her up and look after her. She doesn't want her mom and dad to see her. When you get here, text me, and I will come down and get you," he says to me in a calm, matter-of-fact voice.

Eastern Hospital is on the other side of the city. I quickly put my clothes on and drive for half an hour to the hospital. I text Smith when I get to the lobby. He comes down and escorts me to Heather's room.

Before I go in, Smith grabs my shoulder and looks me in the eye. He informs me, "Listen, it looks worse than it is. I've spoken to two doctors about it. The swelling should go down in about two weeks, with no lasting damage."

With that information in mind, I walk into the hospital room to see Heather. She looks pretty rough, as she's dozing off with both of her eyes swollen shut. Her face is green, blue, and black. It looks like somebody took a ball peen hammer to her face.

I actually wouldn't have recognized her if it hadn't been for the fact that I see her small little hands and Smith telling me it's her. She looks so tiny and vulnerable right now.

"Hey, kiddo," I say to Heather, "how are you feeling?"

Her response still makes me laugh, "Like I went ten rounds with Mike Tyson when he was in his prime!"

As a John and Heather were negotiating a transaction, and when she told him he was under arrest, he tried to run. Heather was wearing her "hooker" shoes and went to give chase. She slipped and fell, and the guy then kneed her in the face several times. To make it worse, he then started to rain hammer blows down on to her face when she was lying dazed on the ground.

Smith was there in about ten seconds, and he arrested the John. Heather was then taken by ambulance to the hospital, where she received a CAT scan and no serious injuries were found.

She doesn't want her parents to see her, but she needs assistance from somebody literally twenty-four hours a day. Her face is so swollen she can't open her eyes. She wants to know if she can stay at my house. "Of course," I tell her.

I tell Heather not to wander off anywhere, and we both kind of laugh at that little joke. I then mention to her that I have to speak with Smith for a minute.

I find Smith sitting on a chair outside Heather's room. He looks at me. "You are going to look after her, aren't you, Dan?" he asks.

"Of course I am. I have one favour to ask of you, though. You owe me one because of this," I point to my broken hand that is still ensconced in a plaster cast.

"Sure," Smith says.

"I want to be in a room with the guy who hurt Heather. Just me and him. No video. No audio. I want to reprogram him. I want to show him what happens when you hurt people," I explain to Smith.

Smith eyes me carefully, "Dan, I appreciate the sentiment. Hell, I want to be in a room with this guy too—but it isn't going to happen. We could all go to jail for that. This piece of shit isn't worth going to jail for. Trust me. He got what he deserved.

I broke his face."

Smith actually broke the guy's face with a single punch. It will require six hours of surgery to put his face back together. Smith hit the guy so hard that he broke his jaw, cheekbone, and nasal bone.

Well, at least I know the guy is suffering for what he did to Heather.

I pull my truck right up to the emergency room entrance of the hospital. Smith and I then help Heather into my truck, and off we go.

Heather and I get home. She can't see anything, so I have to guide her around. When she has to go to the washroom, I have to help her pull her pants down and guide her to sit on the toilet. She's embarrassed and frustrated because she's fiercely independent but now has to rely on me for everything.

It's now about 4:00 am in the morning. She takes her painkillers and asks me for a can of beer, I relent.

We both finally go to sleep. Suddenly, within the first half hour, she starts to shake. I firmly hold her in the dark and call her name. She doesn't wake up. I turn on the lights and realize she is having a seizure.

I am absolutely terrified.

Something is horribly wrong.

I call 911 and explain the situation. An ambulance arrives in about four minutes. The paramedics want to know what happened to her face, and I explain that she got beat up tonight.

Heather and her colleagues are extremely guarded with strangers about what they do for a living. I don't understand it, but I respect it. I leave out that she is a police officer.

The paramedics are quite concerned, and they hook her up to all types of machines. They keep eyeing me. They race Heather out of my house and into the ambulance. I try to get in, but the paramedics tell me that it's against the rules, and I have to drive myself to the hospital.

*That's odd*, I think to myself. I'm pretty sure I've heard of people's families being allowed in ambulances. I race back into the house and try to find my keys. Because I was helping Heather into my house earlier, I completely forgot where I put my keys. I didn't put them down in the normal spot, and it takes me about ten minutes to find them.

I speed off to the hospital, where I inquire at the information desk about where she is. The nurse gives me an unimpressed look.

"Sir, I can't tell you where she is," she tells me in a tone that suggests she doesn't have time for me.

*That's odd*, I think again. It must be because Heather is a police officer. I'm getting a little frantic, so I text Frank and Smith. no response.

I know it's early in the morning, but I'm going to call Frank. He'll know what to do.

I faintly hear somebody yelling behind me. Having a cast on my right hand and dialing with my left hand has been challenging. It's been two months, but it never gets easier. My mind is only focused on contacting Frank about Heather, so I start to walk away from the yelling to find a quiet area to speak with Frank about the details of what is happening.

I'm abruptly slammed into the wall and drop my phone. I'm then roughly thrown to the ground. My cast is underneath me, and my left arm is being twisted behind me. I feel about two hundred pounds on my back.

I'm being told that I'm under arrest and asked to stop resisting. I try to explain that my cast is caught on my shirt, and with an officer sitting on me, I can't get my arm out. I feel my cast being forced from underneath me. The weight feels tremendous on me, and I can barely get a word out. I give up trying to explain why I can't get my hand out.

Suddenly, I feel a tremendous pain in my ankle. A police officer just hit me with his baton for resisting arrest. The sandals that I have on offer little in the way of protection. My hand comes loose. My broken hand is forcibly bent behind my back, and it happens again. The familiar burning sensation of my hand breaking. *God, I love that feeling*, I think to myself. Since I have the cast on, the officer can't get handcuffs on me. So, I get zip tied.

I get hauled to my feet and dragged out to the patrol car. One police officer looks at me and laughs, "I just love these wannabe tough guys. They never want to pick a fight with a man. They go around beating up women. This guy is going to be real popular in jail. I'm sure he'll have many dates!"

I explain to them who Heather is. They know who the H-Bomb is. Apparently, she was their coach officer.

*Thank God. This misunderstanding is over now*, I think. Sadly, it was just beginning.

The two officers look at me. The shorter one glares at me. "So, let me get this straight. You just beat the shit out of Ramos, a female police officer who we have great respect for?"

I respond back, "No, she got hurt today on the job. She was treated at the other hospital in the city earlier today, but she's here again because she had a seizure in her sleep."

Of course, it's far too complex to have a

common computer system that various agencies can use to share and access information.

The two officers don't believe me.

I'm told to stop resisting. My head is slammed into the trunk of the police car a few times. I'm punched in the face and kneed in the groin several times.

I'm told that you never punch a woman, especially not a female police officer. I try to explain what happened. However, they don't listen. They pick me up and knee me in the groin a few more times because I'm resisting.

I'm now lying on the ground like a puddle of water.

I hear them talking. They start to giggle. They inform me that Smith is coming. Smith, I am told, will do a number on me. They tell me he's going to "fuck me up."

Smith shows up a few minutes later. I'm lying face down with my hands still behind my back.

"Hey, Smith, we have the guy who beat

Ramos up. We softened him up for you. Hope you don't mind."

I'm rudely flipped over on my side, a flashlight is shone into my face.

Smith looks at me and informs the two police officers, "That's not the guy who beat up Ramos. That guy is still in surgery. Do you think I would let him hurt Ramos to that extent and not do some permanent damage to him?"

I later learn that their names are Pressfield and Cussler.

"Then, who is this guy?" Pressfield asks as he points at me.

"This gentleman is Ramos' boyfriend, his name is Dan Hayes. I haven't made my mind up about him yet. Ramos really likes him. He's one of Frank's buddies. He's the guy who cooks all the time and brings meals up to the station for us. Cussler, you like his pickles," Smith casually informs them.

"Gentlemen, I will allow the three of you to figure out the current situation yourselves. I'm running off to see how Ramos is doing." And with that, Smith hurries off to the emergency room.

I see Pressfield and Cussler exchange nervous looks.

"What do we do now?" Pressfield asks Cussler. Cussler has a few more years under his belt, and, therefore, he is in charge of the current situation.

"Pressfield, go get a wheelchair. I'm going to uncuff Mr. Hayes."

Pressfield literally runs for a wheelchair. Cussler pulls out his knife and cuts the plastic zip tie off of me.

I am raced into the ER and get checked in immediately. After being x-rayed I find out that my hand is indeed broken again, and so is my ankle. One of my eyes is swollen shut.

I ask about Heather, but nobody seems to know anything. Grace and Smith hunt me down. Grace is working in the ER tonight.

She kindly cleans up my face and gives me some ice for my black eye. Smith whispers something into her ear, and she giggles. She gets another bag of ice and drops it on my crotch.

She smiles at me and whispers into my ear, "It's for the swelling, whitey." This cracks both of us up.

I'm told that Heather is fine, and she's just having an allergic reaction to one of anti-bacterial drugs she is taking.

Smith and Grace are going to wheel me up to Heather's room. Smith asks Grace to give us a few minutes. Grace looks concerned, but Smith reassures her that we're going to have a chat and that's it.

"How big of a problem do you have with Pressfield and Cussler?" he asks me.

I don't know how to respond.

"Listen, it's in your rights to launch a formal complaint. However, they might lose their jobs. What they did was wrong and should never have occurred. In my opinion, they're both good guys, and they both have young families. Ramos likes them, as she was their coach officer. I think they overreacted when they heard Ramos was hurt."

I think about what I asked Smith earlier tonight. I wanted to beat the crap out of the John.

This is karma telling me something. They did what I wanted to do three hours earlier. Two wrongs don't make a right and three wrongs most certainly won't fix anything.

I respond, "I have no issues then."

Smith looks at me. "Dan, I think I have decided that I might tolerate you for a little while longer."

I'm wheeled into Heather's hospital room, and I see that her face is two inches away from Pressfield's face. She has her hands wrapped around the neck of his shirt.

"William, what did you just say you did to Daniel?" H-Bomb has made an appearance tonight.

"We thought he beat you up, and so we broke his hand and ankle and punched him a few times," Pressfield spits out.

"No, William, you did something else. What else did you do to Daniel, William?"

"Um… I kind of kneed him in the groin a dozen or so times, Heather."

"William, Daniel's balls are mine. I own them. They make me feel good. They make me feel happy. I like feeling happy, William. You may punch Daniel in the head or even break his bones, but his balls are mine. I am the only person allowed to touch Daniel's balls. Do I make myself clear, William?"

"Yes, Heather," Pressfield replies.

Pressfield literally runs out of the room after his conversation with the H-Bomb.

Grace checks Heather's vitals, and everything looks good.

Grace and Smith leave us alone for a few minutes.

I ask Heather if she's okay. She laughs.

My wheelchair is close to her bed. She reaches her hand out, and I grab it with my unbroken hand.

"Danny Boy, do you really have all the injuries I have been told about?" she asks me.

"I guess. I am feeling strong though!" I respond.

Heather laughs. "Welcome to our little tribe. There are only eight more people in my platoon who need to break a bone in your body. We are currently running about 33.33 percent, based on my calculations."

We both laugh.

Roughly thirty-four percent of her colleagues, including her, have broken a bone in my body. *I'm so lucky.*

I hear a sound and turn to see Grace pushing a bed into the room. Heather can't leave for twenty-four hours, we are told. The extra bed is pushed against Heather's.

Grace walks over and whispers into Heather's ear for about thirty seconds.

They both giggle.

Grace stares at me for a few seconds. In her sing-song voice, she asks me, "Whitey, do you think you can get your fat ass into the bed?"

With the help of Grace, I get out of the

wheelchair and navigate my way into the bed with my various casts.

Heather and I are lying beside each other in our respective hospital beds.

Grace gives me some pills. I really don't want to take them. I then meet Grace the Warrior.

"Daniel, take the pills. They will help with the pain and swelling. Don't be a dummy," she commands me.

I swallow the pills with some water.

She gives Heather some pills as well.

Heather and I are lying in our beds side by side. She reaches out for my hand, and I take it.

Grace smiles at us, "Good night, my friends. Sleep tight and heal well." Heather and I are both asleep in about two minutes.

It's been a rough night for the both of us.

I wake up around 6:00 am. Heather and I are still holding hands. I hate to break away, but I have to pee. I hobble to the washroom.

After I'm done, I see Grace. She's sitting outside our room, watching over us, protecting us.

I hobble out to see her. She looks at me as I sit down beside her.

She grabs my unbroken hand and stares at me for almost a minute. Then, in her sweet sing-song voice, she tells me, "Daniel, Heather is special. She was placed on earth to do special things. I think the two of you were destined to meet. She likes you in a way I have never seen her like anyone before. Treat her well, as I am watching you."

I stare back at her.

I was scared of Smith's overprotectiveness of Heather, but now, I also know I can't let Grace down.

The next two weeks crawl by. Between my injuries and Heather's, we still don't have enough unbroken body parts to make a complete person.

After the first week, Heather is able open her eyes slightly. She's going stir-crazy. We decide that a trip to the grocery store is in order. To hide her black eyes, she puts on a pair of sunglasses, and so do I.

The lighting in the grocery store is dim, and

we're forced to remove our sunglasses. People stare at the injured couple—a tiny Asian girl whose face is black and blue and a white guy with a black eye and casts on his leg and arm. I bet some people think we're into some really kinky shit.

The cashier who usually checks us out always chats with us. Today, she's strangely silent. I look at her, and with a straight face, say, "You should have seen the eight guys we took on in a fight. They look far worse than us!"

Heather bursts out into laughter.

The cashier just looks at us, shakes her head, and says, "You guys need to be more careful then."

We giggle over how broken we must look for months after.

# 11 HURT BUT STILL IN THE GAME

It's early spring. Both of my casts are removed, and the doctor says I'm able to exercise lightly, as long as I keep on going to physiotherapy as well. I suggest to Heather that we go for a bike ride down by the lake on the paved waterfront trail.

She thinks about it for a minute before responding, "Danny Boy, I need you in one piece. I'm worried about you, since you've just recently gotten better. But, I mean, how much damage can you do to yourself if you're on a paved, flat trail? Okay, let's do it! But promise me you won't hurt your old grandpa ass!"

We're both excited for our mini day trip. Little does Heather know, Mr. Murphy is lurking in the bushes. I'm all too familiar with Mr. Murphy, and I have a feeling he'll pay me a visit today. Heather has met him through me before, she just hasn't realized it yet. If you don't know who Mr. Murphy is, I'll tell you his sole goal in life.

Mr. Murphy has a law named after him—Murphy's Law—which states, "Anything that can go wrong, will go wrong."

I hate him. He is a constant in my life. He usually just hurts me physically, but today, he has something special planned for me. He's going to do something to me that will haunt me for the rest of my life. He is to give me a new nickname today.

I toss our bikes in the back of my truck, and we drive down to where the trail starts. We start riding. It's such a beautiful day. We get to the halfway point near the ice cream stand, and there are children riding around in circles on their bikes and plenty of good friends and couples enjoying the simple pleasure of ice cream and milkshakes.

"If I'm a good boy today, can I have some ice cream, please?" I ask Heather.

She laughs at me and then gives me her signature smirky smile, "Danny Boy, if you're a good boy today, I might even let you lick your ice cream off of me!"

I just shake my head. She's such a tease sometimes.

On the way back, we stop for ice cream at the ice cream stand. We sit on a wooden bench as we take in the breathtaking view of the vast lake. The sun feels good on my skin. I've spent far too much time in casts recently.

"How are you feeling, Danny Boy?" she asks. "Any pain in your hand or ankle?"

"I feel strong. A little sore, but nothing I can't handle," I respond.

She puts her head on my shoulder and holds my hand. I kiss the top of her head. I love the smell of her shampoo. It makes her hair smell like flowers.

For the next hour, we simply enjoy each

other's presence in pure silence as we embrace the nature around us. Just each other's company and the lake. The last six months with her have been one hell of a rollercoaster. It's been intense. But if I had to do it all over again, I would do so without any hesitation.

I am so lucky to have met this woman. I can't imagine being with anybody else.

We get back on our bikes and start riding the trail back to where we had parked.

We're almost back to the truck—it's literally two hundred feet away.

I turn to her and yell, "Race you to the truck!" Heather loves a little physical competition. I start pedaling hard. I'm pulling away from her. I'm going to beat her to the truck and have bragging rights until our next bike ride. Oh man, I haven't had this much fun in awhile.

It was fun while it lasted, but Mr. Murphy decides to make an appearance. And he has plans for me. He's going to make this day special. A day to remember, if you will.

I start pedaling even faster, my vision is locked and fixated on my truck. Nothing is going to stop me. I need the bragging rights, as I have had very little to brag about over the last few months.

I hear Heather scream, "Dan, look out for the…"

I see something out of the corner of my eye. I feel a great weight hit me square on the chest, and then nothing but blackness.

I hear my name being called, there's a bright light in my eyes. I try to open my eyes and wake up, but I can't. I feel like I'm swimming in a thick liquid. My body isn't responding. I go back to sleep.

I try to wake up again. I try to move, but I can't. Now it feels like there's a huge, heavy blanket on me. I try to say something, but I can't. I know something isn't right. My head hurts, my chest hurts, and it feels like I've been hit with a sledgehammer in my chest. My entire body is in agony.

At last, I'm able to open my eyes with tremendous effort, and I see people looking at me and talking. I can't hear them for a bit, but I finally start to hear the conversation.

I realize I'm in a hospital room. Again?!

A doctor is speaking to Heather.

"He likely has a concussion, so he needs to heavily rest, perhaps staying indoors would be best. The CAT scan came back, and we don't see any permanent damage. We also x-rayed his chest and gave him an ultrasound. No bones are broken, and all the organs are intact, but he is heavily bruised. We have also cleaned up all the injuries from when he impacted with the asphalt. We x-rayed his right hand and ankle, given that he recently had his casts removed. They look fine. However, we had to put ten stitches in the back of his head to close that wound and another twenty in each leg to close those wounds. He's very lucky. This is why everybody needs to wear a helmet," he finishes.

I stir a little.

Both Heather and the doctor come over to me. Heather looks absolutely mortified, and she doesn't get scared easily, given the nature of her job. It's very rarely I ever see her like this.

The doctor comes over and looks at my vital signs. "All good, Dan. How are you feeling?" he asks.

"Everything hurts. So, what exactly happened?" I ask.

The doctor responds with a smile. "You had a bit of an accident and fell off your bike. But I'll let your friend tell you the story. The main thing is that you're going to be sore for a few weeks, but you will live. There's no permanent damage. We will likely be able to let you go home today. However, I just want to monitor you for a few hours as a precaution. I'll be back in about an hour to check up on you."

The doctor then leaves the room.

Heather looks at me gently. "Danny Boy, you scared me. I thought you weren't going to make it."

I smile at her. "I'm okay," I say.

Here we go.

H-Bomb is about to make an appearance

154

now, and she is pissed with me.

"Daniel, promise me you will never ever ride your bike again without a helmet. I will find out if you do. You know I will."

Long pause.

H-Bomb isn't done yet. She's just getting warmed up.

*I'm going to be vaporized*, I think to myself.

At least I am already in the hospital.

"Daniel, if you ever hurt yourself again, you better hope you're dead. I mean, really, really dead. Because, if you're not dead, I will successfully finish what you failed to do. You know what, Daniel? I don't like being scared. And today, you scared me. I've never been that scared before, and I don't like being scared. I don't like it, Daniel."

For added emphasis on how unhappy she is, her face is now only about two inches away from my face.

Then comes the longest pause of my life.

She grabs my hand and stares at me with her amazing green eyes and gives me that fierce look that I love. "Daniel, promise me on our relationship that you will always wear your helmet."

I look up at her and say, "Yes, Heather, I will always wear my helmet from now on, without fail."

You never dispute an order from the H-Bomb—she wouldn't like it. Also, my life likely wouldn't be worth living if I did so after she was finished with me.

I ask her what happened.

"Daniel, you are never to race me again on your bike. And you are going to stay away from geese as well!"

I look at her and say, "What the hell happened?"

I am soon told the story. Mr. Murphy really did a number on me this time.

Being fixated on my truck, I failed to see a low-flying goose make a landing. Grown geese weigh between eight to fifteen pounds.

Between my speed and the goose's flight speed, imagine a twelve-pound weight hitting me square on the chest while I'm racing my bike.

The force of the impact thrust me off the rear of my bike. Not to mention, it also knocked the wind completely out of me.

To further complicate things, I wore clip-in cycling shoes. Therefore, my feet were stuck in the pedals. As you can imagine, wherever I went, the bike also went—this made it impossible for me to jump off so suddenly.

My head was the first thing that hit the ground. Due to the impact, it bounced a few times off the asphalt. Next thing I knew, I become unconscious.

Whenever Heather tells the story of what happened, she often jokes to our family and friends that I was lucky that my head got hit first since there's nothing going on inside my brain. I digress.

I fell in a forward momentum as I skidded across the asphalt on my back. My legs were being cut by the bicycle chain and cranks. They were also bending in ways they really were never made to.

I then came to an abrupt stop. There was

blood everywhere. It looked like a murder scene, I'm sure. But what really scared Heather is the fact that I was struggling to breathe since the wind was knocked out of me by the force of the collision with the goose.

Even though I was unconscious, my body was trying desperately to get air into my lungs. I was making all kinds of weird and scary noises. Combined with the blood, I'm sure I looked like an absolute shit show. Heather called 911. They advised her not to perform CPR on me as my chest cavity might be compromised. The ambulance showed up, and I was rushed to the hospital with a very scared H-Bomb following the ambulance in my truck.

While the whole experience was painful—even the parts I was unconscious for—what really hurts are the emotional scars.

Frank still refers to me as "Goose" sometimes.

For a little while, whenever people I know would see me, they would honk like a goose at me.

But what really hurt is the fact that my colleagues started a "How is Dan going to hurt himself next?" pool game. For five dollars per entry, you could enter. Here are a few of my favourites.

"Dan is going to the circus this weekend. He's going to be injured in a stampede of some sort."

"Dan is going to a meeting. A bike courier is going to hit him."

"Dan is traveling in a plane. He will be in the washroom, the plane will hit turbulence, and he will fall upside down into the toilet bowl and be covered with nastiness."

I actually don't blame them for thinking this stuff up. I'm extremely prone to accidents. I mean, really? Who has ever, in the history of all time, been hit head on by a low flying goose while riding a bicycle?

Sadly, this shit only happens to me.

# 12 SAVING WHALES

I have a client who thinks the world of me. They want me to fly out to Nova Scotia to look at their buildings. It's early July, and I have almost fully recovered from Mr. Murphy and his low-flying goose. I ask Heather if she wants to come with me.

Nova Scotia in July is beautiful—no humidity, wonderful scenery, friendly people, great food.

"Danny Boy, I would love to go!" Heather says, flashing that amazing grin at me.

Heather has never been to the East Coast. But I have numerous times, and I can't wait to show her around.

Tankfordian goes to his favourite kennel for the five days while we are out east. The girls at the kennel treat him so well.

We fly out to Halifax, and I spend the first two days looking at real estate. Meanwhile, Heather keeps herself occupied by spending her time exploring Halifax and doing a bit of sightseeing.

We're staying in a luxurious hotel near the casino. After having a later-than-normal dinner, we take a short stroll to the casino. We're both dressed rather casually, likely too casually, but that's okay. As usual, we also had several drinks by this time, and we're caught up in our own little world. I love that about us.

Neither of us are big gamblers, but people-watching is always fun. We wander around, and then I see it—the slot machine that we're going to play. It's a one cent machine, and it's called "Asian Princess."

I whisper into Heather's ear, "See that Asian Princess slot machine? We're going to hit it hard!"

She whispers back, "How about hitting this

Asian Princess hard?" as she wiggles her tight ass in my general direction.

I grin at her and say, "Later. There's money to win now!"

I put a twenty dollar bill into the slot machine. I know the Asian Princess is going to be generous to us.

I press max bet—the bet is about $4.80. I know—we're such high rollers.

I tell Heather to pull the lever, and about ten seconds in, we learn that we just lost our first $4.80.

Heather looks nervous—she doesn't like losing money.

I press max bet, and I pull the lever this time—we always take turns pulling the lever as a way to experiment with our luck (perhaps we are a bit superstitious).

And then it happens. The lights start going off, and people are looking at us. The machine tells us that we just won 99,999 credits. We both look at each other with stupid grins on our drunken faces. Because we both have had a few drinks since we got to the casino, our math skills have diminished. Heather thinks it's $9,999, but I think it's $99.

We wait for a casino attendant to arrive. She looks at the machine and congratulates us on our win. She tells us that she will be back with our winnings and then disappears for a few minutes.

We both stare at each other with our stupid grins. The attendant returns—we've actually won $999.99. We tip the attendant a hundred dollar bill, and she thanks us graciously. Apparently, very few people tip the casino attendants anymore.

We have a few celebratory drinks at the casino bar with our winnings and then head back to our hotel room. Heather is busy texting anybody and everybody about our big win.

We hit the bed and have a sound sleep.

The next morning, we go for a ten-kilometer run at 6:00 am. The streets are still and quiet with minimal traffic. The only sound made in this crisp, airy morning are the calls from the seagulls as they hunt for their breakfast.

We go for a run at Point Pleasant Park—it's

breathtaking.

Heather loves Halifax. She's amazed by the hospitality of the people. East Coast people are a friendly group. No matter where we go, people always ask how we met. A young-looking Asian girl and a salt-and-pepper-haired man—there has to be a story there.

We regale people with our short story. Her version of events is likely more accurate.

"We met at a pub. This loser gray-haired old guy had a crazy shirt on and told funny jokes—he won my heart!"

We run back to the hotel and shower up for breakfast. The weather forecast calls for sun and a touch of humidity today. Heather decides she'll have a pampered morning and get her nails done.

I take off to do some apartment inspections, and I'm finished by mid-afternoon.

I come back to the hotel after finishing work and change into shorts and a t-shirt, then send a text to Heather, *Where you at, H-Bomb?*

No response. *She's likely still at the spa*, I

think. I haven't had lunch yet, so I wander down to the waterfront on the hunt for a pint and some awesome pub fare.

I eventually come across this one pub that has music turned all the way up with lots of university-age kids on the rooftop patio. I then hear a familiar voice singing karaoke. It's the H-Bomb. She's singing "Baby Got Back" by Sir Mix-a-Lot. The crowd definitely approves as they cheer her on.

I go into the building, walk up to the rooftop patio, and head over to the bar. I scan the bar for Heather, and it doesn't take long for her to catch my attention from across the room. She's wearing a white tank top, a fluorescent pink bra underneath, and cut-off jeans shorts that she says are somewhat "scandalous."

I order a beer and tell the bartender that I think the Asian girl who's singing is pretty hot, he concurs. I then ask him if he wants to bet me ten bucks that I can pick her up.

The bartender laughs at me and informs me that men have been hitting on her for the last hour and half. Nobody has had any success. I give him a ten dollar bill and walk over to Heather after she's done singing.

I just smirk at her, and she jumps into my arms. I kiss her nose and spin her around. I look over at the bartender and grin. He walks over and tries to give me a $20 bill. I tell him to keep his money. I would like to buy my new friend a drink though!

Heather has an amazing voice. I, on the other hand, can't sing a song well if my life depended on it.

Heather has about a dozen fans asking her to go up and sing again. She speaks with the DJ and requests a song.

In about ten minutes, the DJ calls her name, and she drags me up on the stage. *Oh crap, here I go*. People cheer us on. She's picked a song that I can at least sing, but not well, mind you. It's "Islands in the Stream" by Kenny Rogers and Dolly Parton.

We both get microphones. She grabs my

free hand and looks up at me with her amazing goofy grin.

*God, I love this girl so much,* I think to myself.

The song starts, and despite my horrible voice, people love it. I suspect it's our dynamic duo energy and primarily due to her voice.

Halfway through the song, I really look deep into her eyes.

I realize at that moment that she actually means the words she's singing, and that she's singing them to me. Her eyes close, and her hand squeezes my hand—her body gently sways to the music.

I'm caught flat-footed. I lose my voice. I can't sing.

Tears start to well up in my eyes. I hate it that I'm such a sucky baby.

When she realizes that I'm not singing my portion of the song, she opens her eyes and wipes away my tears with her fingers. She sings the rest of the song, staring into my eyes

I feel sick to my stomach and joy all at the same time. What an odd mix of feelings!

After the song is over, we walk to the bar to order drinks. Heather holds my hand and looks me in the eye.

"Daniel, you need to learn not to cry so much. It's embarrassing, but in a cute way," she tells me with a grin.

I just smile at her. Heather squeezes my hand tightly, stands on her toes, and whispers into my ear, "Danny Boy, one of the reasons I love you is because you're so in touch with your emotions!" And then she kisses my nose.

We spend the rest of the day at the pub on the waterfront.

Right before we're about to leave, the DJ asks Heather for one more song. They confer briefly on the side of the stage.

Heather looks at me and gives me her best shit-eating grin. I grin back at her.

She jumps on stage, grabs the microphone, and says, "Danny Boy, this song is dedicated to you!"

The young men who are her karaoke fans cheer her on with lots of catcalls and whistles.

Heather has picked a Jimmy Buffett cover of a Bob Marley song, "Waiting in Vain."

Whenever she begins to sing, she amazes me. She can actually sing a little reggae! She even decides to make up her own words to the song. She changes the words to reflect our relationship and how she feels she is waiting for me.

The crowd eats it up. People are up dancing and absolutely loving her performance. I love her energy. That's my H-Bomb!

I'm shocked. I listen to her words, and I'm now concerned about our relationship. I don't understand why she thinks she's waiting in vain for me.

She finishes the song, and her fans call for an encore. The DJ asks her to stay for one more song. Heather looks at me for my approval, and I nod my head. We have no other place to be.

Heather picks "Feel Like Makin' Love" by

Bad Company. She kills it.

I guess my love for cheesy 70s songs has rubbed off on her. It's likely that most people here have never heard of this song before. It sounds totally different when a woman is singing it. She dances during the song, and given the lyrics—her seductive dancing brings a lot of fan approval. Heather also changes a few words to this song as well; she's now singing the explicit version of it.

Her adoring fans just watch and cheer her on. Young men are professing their love for her in extremely graphic terms.

A fan jumps onto the stage suddenly and tries to dance with her. A security person removes him from the stage. It's like we're at a concert. I can't believe how many people think she's singing this song to them. I, on the other hand, know she's singing it to me.

She finishes and has her super shit-eating grin on her face. Blowing kisses to the crowd, she runs off the stage and over to me and suggests that now would be a good time to leave.

I agree. The amount of testosterone and youthful exuberance on the patio is fairly intense after her encore performance. I grab her hand as we leave the bar and head to the best seafood restaurant in Halifax.

Over dinner, I pose the following question to her, "Why do you think you're waiting in vain for me?"

H-Bomb suddenly appears, "Daniel, we've never had a relationship conversation. I want our relationship to be exclusive."

I look at Heather, "Um, you pretty much spend six days a week at my house. I'm not sure if either one of us has sufficient time to be dating somebody else. Unless you and the pool boy are dating…"

Heather reappears, "Good point, Danny Boy, and the pool boy isn't really my type!" she says as she grins at me.

We don't have a pool boy, unless you count Tank and myself.

I raise my eyebrow at her and tell her, "I

always assumed it was exclusive, given my injuries."

Heather smirks and says, "Grandpa, if I gave you a hundred percent of my attention, you likely would be dead in five minutes. You're that old!"

I just grin back at her.

On our way back to the hotel, we have to walk back through the casino. We stop at a few machines and lose about a hundred dollars..

Heather is pissed. I can tell she's getting close to going off on me in the 50-kiloton range.

I then see the slot machine that will make it up—it's called the "Frog Prince."

I grin at her and say, "Don't worry, the Frog Prince machine is going to be more generous to us than the Asian Princess. Because I'm your frog prince!" and I kiss her nose.

I push a twenty dollar bill into the machine and press max bet.

H-Bomb appears, "Daniel, please tell me you didn't just bet $17.25 on a single pull of a slot machine."

I look at the machine and realize then that it is a $0.25 slot machine and not a penny slot machine.

In slow motion, we watch the numbers go by. I am in so much trouble that I don't even want to consider what's going to happen next.

However, today, the luck gods are on my side. We somehow land five lily pads and go into the bonus round. The slot machine asks us to pick three of the seven different options.

I look at Heather and ask her to pick the first one. We win two times our bet.

I then pick the next lily pad, and then things get out of control. I select the grand prize, which means we win 13,700 credits. We don't even begin to do the math, given last night's mathematical issues.

We win $3,425!

We are given this amount in cash, and Heather becomes concerned. Of course, H-Bomb appears.

"We have a lot of money on us, and it isn't

safe. I don't like it, Daniel. It isn't safe to have this amount of money on us."

I smirk at her and tell her not to worry.

She doesn't know this yet, but I always walk around with fifteen hundred-dollar bills in my wallet in case shit happens.

We walk back to our hotel and deposit the money safely in our room.

After a nice, hot shower, I lie in bed watching TV. Heather jumps into bed and snuggles up to me.

"Heather, did you really think our relationship was fairly open, non-monogamous?" I ask.

"No. We just never had the 'official' talk about the dynamic of our relationship. Things just kind of progressed, you know? I need to know exactly where we stand with each other and how we feel about each other," she offers.

I just stare at her.

I'm actually a little hurt she doesn't understand how I feel about her. I thought I've shown my love to her all this time.

Her beautiful green eyes stare into my blue eyes for a few minutes.

She looks at me and grins, "Daniel, I'm just being stupid and insecure. Let's be real, you will never do better than me!"

I just grin at her and nod my head in agreement.

*God, I love this girl*, I think to myself for the millionth time.

The next day, we head to Cape Breton. I've booked a seaside cottage. It's just outside a small town called Judique.

I rented a convertible for the drive. I'm wearing my sunglasses, and Heather has a ball cap on with her hair in a ponytail. I feel like we're back in our early twenties as we coast along the highway without a single care in the world. She looks stunning, as always.

The geography of Nova Scotia is spectacular. Neither one of us strikes up a conversation, and I think it's beautiful just being in this moment with each other. Just me and Heather, being our complete natural selves as we listen to the music on the radio and watches the beautiful scenery go by through the windows. As always, I have a cheesy 70s station on. Satellite radio has a few stations that I enjoy.

A beauty comes on, and it's one of my favourites. I grab Heather's hand and grin at her. She puts her head on my shoulder, closes her eyes, and starts humming along to the song.

The song is by Don Williams. It's called "I Believe in You."

I kiss the top of her head—her hair smells good.

I wish I could convey to Heather how I feel during the song. Words escape me. The warmth of the sun, her hand in mine, what I feel when she squeezes my hand, the love we feel for each other. To the day I die, this will most likely be the highlight of my life.

We take our time driving to the cottage we rented. We don't really have any solid plans for the next few days other than a whale-watching tour that we signed up for. There were many different options to choose from, but we thought this would be a fun and unique experience.

We stop at Port Hawkesbury and grab lunch at a food truck. We both order fish and chips and find our spot at a picnic table. Heather grabs several whale-watching brochures from a tourism booth and examines them intently.

I love the fresh air, the smell of the ocean, and the sounds of the sea birds crying in the background. It's so peaceful.

I then feel a tremendous pain in my arm and let out a yell. My arm feels like it's being amputated! I see some sort of bug on my arm, and I try to hit it off, but it's too late.

Heather gives me a concerned look, "Are you growing weak in your old age, Grandpa?" she asks.

"A bug bit me, and it really hurt!" I tell her.

Heather looks at me, shakes her head, and goes back to reading her brochures.

Thirty seconds later, she shoots straight up and screams out, "Holy fuck! That does hurt!" as she rubs her leg. She has also been bitten now.

"I know, right!" I say to her.

We rapidly eat our lunch and, luckily, we avoid any additional amputations. We drive the last fifty kilometers to our cottage. Despite the distance, the drive doesn't feel long at all. We've already arrived. The lady who owns the cottage checks us in and informs us that the deer flies are really bad this year, and she kindly leaves us a container of bug spray in the cottage.

We both agree with her that the bugs are bad—Heather has a tremendous welt on her leg now, and my arm is swelling up.

Our cottage is quaint. It overlooks the beach and, while it's small in size, it totally suits us.

I had packed a cooler full of beer, water, and food, which I have now unpacked into the fridge. We sit at the dinner table inside the cottage and gaze at the ocean. Heather has an almost frozen can of beer resting against her thigh where she was bitten, and I have a cold can of beer resting against my arm.

I grin at her. "Welcome to the great outdoors!" I say.

"Danny Boy, this is horrible. I'm scared to go outside. Those bugs bite!" she tells me.

Little do we realize that Mr. Murphy is also vacationing with us. At least the good news is that if Mr. Murphy is also vacationing, so he won't cause me any further injuries. I should be scared, but at least I won't be injured.

The property we are staying at has several cottages. We see people on the beach, and all of them are pointing at the ocean. We're both intrigued and drench ourselves in commercial grade bug spray and decide that we'll go outside our cottage.

We walk hand in hand down to the beach. We then see whales in the ocean. They're within fifty feet of the beach. There are about twenty of them. We watch them for about fifteen minutes, it's amazing to see them swim around and jump in and out of the water. They appear to be such gentle creatures just enjoying a beautiful day.

The owner of the cottages appears and tells us that what we're seeing are pilot whales and that they appear almost every afternoon. They weigh about 2,500 pounds and are friendly toward humans.

Heather and I both smile at each other. We feel the whale tour tomorrow is going to be amazing.

We end up meeting a few of the people from the adjacent cottages, and they all seem to be pleasant people. The majority of them are from our city.

Heather is sitting on the picnic table looking at the ocean as I prepare dinner. Tonight's dinner is BBQ steaks, Caesar salad, and an assortment of grilled veggies.

As the sun is setting to the west, I take a picture of her. She's wearing one of my golf fleeces. The wind off the ocean tonight is chilly. The picture is amazing—it's her and her silhouette by the Atlantic Ocean with the sun setting in the background.

We eat dinner inside as the bugs are far too intense. Tonight, we dine in silence. We both watch the everchanging seascape through the bay window.

After dinner, I clean everything up and wash the dishes. Heather relaxes in a chair and stares intently at the ocean. She has never seen the ocean before, and she looks deep in thought.

I wonder what she's thinking.

It's now 9:00 pm, and I am exhausted. I look at Heather, and she's actually sound asleep in her chair. I try to wake her up, and she mumbles something about the fresh ocean air and how she's so sleepy. I pick her up and carry her to the bedroom. She's so exhausted that I have to help her undress. I help her under the blankets, and that's that. I can't wait to be sound asleep as soon as my head hits the pillow, it's been a long day.

I'm suddenly awakened by a not-so-gentle slap on the face by the H-Bomb. She's partially on top of me, screaming at me.

"Daniel, it's 11:00 am, and we never sleep

in this late! There has to be a carbon monoxide leak, we need to leave the cottage. It's not safe. Wake your fat old grandpa ass up, Daniel!"

I groggily wake up and start to comprehend what she is saying.

I'm slapped again in the face, much harder this time, "Daniel, we're slowly suffocating to death—we need to evacuate the cottage. We've slept in so late so there must be a carbon monoxide leak. Wake up!"

I burst into laughter.

Heather is now fully on top of me, and her face is two inches away from mine.

She then begins to pout.

"We aren't dying, are we?" she asks. She sounds disappointed somehow.

"No, H-Bomb, we aren't dying," I manage to get out between my laughs.

I explain to her that the cottages are seasonal, and they have no heat. Also, all the windows are open, so a beautiful breeze is blowing into the cottage.

I then explain to her that we are in a comfy king-size bed with a warm duvet and that the fresh air makes people tired. But the primary thing is that there is no noise. No cars driving by. No airplanes flying over. No people. Nothing but the gentle sound of the ocean.

Heather calms down, lies down beside me, and snuggles her tiny body against mine.

"Danny Boy, I was terrified that I didn't have your wheelchair with us so I would have to carry your fat old grandpa ass out of the cottage," she whispers into my ear and gives me a sleepy grin.

I slowly run my fingers through her hair. It relaxes both of us—we are both so sleepy. Sleeping in is also pretty great. I can tell by Heather's breathing that she has fallen asleep. I too fall asleep soon.

An hour later, we are abruptly woken up by screams of panic and fear just outside our cottage.

We hear, "Oh my God, what are we going to do?!"

"Somebody, please, call 911!"

We both jump out of bed and dress. We then grab our sunglasses and our phones. We're out of the cottage within thirty seconds.

I have learned a few things about police officers. Dark sunglasses are their friends. It allows you to look at a person or their surrounding environment without anyone knowing what you're looking at. It also allows you not to make direct eye contact with a person, which is considered an act of aggression by most animals.

The screams are coming from the beach. We walk down to the beach and see a crowd of about twenty people. There, fifteen pilot whales have somehow beached themselves. Some of the whales, because of the way they are shaped, are upside down and are slowly suffocating because their blow holes are in the sand.

The whales that are suffocating are spasming as they are in their death-throes.

Heather is in tears as she looks at me completely devastated.

"Daniel, we have to help the whales. It would break my heart if they died."

"Roger that, H-Bomb!" I wholeheartedly agree.

I grew up in the country on a farm. These whales are bigger than cattle, but not that much bigger. *I need to find a rope,* I think to myself.

I spot an old boat that is too far inland for the tide to touch. In it, I find two pieces of rope that are suitable both in length and strength, and I race back to the beach with them.

I grab Heather, and we race to the ocean shore and get to the first whale that is struggling. I manage to wrap one of the ropes around the tail of the struggling whale.

I stand right behind the whale, and Heather and I start pulling it off the beach and try to bring it back into the water. We can't move the whale—it weighs about 2,500 pounds.

I scream at the people watching us to help pull on the rope. They all look nervous. However, I appear to know what I am doing, and a few brave souls come down to help. With our combined strength and motivation, we are finally able to move the whale into water deep enough for it to be rolled over!

For some reason, I end up at the front end of the whale near its mouth. I look into its eyes. This whale's eyes are intelligent—he knows we are helping him. I pat the whale and talk to him. I tell him we got his back and that he's going to make it.

We have to drag the whale about four hundred feet out into the water so that it is deep enough for it to stay afloat. It's just Heather and me now, treading in the water. People want to help, but not in the deeper water. The water is about ten feet deep.

I swim to the back of the whale and untie the rope. Heather talks to the whale—she also notices how intelligent the eyes of this animal are. I swim back to the front.

The whale looks at us and lets out an unhappy yell. Heather and I look at each other—this may not have been the brightest thing we have done in our lives. We are with a large wild animal in ten feet of water.

The whale then starts to bump us back toward the beach.

We get the idea, Mr. Whale—go rescue your buddies. Roger that!

We spend the next four hours rescuing as many whales as we can. Sadly, two of the whales can't be saved.

As we drag each whale out into deeper water, the whales that have been rescued before come in and swim next to the newly rescued whale.

These animals could crush us by mistake, but they only make minimal contact with us. I feel deep down in my heart that they know we are helping them.

We drag the last whale out into the deeper water. I untie the rope around its tail; Heather is treading water beside me.

Then, a whale appears beside me and starts talking to me quietly. He gently bumps Heather and me a few times back toward the beach. We have no idea what he is saying. We both hope he isn't angry.

Heather and I are both a little concerned, so we start swimming back to shore.

The whale gently chirps at us and disappears.

We both look at each other in amazement as we swim back to shore.

When we get into shallow water, people clap and yell their approval. High fives are given all the way around.

We exchange emails with people who have taken pictures of us swimming with the whales and helping them off the beach.

We are both exhausted. We spent the last four hours in the cold Atlantic Ocean, and we have not eaten or drank anything today.

We stagger back to the cottage. Heather is cold and takes a hot shower for about thirty minutes. I change into dry clothing and try to create a meal out of our limited supplies. We had planned on grocery shopping for a few things today, but we are far too exhausted.

So, tonight, we are having a poor man's charcuterie plate. I find some beef jerky, pickles, generic cheese, a few packs of crackers, and some hot sauce.

I had put a six pack of beer in the freezer when Heather started her shower. The cans are ice-cold now.

I grab two, give her one, and take one for myself. We open them at the same time and clink cans.

We stare at each other for a few minutes as we drink the cold beer.

We're both grinning at each other. This shit could only happen to us.

As we nibble on our combined breakfast, lunch, and dinner, we both remember the craziness of the day and are strangely silent. We finish our meager meal, and I jump into the shower.

It's about 7:00 pm when I finish my shower and come out.

I walk into the bedroom and see that Heather is curled up in the bed under the duvet and sound asleep. She's actually snoring. When I hear her gentle snores, I know she is super tired.

I walk into the kitchen and grab another beer and find another small package of crackers.

I sit down on a chair in the bedroom and silently eat my crackers and drink my beer as I think about the day.

*I guess we don't need to go on a whale-watching tour now*, I think. I am pretty sure that we will never be any closer to whales than we were today.

Mr. Murphy was most certainly involved in today's events.

Heather is mumbling, or it might be the H-Bomb—they are both exhausted, so I'm not sure who is speaking—the voice is clearly tired and very quiet.

"Daniel, it was so hot that you took charge today, you need to be rewarded…"

I smirk at her and don't move. Within thirty seconds, Heather is sound asleep again. I get into the bed after I finish my beer and drift off to a very well-deserved sleep.

We sleep the best sleep of our lives—a well-deserved sleep for the champions.

I wake up, it's now 6:00 am. I hate being middle-aged. A washroom visit is imminent in my very near future.

Heather is exhausted. She's not going to move out of the bed any time soon. I make some coffee and walk outside.

I'm left with my thoughts as I sit on a picnic table looking at the ocean. I do this for two large cups of coffee. I contemplate many things—I work too much, I don't spend enough time with my aging family, I don't spend enough time with my friends.

Being away from work, emails, and cell phones are cathartic.

It's now 7:30. H-Bomb appears in her ninja dust manner. She has a blanket over her, and she sits on the picnic table. She grabs my coffee and warms herself from the cup.

We sit on the picnic table looking at the ocean. She has her head against my shoulder and slowly drinks my coffee.

I think to myself, *I am so lucky that I got to meet this girl. She makes my life so much better. I can't imagine not having her around.*

Sadly, my tears start flowing.

Not a lot though, just a bit.

Heather doesn't look at me, but offers this, "Daniel, I see and hear those tears. Whatever you're thinking about, stop it."

Long pause.

"I have something that will make you happy. I have nothing on under the blanket!"

I look at her, and she gives me her super shit-eating smirk.

"Danny Boy, that should stop the tears! Stop being an old man!" I'm told as I'm dragged back to the cottage by the most beautiful girl in the world.

That day, we drive around the Cabot Trail. The landscape is breathtaking. On one side of the road are mountains, on the other side is the ocean.

We return to Toronto without any further incident.

# 13 TRIP TO DISNEY WORLD

It's early November, and the weather is miserable—cold rain and wind. Trees have lost most of their leaves, and the landscape looks dreary and gray. I'm not a huge fan of March or November for this very reason.

The days are getting noticeably shorter, and when daylight-saving time kicks in, the days become darker sooner.

The last yearly quarter is my busiest time of year. I keep flying across the country to look at buildings, writing reports and communicating with clients. I'm literally working from 4:30 in the morning to 10:30 at night.

This year is different. Heather is essentially living at my house now. Unfortunately, she's working nights this week. She starts at 6:00 pm and finishes at 4:00 am. I normally get up at 4:30 am, but now I get up at 4:00 so that she has a nice breakfast waiting for her when she gets back to my place after work.

I wake up at 3:30—it's pouring rain, and it's super windy outside. *Just a miserable day*, I think to myself. I lay in bed, and Tank is snoring up a storm beside me. Tank sleeps in funny positions. This morning, his head is at my feet. He's lying on his back and is exposing his most intimate parts to me. I've never seen a dog sleep this way before, and he does it all the time. Obviously, he's incredibly trusting and comfortable with me and Heather.

All I really want to do is sleep in, as I've been burning the candle at both ends. However, I know it wouldn't be fair to Heather if I did that. I've promised her a delicious meal after such gruelling shifts.

I get up and start making breakfast for her

and decide on homemade tomato soup and grilled cheese, bacon, and spicy pickle sandwiches. They're Heather's favourites. The weather channel tells me that with the wind chill, the temperature is -3°C. It's an absolutely gloomy mess outside.

The soup is simmering, and the sandwiches are ready to be baked.

The front door opens, and a very wet and cold Heather enters the house. The walk from the driveway to the front door is only about forty feet. Heather is soaked from the rain, and she looks cold and miserable.

"Danny Boy, it smells so good in here! I'm soaked beneath the skin—it's pouring outside! The walk from my car to your front door is too far," she pouts.

I'm ready for this. I have a towel and some clothes for her at the front door. I help her out of her jacket, and then I start removing her pants—they're soaked from the rain.

"Oh, Danny Boy, what do you have in mind?" she purrs into my ear.

I just smile at her, "You, sitting in front of the fire with dry clothes on and a warm blanket wrapped around you!" I tell her.

Heather looks disappointed and puts on her pouty face. "Breakfast better be good then."

I take all her wet clothing down to the basement and hang them up to dry. It always amazes me how small her clothing is compared to mine.

Heather is sitting on a reclining chair and still pouting as she stares into the calming flames in the fireplace.

Today is her swing shift. She gets one day off, and then she works day shifts for five days straight. I have no idea how she does this—I could never. Her game plan for today is to stay up until 7:00 or 8:00 pm and then sleep through the night. Hopefully, her internal clock will recalibrate for the upcoming day shifts.

I ask her what she wants to drink. She asks for my special hot chocolate, which has peppermint and cinnamon liquor in it. It's roughly 4:30 now, this is her after-work, wind-down time. I make the hot chocolate for her and bring it to the living room.

Heather literally chugs the hot chocolate down and tells me she wants another one. I know my H-Bomb—I'd made two at once, and I immediately give her the next steaming cup.

She flashes her beautiful smile at me, "Danny Boy, you're learning!"

I just grin at her. I sit down on the floor beside her as we both stare into the fire. Heather runs her fingers through my hair as I lay my head on her lap. I find this so relaxing, I'm almost asleep. The warmth of the fire and her fingers running through my hair puts me into a trance.

I love this girl so much.

We spend the next half hour doing this. Tank is in front of us, his back against the warmth of the fire, and the only thing we hear are his gentle snores. I'm so sleepy. Heather's fingers gently run through my hair as she takes another sip of her hot chocolate.

It's one of those moments she and I

frequently share. I've never had them before or after Heather.

Her phone beeps once, and then it goes crazy. Beeps are occurring faster than the phone can beep. *Something big is up,* I think to myself.

Then, H-Bomb appears. "This is such fucking bullshit!" she exclaims.

I look at her quizzically—she looks furious. I wouldn't want to be on the receiving end of her wrath right now.

"Daniel, please get me my laptop right now," she commands me.

I jump to my feet and get her laptop from the dining room table. I then watch her type as fast as she can on her computer with one hand while sipping her hot chocolate. I now know Heather well enough that when she goes off like this, it isn't directed at me. I let her do her own thing. I'll find out what the issue is soon enough.

After she's done with her angry typing, I get the low-down of what's going on. Due to budget considerations, all vacation time must be used up by the end of the year, versus being carried over into the following year. If you don't take your vacation, you'll lose it.

I don't understand government bureaucracies. As an effort to "save money," they force their employees' hands. This is a prime example of what not to do. In this circumstance, any police officer who has any vacation time left will immediately book their vacation in the final six weeks of the year. In this particular year, because so many people have unused vacation time, the police service is forced to bring in people on double overtime, as they are short-staffed. So, as opposed to paying it out on a one-to-one basis, they pay it out on a two-to-one basis. Brilliant!

It's now about 6:00 am—it's time for me to start working. I head upstairs to my office and start going through my e-mails. I hear Heather downstairs. It sounds like she's cleaning the kitchen.

A few moments later, I sense her presence behind me. I don't turn around and look at her, but I say "Whatcha doing, H-Bomb?"

My chair is abruptly spun around. "How did you know I was behind you?" she demands. Her face is now two inches away from mine.

"I just did. I don't know, Heather."

Once again, she begins to pout. "Your old age is rubbing off on me, Grandpa. I'm losing my edge. I used to be stealthy, now I'm old and washed up like you!" I'm told.

I raise an eyebrow, "Heather... what have you done?" I ask her.

"I hope you aren't mad, but I booked us a trip to Florida. We leave in eight days." She's staring at me with puppy-dog eyes, the same kind of eyes as Tank when he's done something mischievous.

Heather and I fight infrequently. She knows this is my busiest time of year. I also know that I work far too much and could likely benefit from some sunshine and less work. My flash of anger passes. *Who wouldn't want to go to Florida with a pretty girl?* I think to myself.

I rearrange my work schedule and pack my laptop with me—just in case.

Two days before we go, I get dragged out on a shopping trip for clothes. Heather wants to buy a few new bikinis for the trip. As always, I get a few photos. The bikinis are pretty small, and they leave little to the imagination. She looks stunning.

I am now super excited about the trip. The sunshine, the beach, exploring with Heather—this is going to be fun. I can't wait!

The plan is to spend four days at Disney World and four days at the beach. Heather has never been to Florida before, but she has always talked about wanting to visit.

I haven't been there in years.

The first day we're there, I discover something. In my youth, I had loved roller coasters—but not so much now. I'm terrified. While we're on our first ride, I actually bruise both of my palms because I'm literally hanging on for dear life.

I try to hide my fear, but Heather notices it.

"Grandpa, are you scared of the rides?" she

asks.

I try to act brave. I know the rides are safe and nothing bad is going to happen to me. However, my lizard brain is telling me not to get on the rides as an act of self-preservation.

The next ride terrifies me. It's indoors and almost completely dark. You can't see which way you're going because you can't see anything—all you feel is being tossed left, right, up, down, on your side or upside down.

Heather senses my fear and grabs my hand before the ride starts.

"Danny Boy, your hand is shaking. Are you that scared?"

Before I can answer her, the lights go out. For the next three minutes, we scream through the entire ride. We're most likely going at a hundred kilometers an hour. I close my eyes and think to myself that I will get through this ride without vomiting or urinating in my pants.

The ride comes to an end. I'm still shaking, and I have a hard time walking down the staircase—that's how frightened I am.

My fear has not gone unnoticed. The H-Bomb is all-seeing and all-knowing, and she isn't happy with me.

"Daniel, why didn't you tell me the rides bother you that much? I wouldn't have asked you to get on them if I knew how much they bothered you. Daniel… Daniel, we're in a relationship and I don't want you to hide things from me. I am all-seeing and all-knowing. I will find out. I always do."

I respond with my standard "Yes, Heather," as I stare at my shoes. I just want to keep her happy, that's all.

Heather grabs my bruised hands and stares up into my blue eyes with her green ones for about twenty seconds.

She slaps my ass and gives me her wonderful goofy grin, "Grandpa, I knew I should have packed adult diapers for the trip because you're so old!" We then walk around the park, enjoying the beautiful weather.

When Heather finds a ride she wants to go

on, we stand in line together, and then I let her go off on her own. I don't mind watching her from afar, she looks funny upside down.

She's a super good sport about it, but I'm teased.

While we eat our lunch, I see her looking at her phone and then looking up at me with a mischievous grin on her beautiful face. I know she's up to something. My phone beeps.

Heather has texted the gang a picture of me from after we got off the last ride I was on. I don't look good. I'm flushed and sweaty. I also appear to have a lovely tinge of green to my skin and look like I am about five seconds away from vomiting all over myself.

The picture is followed by this text, *This is Dan after the second ride of the day on day one of our vacation. I'm pretty sure he wet himself, he was that scared. He is sooooo old that he can't handle roller coasters anymore!*

Of course, the boys pile on. Within thirty seconds, everybody suggests that I'm likely eligible to be in a nursing home. To make things worse, they even tease that people are going to buy shares from the company that makes adult diapers.

I do receive one text from a friend who will remain unnamed—he also shares a dislike for roller coasters now. Funny thing is, he's actually twelve years younger than I am.

For the next four days, we spend all day walking around, sampling food, and enjoying the sun. Maybe I'm old, but it's better than being upside down until I turn green!

On the fourth day of our trip, we decide to spend the morning at the waterpark. The forecast is calling for sun and heat, which, combined with the waterpark, likely means we're in for an amazing day.

We're in the hotel room and are getting ready to go to the water park. Heather puts on one of her new bikinis and stares in the mirror.

She looks ridiculously hot, and there really isn't a lot covering her. The one thing that intrigues me about her is that despite her confidence, she has moments of self-doubt.

"I'm not sure if I can pull this bikini off," she says as she turns around and examines her body from all angles in the mirror.

I'm not sure if she is speaking to me or talking aloud to herself.

I start to clap—she gives me a fierce H-Bomb look.

"What are you clapping about, Grandpa? Are you stroking out over there?"

I burst out laughing, "Heather, you look so fucking hot. And, yes, you are causing me to have a stroke!"

Heather beams back at me.

"Okay, Danny Boy, stroke-causing is the look I'm going for! Why don't we play dress up, and we can finish with you deciding what I am going to wear today?" She smirks at me.

I choose a pair of cut-off jean shorts and a white shirt tied-up, a total Daisy Duke style. The white shirt contrasts with her tanned skin beautifully. To that, I add her aviator sunglasses.

I take a step back and admire my clothing selection. Heather looks incredibly sexy today. Her flat stomach is on display and shows more than a hint of her six-pack abs.

From our hotel, it's about a thirty-minute walk to the water park. Heather gets stared at the entire time—eyes follow her everywhere we go. There's literally a crowd of men following us.

When we first started dating, the unwanted attention directed at her sort of bothered me. We had a serious conversation about it.

"Danny Boy, I've been dealing with this my entire life. And yes, sometimes it does bother me. But I would rather have the attention than the alternative in which men run away from me because I repulse them. For our relationship to work, you'll have to put your insecurity and male bravado aside and always remember one thing. I am with you, not them. Always remember that, Danny Boy—I go home with you everyday," she'd reassured me.

It's a sound strategy. From that point in time, I didn't let other people's actions bother me.

However, today is one of those challenging days.

We stake out two chairs close to the lazy log ride. It's now about 10:30 am, and we're going on the first ride of the day. We both enjoy the lazy log ride. It takes about half an hour to float back to our chairs. We comfortably sit there, minding our own business, and then it begins. A bunch of men in their late twenties and early thirties start catcalling Heather.

"Hey, baby, why don't you come over here and sit on my face, and I'll guess your weight!" the leader of the group yells at Heather.

We both choose to ignore them in hopes that the off-side comments will cease.

For the next hour or so, the group keeps on getting louder and more obnoxious. It's clear to me that they've been drinking heavily, and it's still morning. Between the sun, alcohol, and lack of food, I suspect they're probably resistant to pain.

My gut's telling me that this isn't going to end well. I suggest to Heather perhaps we should move and get away from them. She agrees. We pick up our stuff and find a quiet corner at least a ten-minute walking distance from the group.

We're now sitting near a waterslide that drops almost 150 feet straight down. People come zipping out of the slide and skip across the water like a stone that's being thrown.

It looks like a lot of fun, so we proceed to go down the slide a few times. We're both killing ourselves laughing.

All of a sudden, Heather has an odd look on her face. I know exactly what is wrong. It's noon, and she's hungry.

"I'm starved!" I'm told. "Come on, Grandpa, I'll buy you lunch! Because you've been a good boy today, I'll even let you have a cheeseburger with fries and an ice-cold beer." She flashes her goofy grin at me.

We sit in the shade while we eat our lunch and drink our beer.

"OMG! That beer was so good, I sure could have another one!" Heather informs me.

Off I go to buy two more ice-cold beers. As

I'm being served, I hear a commotion behind me. I pay the bartender and slowly start walking back to the table. Heather is now standing—it's not Heather though. It's the H-Bomb, and she's pissed. If I had to hazard a guess, based on the vein in her head, she's going to go off in the 75-kiloton range.

It's the group of men who were giving Heather a hard time earlier.

I didn't catch what the leader of the group said, but it clearly ticked off the H-Bomb. I stand back to watch the gong show that's going to occur. You never want to go into a battle of the wits unarmed. This guy is clearly unarmed, and he's going to be slaughtered.

It always amazes me that people think they can out chirp a police officer. Police officers bear the brunt of so many insults that it usually rolls off them no problem.

I have no idea what this man has said to Heather, but I know she's going to vaporize him.

"What's your name, honey?" Heather asks the guy.

He thinks he's got it made—his crew catcall at him and cheer him on. I know where this is going, and it isn't going to be pretty.

"It's Greg, baby. I want to smash your hot little body. Come on, baby, let's party!" and he reaches out and attempts to grab Heather's ass.

*Greg, that's a painful mistake you just made*, I think to myself.

Before his hand could even reach close to her rear, Heather grabs his hand and starts twisting it in a submission hold. Greg drops to his knees, he's in tremendous pain, and he's screaming. His crew are now strangely quiet.

Heather then lays into him verbally, "Greg, baby, let me tell you something. Men who talk the way you do always have small cocks. I mean really small—gerbil-like. You talk a good game to make up for your lack of size. I get it, no man wants to admit they have a small tool, and I mean a really small tool. That's okay, though. You see, I'm so hot and way out of your league, that it really doesn't matter. You don't stand any kind of chance with me."

Heather is just getting warmed up now. I take a sip of beer, enjoying the gong show in front of me. Heather has lessened her grip on Greg's arm. He's now able to talk.

"Let go of my hand, you fucking little Asian bitch!" he spits out at Heather.

Ah! Greg, my friend, that was a fatal mistake.

Heather cranks his hand one more time, and Greg yells out in pain.

"Greg, baby, you have no game and potentially have the smallest cock that the world has ever seen. You should never speak that way to anybody. You're acting like a bully, and I fucking hate bullies!"

Heather begins to crank Greg's hand even more. He's once again screaming in pain. His buddies are in shock. They don't know what to do. One of them takes a step toward Heather but decides against trying to help his friend.

"Greg, baby, you need to be punished for

your behaviour today—it was rude. Greg, admit to me you have a small cock."

Heather starts really twisting Greg's hand. He's in agony.

Heather turns to his friends, "You guys better film this. Today, Greg is going to tell us the truth about how small his cock is."

His friends pull out their phones and start filming.

Heather then gets Greg to admit to a lot of his failings—small cock, low intelligence, bad posture, and dirty teeth. The last thing he does on film for his buddies is the best. Heather has let go of his hand, but by now, she's in charge of the situation. Greg begins to recite and act out "I'm a Little Teapot." You know how the song and the moves go. Kids eat this song up. I'm killing myself laughing.

Heather then tells Greg, "Greg, baby, please go away with your small calibre weapon. Last thing, you better hope I don't see you again." She then blows him a kiss.

Greg looks crushed.

Greg and his crew scuttle off with their tails between their legs. I just look at Heather and laugh and tell her what an impressive performance it was.

I make a toast to her, "To the most badass person I know!" She grins at me and drinks her beer.

The H-Bomb strikes again.

# 14 A DIRTY WEEKEND AWAY

Heather still has a few days of vacation she needs to use up. We plan a trip—a four-day mid-week trip to a ski resort in Vermont. Neither of us ski, but the idea of being at a ski resort and walking in the woods, snowshoeing, snow tubing, and drinking hot chocolate sounds like fun.

Both of us are still quite tanned from our time in Florida. From my place, it's about a nine-hour drive to the ski resort where we're staying.

We've never been to Vermont. Based on our little research, it's extremely scenic and quite mountainous—the views appear promising. We luck out, as the weather Gods are on our side. For the entire duration of the drive, we have sunshine and clear roads.

We arrive at the resort, check in, and decide to have dinner at the lobby bar.

Heather, as always, looks stunning. Tonight, she's wearing pink runners, a pair of tight jeans, and a white sweater. Her hair is down, and she's wearing her usual amazing, toothy grin. We stroll out of the elevator holding hands and walk over to the lobby bar. As we expected, it's rammed with skiers and snowboarders trying to unwind after a beautiful day on the slopes.

We find a table for two beside a fireplace. Heather has brought the hotel amenity guide with her and is intently researching things to do over the next few days.

Our drinks arrive, and Heather continues her research as I stare into the flames. Unwinding after the nine-hour drive, I'm having a Zen moment. Being warm and cozy with my favourite person in the world right now, I don't have a single concern in my mind.

A few minutes later, I'm snapped out of my

state of trance. Heather suddenly grabs my hand.

I look up at her, and she looks absolutely thrilled.

"Oh my fucks, Dan, they have a heated outdoor Olympic-size pool!" she exclaims.

"Well, it's a good thing we brought our beach gear," I respond back.

"Oh, I want to go tubing! And then I want hot chocolate outside around the bonfire. Oh, then we'll go snowshoeing, and then…"

I just grin at Heather. I love it when she gets excited about doing something. I grab her small hand and give it a squeeze.

Heather looks up at me and gives me her super shit-eating grin. "Too much?" she asks.

"No, of course not. It all sounds great!" I respond back.

Dinner goes as usual—we enjoy ourselves over casual conversation and delicious food. The heat from the fireplace makes both of us sleepy. We pay our bill and head back to our room, crawl into bed, and are quickly asleep.

We get up around 6:00 am and hit the gym. Nothing too strenuous, just light weights and a quick run on the treadmill.

We shower and grab breakfast around 7:30. I never understand hotel breakfast buffets. They're expensive for pretty basic items, and I never get my money's worth. Heather, on the other hand, does get her money's worth. She kills a breakfast buffet like nobody I know.

I always make fun of her "Asian belly," as I call it. One Thanksgiving, I made a full-on turkey dinner for her family. Turkey, stuffing, roasted root vegetables, scalloped potatoes, salad, and a huge selection of appetizers. I even planked brie cheese with sun-dried tomatoes, olive oil, honey, garlic, and a variety of berries on a BBQ.

There were no leftovers!

Heather's dad was super impressed. From that point on, I was in charge of "western cooking," as he called it, for her family functions.

Today, Heather has us booked for a couple's massage in the morning. I've never been to a spa before. What an amazing experience, this is the most relaxed I've ever been.

While we're at the spa, we're served lunch and a few drinks.

It's about 2:00 by the time we finish at the spa. Heather wants to travel to the peak of the mountain, and I definitely think that it's time for an adventure after our pampering session. *I wonder what it'll look like from the top,* I think to myself as we hop on the chair lift.

Today, it's extremely cold—almost a new cold record is set. We're dressed appropriately, but we're absolutely freezing on the chair lift as we're moving further and further away from the ground. Halfway up the mountain on our ride, we run into a fog bank. The fog is so thick, I literally can't see Heather although she is sitting less than a foot away from me.

It's like we're on an alien planet, I'm sure there are plenty of skiers and snowboarders just below us, but it really feels like there are no other signs of life besides us. The fog muffles all sound, and it is a little eerie. Heather slides over to me and snuggles up against me. She whispers into my ear, "Danny Boy, do you want to make out?"

I just look at her and grin.

I kiss her nose, and she grins back me.

We reach the summit, and it's odd. We're now above the cloud line, and the fog has pretty much cleared. We look down at the clouds, and we can't see the base of the mountain. We wander around the peak of the mountain, taking in the sights and watching people ski and snowboard.

About an hour later, we take the chair lift back down the mountain. The both of us are starting to get really cold.

"H-Bomb, why don't we hit the heated outdoor pool?" I ask her.

"Danny Boy, you are in for a treat!" she declares.

"Why's that, H-Bomb?"

"I am going to rock a special bikini for you!" I am informed.

We just grin at each other.

We head back to our hotel room and change into our swimwear. Heather emerges from the washroom with the hotel-supplied fluffy housecoat on.

She just smirks at me.

We head down to the outdoor pool and are surprised to find that the stone area surrounding the pool is also heated. This resort has really thought of everything. I put our towels down on a chair, and Heather hands me the housecoat she's wearing.

I just grin stupidly at her.

She's wearing a white bikini that I've never seen before. I'm pretty sure the amount of material it consists of likely wouldn't cover one of my hands. Because she's still so tanned from our Florida trip, the bikini contrasts dramatically with her skin.

Heather immediately races toward the pool and yells, "Cannonball!"

As she surfaces, she playfully splashes at me, "Danny Boy, the water is so warm. Jump in!"

I dive into the pool, and I'm shocked at how

warm the water is. It's almost a hot tub type of heat.

We're in the pool for about five minutes when a waiter approaches us.

"Would you like anything from the bar?" we're asked.

Heather immediately pipes up, "I'll have a Cosmo, and the old guy over there will have a beer!"

The waiter scuttles off and returns with our drinks in plastic cups.

Heather and I both grin at each other. This is awesome—being outside on a cold day in a heated pool by ourselves with bar service!

Could life ever get better than this?

We spend the next half hour swimming around and chatting about nothing, as we often do.

The temperature suddenly dips. According to the display board, we're at -20 degrees Celsius.

Because the water is so warm and the air so cold, fog begins to develop as the two elements meet. We can't even see the other end of the pool.

Our waiter has disappeared. I guess it is too

cold for him to come out.

Being the gentleman that I am, I offer to go inside and get us more drinks. Just as I get inside the door, the waiter appears and asks if we would like another round. I tell him we would and then go back outside.

The fog from the pool has intensified, and combined with the setting sun, I can barely make out Heather's form in the pool. As I walk back, she surfaces from the water and grins mischievously.

"Danny Boy, somehow, my bikini fell off my body. How do you feel about that?"

I just grin at her, and she treads water in front of me as I enjoy the view.

As we're both lost in each other's stares, the moment is ruined shortly thereafter when four twenty-somethings show up at the opposite end of the pool.

We hear them scream, "Cannon ball!" and splash into the water seconds later.

H-Bomb appears then.

"Oh my god, Daniel! You need to find my

bikini, I think it's floating in the pool. I need my bikini! Do you understand me, Daniel?!" she commands me in a state of panic.

Of course, Heather's bikini is in the shallow end of the pool right beside the four twenty-somethings.

I retrieve her swimsuit, but not before the young men stare at me with disbelief.

"Gentlemen, my friend apparently had a tragic wardrobe malfunction," I tell them.

I give Heather her bikini, and she now struggles to put it back on while treading water in the deep end of the pool.

She quietly curses me to no end. I just grin at her.

To add insult to H-Bomb's injury, we have to walk by the guys to get back inside the hotel.

One of the guys looks at us and says to his buddies, "Damn, I wish I could have seen that tragic wardrobe malfunction."

I just grin at her—she looks angry for a split second and then flashes her goofy grin back at me and gives me a high five.

"Quick thinking, Danny Boy!"

We're both exhausted. So, we decide to have room service dinner in our hotel room. The food is fantastic. We sit in front of the fireplace as we eat silently while watching a replay of last weekend's football game.

I've always felt that if two people can sit in silence and not feel pressured to speak, it's likely a solid relationship.

Tomorrow is our last full day at the resort before we leave for home. We have a lot planned. On the other hand, Mr. Murphy has something else planned for me—we're going bowling, and, sadly, I am going to be the pin.

The day starts off innocently enough. Good breakfast, hot coffee, and wonderful conversation.

After breakfast, we go back to our hotel room and get ready for the day.

Today, Heather is feeling mischievous.

She's wearing her cute pink and white winter boots, black snow pants, and a colourful winter jacket. She looks extra adorable in her bunny hat that her mother knitted her.

Her mother is ingenious—she buys fleece hats and then knits a cover for them and sews them together. You get the warmth of a good hat combined with a cute animal for fashion. Because of her attire and her youthful appearance, she appears to be much younger than she is.

We go outside and head over to the tube run. The tube run is a decent-sized hill with a track carved into it. Riders get into a tube and shoot down the hill through the course, stopping at the bottom. The ride lasts for about three minutes, and it's lots of fun.

We stand in line to rent our tube. I thought Heather would want each of us to have our own tube due to her competitive nature, but we eventually decide on a two-person tube so we can experience the fun together.

As we get to the front of the line, I recognize the rental cashier at the tube station. He's one of the kids from the pool last night when Heather had her "tragic wardrobe malfunction."

He smiles at us. "Good morning, folks, it's a lovely day to be out on the slopes."

I ask for the two-person tube and pass the money for it to the kid.

He then states positively, "Sir, I think it's such a nice thing for you to be taking your adopted daughter out tubing today."

I can't tell if he's being cheeky or if he's actually serious. I look at him and ask him how old he thinks my "adopted daughter" is.

"Perhaps twelve," he states.

H-Bomb isn't having anything of this.

She takes off her hat and literally stomps her feet.

"I'm thirty-two years old! What's wrong with you?" she asks him.

The kid and I start to giggle, and Heather looks me dead in the eyes.

"Daniel, you aren't helping. Stop giggling!"

The kid then has the ultimate a-ha moment. He remembers us from last night.

He doesn't know what to say. He's turning red. He then sputters out, "I'm so sorry. I remember you from the pool last night. You are so hot!"

I burst out laughing.

Heather just glares at him.

*Poor kid didn't realize he was teasing the hot girl he saw from last night*, I think to myself.

He gives us the tube, and we sit down on the chair lift and head to the top of the hill.

We spend the whole morning speeding down the hill and then heading back to the summit with lots of laughs and grins at each other.

Heather informs me that she's feeling a little cool would like this to be the last run of the day before lunch.

We complete the last run, and as we're walking back to return the tube, she's a few steps ahead of me. She looks at me and says, "Wait, Grandpa, I think I see a cool photo. Stop right there."

Heather whips out her phone and says, "I want a photo of you putting your finger on top of the mountain peak."

You know those photos that people take? It looks like the person is either holding something up or pushing it down. It's kind of lame and cheesy, but hey, why not.

It's a simple request, so I put the tube down and start taking directions from Heather.

"Danny Boy, back up a few steps and turn a bit to the left... no, the other left. Move your hand up a bit, not too much... down a bit."

This goes on for about thirty seconds. I'm hungry, and my patience is wearing thin.

"Heather, for the love of God, just take the photo, will you? I am hungry!" I tell her.

Mr. Murphy is lurking at the ski hill today. He doesn't like the tone of my last statement, and he's going to teach me a lesson on how I need to be more patient when dealing with the most beautiful girl in the world.

Today, Mr. Murphy is going to teach me to be more respectful to Heather.

I'm going to learn this in one of the hardest

ways possible.

Despite my less-than-ideal patience level, Heather is able to snap the perfect picture.

It's now Mr. Murphy's turn.

A split second after Heather takes the photo, a group of kids on a tube collide with me. I'm tossed in the air, and I land on my head.

I'm knocked unconscious.

I wake up to members of the ski patrol and Heather looking at me as they wait for an ambulance.

Heather looks worried.

I try to sit up, but I can't move. I've been immobilized on a backboard in case I've broken my neck. I struggle to get up. I'm told not to make any movements as I have a serious injury.

H-Bomb takes charge.

"Daniel, stop moving. You've been unconscious for almost ten minutes. You've been badly injured. Badly injured, Daniel. Stop moving and sit still or I'll get mad. I know you don't want to make me mad. Daniel, please stop moving."

I look up at Heather and see a few tears streaming down her face.

I've been injured before and seen her looking concerned. But I've never seen her in tears before.

*I better listen to her*, I think to myself.

I stop struggling and lie still like a good boy.

The ambulance appears, and I'm stretchered over to it.

Heather jumps into the back of the ambulance and holds my hand as we're rushed to the hospital.

As I lie in the back of the ambulance pondering that I might have broken my neck, I do a body scan. I can wiggle my toes. I can feel them pushing against the inside of my boots. I know I can move my fingers as I give Heather's hand a squeeze.

I look up at her and tell her, "I can move my toes and fingers, so that's a good sign. Right?"

Her green eyes stare into my blue eyes, and I see more tears streaming down her face.

I think to myself, *I better man up here.*

"Heather, I'm fine. I likely have a concussion. I feel pain but I can move my fingers and toes," I tell her.

Her eyes then avert mine. That's not like her. I give her hand a squeeze and ask her, "Kiddo, what aren't you telling me?"

The ambulance attendant shakes her head at Heather.

"Nothing, Danny Boy. Nothing. Have I told you how much I love you today?"

Heather then looks away from me because she can't maintain eye contact. She starts sobbing.

*Oh shit,* I think to myself. *I'm seriously fucked up.*

I keep occasionally squeezing her hand and telling her not to worry about me.

What they're keeping from me is that my head is at about a 45-degree angle from where it should be. It can't be straightened.

We arrive at the hospital after a thirty-minute ambulance ride.

I'm rushed to the emergency room, and several doctors and nurses cut off my clothing. I find myself now lying naked in front of a group of people, the majority of whom are females.

I'm not really too concerned about my neck at this point in time. My concern relates to the size of my penis. I'm not overly blessed with girth or length.

This is embarrassing to no end. Why does this shit happen to me?

The doctors and nurses appear to be speaking a different language, it seems to me. While at the same time, they're speaking English. They follow whatever protocol they're supposed to follow with a neck injury.

I occasionally glimpse at Heather in the background. To say she looks concerned is an understatement.

"Check if the patient can wiggle his toes."

I'm asked to wiggle my toes.

"Check if the patient can squeeze his hand."

A doctor holds my hands and tells me to

squeeze her hands.

I'm asked where the pain is.

I jokingly tell them this really is a pain in my neck and that I would like to leave shortly.

My attempt at humour falls on deaf ears.

I'm then taken for a CAT scan and an MRI.

I learn that I have a concussion and, wait for it...

A dislocated spine.

I didn't realize a person could dislocate their spine.

It's as painful as it sounds.

The emergency room doctor calls the on-call chiropractor, and they review my MRIs.

Heather and I are told the good news—no lasting damage, but they have to adjust my spine so that it resets properly.

They can't give me anything for the pain, but to say that adjustment was painful is an understatement.

It's difficult to accurately remember everything that happened. There was a searing pain in my neck and a loud pop, and everything was back in place.

Heather would later tell me she knew it really must have hurt because I turned pale and grunted.

We are now faced with our next challenge. All of my clothing had been cut off of me. All I have on is a hospital gown. Even my boots were cut off.

There's only limited taxi service in this small town, and it's now past 8:00 pm at night. The cab company closes at 9:00 pm, we are informed.

Heather races down to the hospital gift store and finds me a pair of shorts. Unfortunately, they are an extra small. I most certainly don't fit properly into a pair of extra small shorts. She also purchases a pair of grandpa slippers, as I call them.

As I get dressed, I look in the mirror of the washroom. I look strong. Hospital gown, check. Shorts that look like they're gym shorts from the 1970's, check.

The pièce de résistance is my cute grandpa

slippers.

We manage to hail a cab and get a lift back to the resort.

The cab driver asks what happened.

Heather pipes up, "Tragic photography accident."

The cab driver just stares at us from the rear-view mirror.

My phone buzzes. It's a text from Frank.

*Brother, are you okay? The H-Bomb scared the shit out of a bunch of us today. How the fuck did you dislocate your spine?*

I can't tell the boys it was a tragic photography or a tubing accident.

I make up a lie. It's legendary. I'm not sure if anybody ever questions Heather about it, for obvious reasons.

"Man, don't tell anybody this. She's a freak in the bedroom, and I couldn't remember my safe word," is my response back to Frank.

Frank responds back with "Ah, man, take care of yourself. You're getting old, lol!"

## 15 I NEVER HAVE BEEN TO SPAIN

Heather is gradually spending more time at my house than at her condo. According to her, the primary reason she's coming over is that I know how to cook, and she loves Tank.

If those are the only reasons she's hanging around, I don't really believe her.

Heather really hasn't traveled that much other than our trips together, so I decide to take her on another vacation. I've decided on a ten-day trip to Spain.

I've planned five days of touring and five days of sitting on a beach on the Mediterranean. Heather rocks a bikini like nobody I know. I'm grinning just daydreaming about her in a bikini, and we aren't leaving for another six weeks.

As I'm packing her lunch, I write the following on a sticky note, "Well, I never been to Spain." It's a song by Three Dog Night.

On the back of the note I write, "Do you want to go? Open the envelope." In the envelope are our tickets. I put all of this into her lunch bag.

Around 10:30 am, I get a text from her. It reads, *Are you serious?*

I respond back, *Those are real tickets, so, yes!*

I get a happy-face text back and, *I'm so excited! I haven't been to Europe before. I am going to need to go shopping for pretty things.* For a woman whose job requires her to be both physically and mentally tough, Heather likes to maintain her soft feminine side.

Shopping with her is always an adventure. I always get a few snapshots from the changing room. The first time we go lingerie-shopping together, she sends me a photo of her wearing a cute coral pink bra and a matching thong. God, she looks so hot, she really could be a model.

The picture was followed by this text from the H-Bomb:

*Daniel, this picture is for your personal enjoyment only and is not to be shared with anybody. If I find out you have forwarded it to anybody, I will insert my collapsible baton in every body orifice you have. Daniel, do you understand what I am saying?*

I respond back with, *Not to be shared with anybody else. Roger that, Heather.*

She then responds back with a happy face and sends me a few more photos.

I grin.

Her next text is a not-so-subtle reminder, *Daniel, not to be shared, especially with Frank. My baton in your orifices. I will find out if you do.*

There is no doubt in my mind that she would find out. It must be the police officer in her. She finds everything out. I'm an open book with most people I know, but Heather knows me inside out.

The trip to Spain goes well. We have a ton of fun exploring the countryside. However, the trip is marred with "The Incident", as Heather and I call it.

One afternoon, it starts raining, and we spend it having lots of fun in our hotel room. It's getting close to dinner time, and I decide I want to take a shower. The shower is so large, you likely could get six or seven people in it. The look and feel of it is super modern, and the walls are all glass.

The night before, I watched Heather shower. She knew I was watching her, and she put on a bit of a show for me.

I start having a shower, and all of sudden, she joins me. I have shampoo in my hair and my eyes are closed. She's timed this perfectly. She starts lathering my body with soap, and things progress from there.

After we finish showering, she tries to open the shower door, but it won't open. It appears to be stuck. Heather, being strong-willed, isn't going to be defeated by a shower door. She pulls really hard on it, and the door comes past the plastic that prevents it from swinging inward. At this point, we both realize that the door is supposed to be pushed open and not pulled open.

We are now trapped in the shower.

She turns to me, "Daniel, you need to figure out how to get us out of the shower. If I turn into a prune, I will not be happy."

She then goes into the corner of the shower and pouts.

*Just lovely*, I think. *I'm trapped in a shower with a beautiful naked girl, and she's unhappy. Story of my life.*

I spend the next hour scheming on how to get us out of the shower. maybe I can lift Heather over the glass closure. No, that wouldn't work, I'm not tall enough.

I try pushing the door in both directions. It won't move.

Heather is looking less happy as each minute goes by.

We have only one option. We need to force

the door open and likely break the glass, if necessary, to get out.

I explain my plan to Heather. I'm going to push hard enough on the door so that it either goes back past the plastic tabs or it breaks. I get her to stand as far away as possible from the shower door. I will sacrifice my feet for hers.

I start slamming my shoulder into the door. All the glass panels are rattling violently. I look back at Heather. She looks really nervous.

"I am going to hit it really hard this time," I tell her.

I walk back as far as I can in the shower and lower my shoulder. I'm literally doing a football block. I smash into the door, and it gets past the plastic stops. Shockingly, it does not break.

My shoulder hurts quite a bit, and it's bruised for the rest of the trip.

Heather casually strolls out of the shower, grins at me, and slaps my ass. "Good save, Danny Boy!" I'm told.

# 16 FIGHT NIGHT

One evening after dinner, Heather and I are cleaning up in the kitchen, and she looks over at me with a mischievous smile.

"Danny Boy, I may have volunteered you for a fundraising event in three months. I hope you don't mind helping."

"Anything for you, Heather. What will I be doing?" I ask.

Her smile gets bigger. Whatever she has planned for me, she's super excited even just by the thought of it. I get excited just watching her get excited.

She claps her small hands and gives me this

big grin, "We need somebody to box at 155 pounds in the annual Police Charity Boxing Event!"

I then learn a valuable life lesson. Never agree to volunteer for something until you know what you are volunteering for.

For the next three months, I train like a madman to make weight. I normally walk around at 180 pounds, but I actually manage to get down to 155 pounds fairly easily. One day, while I'm in the shower, Heather joins me. She's looking at me. I now rock a nice six pack.

"Daniel, I love your six pack. But you're all veiny, and you have no ass. I don't like veins, Daniel. It looks like you need to be back in the morgue shortly," H-Bomb informs me.

"I'm not sure what I can do about that, H-Bomb. You volunteered me. You've been training me," I point out.

Heather returns. "Good point, Danny Boy." She slaps my ass and gives me her amazing grin.

I train really hard, day and night, on my own and with Heather. I've been participating in mixed martial arts for about ten years now. I've sparred before, but I've never really fought. I'm way too accident-prone to actually fight.

At the age of forty, I'm about to have my first amateur fight.

My opponent is a well-meaning person from the ambulance service. On the night of the fight, he can't make weight. He sees me, and just doesn't want to fight. I'm cool with that. I really don't want to fight either.

Heather is bitterly disappointed. She wanders over to one of the officials, and I see her having an animated conversation with him. The official looks a little confused—he looks at me and shakes his head.

Heather comes back and informs me that she's off to find me another opponent. Then, she's gone. I don't see her for a little while.

Meanwhile, Frank keeps me company. He's bored. He's texting on his phone. We hear fans cheering. There are about 2,500 people out tonight to raise money for a variety of worthy organizations. Frank wants to be out there watching the boxing and not stuck back here with me.

My hands have been taped and my gloves are on. I'm not a boxer. I'm more of a Muay Thai fighter. "Fighter" is likely too strong a word for what I am. In any event, I'm fighting barefoot tonight, and boxers wear shoes. I'm hoping for an intimation factor, I guess. Or I could be wrong, who knows?

My fight is scheduled to be one of the last fights of the night. I still have about an hour and a half wait.

Frank's phone starts beeping—he's getting a bunch of texts in quick succession.

I hear him muttering, "Fucking Ramos—that girl is stacked!" I later learn that Heather has asked him to run out and buy her a sports bra and short shorts.

"Okay, Dan, I have to run out and go buy a few things." He then gives me a big hug and says, "Brother, I love you. Just remember I am not involved in this."

He runs off. *That was a very odd goodbye*, I think.

Then, Smith shows up. His fight lasted about six seconds. He punched his opponent once in the face and it was over.

He has this strange smirk about him.

"I volunteered to fight you, but everybody said that would be unfair. Heather found you a new opponent. I'm pretty sure your new fight isn't going to be any fairer. Do you have your MMA gloves with you?" He asks.

"I do, but what's going on?" I'm now getting a little worried. I know a little of everything, but I'm an incredibly inexperienced and very old white belt in Jiu jitsu.

"Take your boxing gloves off, and I'll re-tape your hands for your MMA gloves. We don't have a lot of time. You're up after the next fight." Smith rapidly tapes my hands.

"Who am I fighting?" I ask.

Smith just smirks. "This is going to be fucking epic! I can't wait to watch the gong show that's going to happen," he states.

I'm taped up and have my MMA gloves on now. An official comes back and asks me if I'm ready.

I confirm I am.

There is a hierarchy at these events. As they are police events, the police fighter always enters last. There are entrance songs and everything—they go all out for this event. The front row tickets get sold for almost a $1,000 each.

I'm advised that I am no longer entering last. I'm entering first. I now know that I am about to face a police officer as my opponent. I'm asked what entrance song I want played, and I say none. I'll walk out without music and by myself.

Where are Heather and Frank? I fear I'm about to walk out by myself. I'm beginning to feel nervous, but I'm also getting revved up. I feel everything at once, all at the same time.

My adrenaline is surging. An official holds me at the entrance of the door. He'll give me the signal to enter the room.

I hear the announcer, "Ladies and Gentlemen, we have had a change in our fight card tonight. I am pleased to announce that the last fight of the evening will be a mixed martial art fight in the open division!"

The crowd roars. This is something new and unexpected. The crowd is on their feet. People are screaming for more blood and action.

For those who don't know, the open division is an unlimited weight class. You can have somebody my size fighting somebody Smith's size.

I know this isn't going to end well for me.

I really don't like this. I have butterflies in my stomach. I have a feeling I'm going to be fighting Smith.

I think to myself, *where is Heather*? Frank suddenly appears beside me, and he's out of breath.

"Sorry, Dan, I've been running around buying some stuff. Don't worry, you aren't walking out by yourself."

The official tells us to go. The crowd is screaming. People high-five me as we walk out.

The crowd is excited. Open weight class fights don't happen very often. I walk up to the ring.

The officials want to see my mouthguard. Check.

"Do you have a soft jock on?" I'm asked.

I nod, and then I'm up inside the ring by myself.

Frank is up in my corner—he looks nervous. He's giving me some water, and I have my back to where my opponent is going enter.

The lights get turned down low. A familiar song starts.

I hear drums.

Boom. Boom. Boom.

The crowd is going crazy. Based on the way they're losing their shit this late in the evening, I'm pretty sure the alcohol is helping.

Then, a scary-sounding guitar entrance is heard.

It's "Iron Man" by Black Sabbath.

I now know exactly who I will be fighting tonight. It's Smith. I'm going to be destroyed by him. I'm going to have a broken face.

Fuck. Why would Heather let this happen?

I look at Frank. He looks back nervously at me and says, "Hey, Dan, they put me up to this. This isn't fair to you, I know. But it's her, man. I'm so sorry."

I don't turn around. I already know it's Smith. I just look down at the ground. Frank puts a bag of ice on the back of my neck to keep me cool.

Then, the lyrics to the entrance song start. It's a familiar voice. It's mine.

I am singing her entrance song. The crowd thinks it's Black Sabbath's Iron Man—however, I know it's me. The opening verse starts this way:

I am the H-Bomb

I am very fine looking.

I am all-seeing and knowing

She can shop at the mall,

Or online if she feels like it.

I made this song up when I got my new computer. I did a little remixing for Heather and created it. She loves it. It's on all of her playlists.

I turn around, and I see her racing out of the entrance to the ring. Smith is her cornerman. He's trying to catch up. Holy shit—I'm fighting Heather.

The crowd is going into a frenzy. I can't believe I'm about to compete against the H-Bomb, in a fight! I'm not sure how this is going to go down, but I really don't want to fight her. I'm at least seven inches taller and fifty pounds heavier than her.

I don't stand a chance.

I turn to look at Frank, "I'm not fighting her, Frank. No way, man. Not going to happen."

H-Bomb knows I won't fight her. She's all-seeing and all-knowing.

She has prepared for this eventuality. Frank shows me his conversation with Heather on his phone:

"Heather, he won't fight you."

"Franklin, Daniel has a choice. He can fight me here with a referee in charge or tonight at home with no referee. The decision is his regarding where he wants to fight. But we are fighting tonight, one

252

way or the other."

The H-Bomb has spoken.

Frank looks at me and whispers, "I am so sorry. Good luck!" He jumps down and off the ring.

The announcer starts with his shtick.

"Let's welcome the fighter in the red corner... this man is making his debut fight tonight! He's a mixed martial arts fighter. He's from Caledon East. He weighs 155 pounds and stands at 5'9" – Dan Hayes!"

The crowd is fairly quiet. Then, the announcer gets his best big fight entrance voice.

"*This* woman has a black belt in Jujitsu. She is also a Muay Thai fighter. She has a professional record of 3 wins and 0 losses, all by knockout. She stands at 5'2" and weighs 102 pounds – Heather 'The H-Bomb' Ramos!"

I would say that at least half the people here tonight know her. Chants of "H-Bomb" are roared and echoed throughout the stadium.

She just stares at me. She looks angrier than I have ever seen her before.

I have developed a rating scale on her level of anger by judging the vein on her forehead. It's off the charts tonight. I often joke with Frank about her levels of anger. Normally, Heather is at a five-kiloton explosion range or at a maximum of 15-kiloton explosion range. Tonight, she's off the top end of the scale. She's well past the 100-kiloton explosion range.

We meet in the middle of the ring. The referee explains the rules. It's going to be five three-minute rounds.

Heather just glares at me.

I smile at her. I attempt to touch gloves with her, she won't even do that.

The referee directs us back to our respective corners. The crowd cheers, but I don't hear this. In my head, my thoughts are consumed by how angry I am with her. I hate this predicament she's set us up for. *Why do this to me?* I think.

I don't want to fight her, but what choice do I have?

You never want to give somebody no option,

no way out. Heather has made a mistake in her game plan. I realize I have no option. I must go out and fight her.

The fight is going to start in a matter of seconds. I start slowing my breathing as I have been trained to do for years.

My game plan develops. I'm going old school on her. I'm going to force her to move my weight around, which will tire her out. I'm going to stay out of her range or be uptight real close to her and I'll lean on her. I'll use my weight and reach advantage to tire her out.

The referee asks each of us, "Are you ready?" I nod. She nods.

"Fight!"

We approach slowly. She knows how I would normally start a fight. I have it choreographed. A few left jabs to my opponent's face, not really making contact, a right cross to the head, a side-step to the left, left hook to the liver, right hook to the belly, another left hook to the liver and a left jab back out.

She's waiting for this—I throw two left jabs,

and she's ready to knee me when I drop down for the liver shot. Her lead leg is planted firmly. She's anticipating what I will do. I have a few tricks up my sleeve. I launch a short kick, and my shin collides with her inner thigh.

The sound of my shin colliding with her thigh is a solid slap.

I look at her. She grimaces—I know that it hurt.

I start moving forward, using my reach advantage. I continue to give her left jabs and right crosses so she can't touch me. I start pushing her toward the corner.

Smith is screaming at her, "Take him to the ground, take him to the ground!"

I get H-Bomb backed into the corner, and I start leaning on her. She starts trying to knee me in my legs, and because I'm taller, it's easier for me to block her knee strikes.

People who have never trained don't realize that there's a lot of math involved in fighting. Leverage is very important. My body is just longer than hers, so I win the battle of leverage naturally.

We continue to exchange blows. She then tries a roundhouse kick to my head. I get my arm up to block it, and there's a big slapping sound. She's head hunting now. If that kick had made contact with my head, I likely would have been knocked out.

The round ends. I go to my corner where Frank is. He gives me water and puts ice on the back of my neck. He's screaming at me, "I can't believe you made it through the first round! You got this! You can beat her!"

Round two starts, and I follow the same game plan. I can tell she's getting tired. We both exchange blows again. I see an opening, and I kick the thigh of her planted leg where I had kicked her in the first round. This time, it really hurts her, and she changes to a Southpaw stance, which is left-handed. I know that her leg is really sore now. I back her up into the corner. I start attacking her hurt leg. I lean on her.

The bell rings and we go to our respective corners.

Frank greets me with a hug, "Oh my God,

Dan, this is the best fight I have ever seen. You guys are just whaling on each other!"

I'm beginning to feel tired. Secretly, I'm enjoying this in a weird way. I'm literally having the shit beaten out of me by a girl I love.

People are screaming and yelling their approval.

I look at Heather. She looks exhausted. Smith is speaking into her ear. I know what the plan is—she's tired but she still wants to go to the ground, where her skill set is far stronger than mine.

But I have a secret weapon that she doesn't know about. For some reason, I excel at sprawl drills. A sprawl drill is when one fighter lunges at the other person's legs. The defender pushes his legs back and then leans on the attacker.

Given my size and reach advantage, she won't be able to grab my leg or arms, and this should minimize her superior ground skills.

Round three starts as expected—she lunges at me and I sprawl on her. I lean on her for about ten seconds. If you have never rolled (Jiu Jitsu training), you can't even begin to understand how exhausting it is for the person struggling. She's struggling with literally 150% of her body weight on top of her.

This goes back and forth for the next two minutes. I transition to side control, and I quickly place my elbows on her left side, one on her hip and one just under her underarm. My left knee is against her hip on the right side. I then begin to knee-strike her with my right knee—not super hard, but hard enough that I feel the wind coming out of her each time my knee makes contact with her ribs.

The bell rings then, and that's the end of Round three.

I go to the corner—Frank is now losing his shit. "You have her! You have her! Oh my God, H-Bomb is going down!" He's yelling and screaming out of joy.

I sit on my stool. I'm so exhausted I can hardly sip my water bottle. I look at Heather, she looks as tired as I am. Smith yells into her ear, because the crowd is so loud.

We make eye contact. She gives me her super

shit-eating grin. I smile back at her. We're good.

Round four starts. We get to the middle of the ring, and she holds her hand out to fist bump. We fist bump and go at it. Round four starts and finishes similar to Round three, except my nose is now bleeding a bit, and I have a small cut on my forehead from Heather's leather gloves.

I sit down on my stool, and Frank is putting ice on my neck. He isn't saying anything, which is unlike him. However, I know he's confident in me. He looks at me and just shakes his head and laughs, "Go get her, champ!"

Round five starts. We're both exhausted.

My sprawl drill is crazy weak now because of how tired I am. We go to the ground, and she grabs my arm, and I end up in an arm bar. Heather cranks my arm until it's ready to break. She screams at me to tap out. I won't though.

I know another secret of hers. She will never break my arm.

I struggle and land a few punches on her stomach. She curls up a bit and briefly lets go of her grip on my arm.

Sometimes, when we're in bed, we wrestle. My ground game has improved dramatically over the last year.

I somehow end up behind her in the rear-naked choke position. There is no way for her to get out. Even though I'm tired, I could choke her out.

I feel her body sigh. She knows I'm going to choke her out, but she won't tap. She's prepared to be choked out. I start tightening my grip—I am lying on my back, and she's on top of me. My arms are wrapped around her neck and head, my legs are pinning her legs down. It's the perfect setup. I likely could choke her out in seconds.

But I don't.

I roll over, and she is now below me. I stand up and walk backward a few steps and tell her to get up.

There are thirty seconds left in the fight.

She gets up, and she's a little pissed that I didn't choke her out.

Then, for the next thirty seconds, we punch,

kick, knee and elbow each other.

The bell rings. We're bruised, bloodied, and exhausted.

We collapse to our knees and start making out in middle of the ring. The crowd goes crazy.

We wait in the middle of the ring with the referee for the official announcement.

The announcer says, "Ladies and Gentlemen, the 1st judge scores this match a draw. The 2nd judge also scores this match a draw, and the 3rd judge also scores this match a draw. This fight has been scored a unanimous draw."

*Wow*, I think to myself, *we tied.* That rarely ever happens. Heather grabs me, and we start making out again. She whispers into my ear about how turned on she is and the things that she wants to do to me later on at home.

At that precise moment, our photograph is taken. The picture is amazing. It has a special spot in my picture collection.

We win fight of the night, and we donate the $1,000 prize back to the police charity.

# 17 CAMPING

It's mid summer, and Heather and I both have some vacation time left to use up. On a beautiful Sunday afternoon, we head over to our favourite pub and sit on the patio.

Our plan is to discuss our options in vacation destinations.

We have a few drinks and blue-sky a few ideas. Our vacation ideas vary widely. A trip to Europe would be fun again, or perhaps a trip to Asia.

I've brought a pen and some scratch paper. I scribble down all our ideas.

I have a brainstorm. As we can't make up

our minds, I suggest taking the decision-making out of our hands.

I fold up each piece of paper with a destination on it and put it into a glass that the bartender has provided us.

We then ask the bartender to pick one piece of paper out of the twenty or so in the cup. He draws out one and reads it aloud.

"Camping at Large Bear Park," he proudly announces.

Heather and I both grin at each other.

"Danny Boy, I've never camped before! I am super excited to be camping with you!" Heather tells me excitedly.

We then start preparing for our camping trip.

I haven't camped in more than a decade. I've either given away or lost most of my camping gear. I decide that we should buy new gear.

Heather and I decide to visit an outdoor store to pick up some items. The selection of camping gear there is huge. There is one problem though.

Heather is super precise about selecting new camping gear. The colours of all the gear need to coordinate with one another. Whenever Heather goes shopping, she buys outfits in a colour coordinated fashion. From her panties and bra to her shirt, pants, and shoes. Everything is purchased together and are normally only worn as the complete outfit. Rarely are they mixed and matched.

Heather's condo is literally a walk-in closet.

At one point in time, we have six different tents and eight sleeping bags in our cart. After six hours, we finally decide on a tent, our two sleeping bags, along with other items. Heather is satisfied that our choices are sufficiently colour coordinated according to her taste.

We end up purchasing almost $1,200 worth of new gear.

Heather turns to me and says, "Who knew it was going to be so expensive to get colour coordinated camping gear?"

I just shake my head and grin at her.

"Danny Boy, there isn't enough time for me to buy my new camping outfits today. We will have to do that tomorrow," I am informed.

It's now early autumn, and we've booked a site at the park.

We take Tank to the kennel, and I then pack my truck. We have all our camping gear plus our mountain bikes in the back of my truck. I ensure everything is secured, and off we go.

Large Bear Park is a four-hour drive north of where we live. The weather is beautiful for early autumn. According to the park's website, the water is still warm enough to swim in.

As we check in at the park, Heather picks up a few brochures. We drive to our campsite, where H-Bomb shows up, and she isn't happy with me.

"What the fuck does "be bear smart" mean? Please tell me there aren't large bears in the park. I don't like bears, they eat people. I'm so small, I'd likely be just an appetizer for a large bear! I don't like bears, Daniel," I'm informed.

"Um Heather, why do you think it's called

Large Bear Park?" I ask her.

Sometimes, people can't see the forest for all the trees.

Heather just pouts, glaring at me.

"Stupid whitey with his camping idea—now we're going to be eaten by bears in the wilderness. It's a good thing I can run faster than he can. He's so fat, it'll take a bear at least a day to eat him."

I don't say anything to Heather. I know her well enough to let her pout for a little while and get over it.

I find our campsite and begin to unload our gear. Heather has disappeared. After a few minutes of searching, I find her.

She's is standing on the picnic table in our campsite with a scowl on her face Every few seconds, like a hawk, she rotates around like she's on watch.

I am now struggling to set up our tent. It's a two-person job at best.

"What are you looking for?" I finally ask her.

"I am on the lookout for bears—large bears. Some idiot took me camping where there are large bears. Do you know who that idiot is? This girl is not going to be eaten by a large bear."

I grin at her.

Heather begins to pout once again. "We aren't in danger of getting eaten by large bears, are we?"

"No, H-Bomb. We aren't in any danger as long as we're smart about making sure our garbage is disposed properly and we store all our food in the cooler in the truck," I tell her.

Heather slowly descends from the picnic table. I suspect she doesn't believe me, but I'm sure she will, soon enough.

It takes us a few hours to set up the campsite to our satisfaction. We have a cooking area near the fire pit. The picnic table serves as an eating and food prep area. Our lawn chairs are set up, and the firewood is neatly piled near the fire pit. Everything looks shipshape.

Because it is fairly late in the camping year,

the park is only about ten percent full. We don't see any other campers in sight.

It's now halfway between lunch and dinner. I suggest to Heather we go for a bike ride around the park. We ride through the park checking out the various sights, and out of the corner of my eye, I glimpse a streak of white.

I stop my bike and motion Heather to stop and be quiet.

She glares at me and whispers, "Daniel, you promised we wouldn't be eaten by large bears. You see a bear, don't you?"

I make a shushing sound at her.

After a minute, Heather sees what I see. Four whitetail deer appear out of the forest and are now walking toward us.

Because we aren't moving, they get so close we can almost touch them.

I look at Heather, and she has a look of amazement on her face. She's never seen a wild deer before. As for myself, I saw all types of animals growing up in the countryside, but I've never been this close to any type of deer. We spend almost thirty minutes silently watching them. The deer are stocking up on food for the long winter ahead of them.

In her ninja-like manner, Heather slowly pulls out her phone and takes several closeup photos of the deer.

The deer now sense that more humans could be near them and they wander back deeper into the woods to hide for a little while.

Heather has a big goofy grin on her face, "Danny Boy, that was amazing! I love camping!"

I smile back at her, and we head back to our campsite.

I start prepping food for an early dinner tonight, as we haven't had lunch yet.

Heather gets two cans of beers out of the cooler and opens both of them for us.

For tonight's dinner, I'm making barbecue cheeseburgers with an Asian salad with sesame ginger dressing and two different types of nuts in it.

Heather sits at the picnic table and watches

me prepare the food, and all of a sudden, she hisses at me, "Daniel, there's a striped, brown rat sitting on the picnic table, and he's watching us. I don't like rats!"

I look over and see a friendly-looking chipmunk staring at us. I'm sure he knows I'm an easy score.

I explain to Heather that it isn't a rat but a chipmunk, and they are super friendly little guys. I name him Chipper the Chipmunk.

I gently roll a few nuts his way, and he gladly scampers over and stuffs his mouth full of nuts, almost to the point where it looks like his mouth is going to burst.

Heather howls at him, "Danny Boy, oh my God, Chipper looks ridiculous! How can he stuff any more nuts into his mouth?"

Chipper scampers off and hides his new-found treasures. He returns in about five minutes. I greet him with a "Hello, Chipper!"

Heather is suspicious. "Danny Boy, how do you know it's Chipper? He likely told his chipmunk buddies that you're an easy mark, and now there'll be a lineup of chipmunks seeking welfare nuts!"

I respond back, "See that scar on his right hind leg? That's how I know it's Chipper. He likely got into a fight with another animal that wanted to eat him, but he managed to escape."

Heather looks at me and then at poor Chipper. Heather likes to protect people and animals—while it's her job, it's also who she is.

I know what's going through her mind—she wants to look after Chipper to the best of her ability while we're here.

Before I start dinner, I show her a trick.

I sit on a lawn chair and place a nut on my hiking boot, a nut on my knee, and a nut on my hand while it rests on the top of my leg.

Heather looks at me, puzzled.

I tell her to just watch how smart Chipper is. In about thirty seconds, Chipper takes the nut off my boot and puts it in his mouth. He then climbs up my leg and stuffs the nut resting on my knee into his mouth, then he scampers up and sits in my hand

and starts munching on that nut.

Heather looks amazed and impressed. Chipper even lets me scratch him between his ears. He's is content with sitting in my hand for a few moments.

Heather asks me if he would do that for her. First, I show her how to place the nuts on her leg. A few minutes later, Chipper is eating nuts out of her hand. I take several pictures of her and her new furry friend.

In the photos, Heather has this look of amazement and wonder. It's like she's a little kid again. She immediately emails the photos to a few people—her parents think that Chipper the Chipmunk is hysterical.

I goofily grin at her, and she responds back with her equally goofy grin.

Chipper the Chipmunk and Heather become good friends over the next few days.

After dinner, we sit in front of the bonfire and stare into it. Both of us sit silent for about an hour, enjoying the smell of wood smoke and the crackle of the flames. Around 10:00 pm, we both start yawning and head into the tent.

Having camped before, I know the best way to set up the tent. I've inflated a large air mattress that essentially covers the entire floor. We both get ready for bed in the dark. I've positioned my sleeping bag on the right side of the air mattress and Heather's on the left.

In the dark, as I attempt to navigate into my sleeping bag, and find the most beautiful girl in the world has stolen my sleeping bag! *Not a big deal*, I think. I turn to move over to her sleeping bag, and I hear this.

"Danny Boy, what are you doing? I have a gift for you inside your sleeping bag... me! And I barely have anything on!" she teasingly informs me.

Unfortunately for me, I had bought winter-weight sleeping bags that are only made for one person. I spend about a minute struggling to join Heather in my sleeping bag and sadly realize that the both of us won't fit into it.

"Don't worry, I have a plan." I tell Heather.

I unzip both sleeping bags and lay down one the bottom and use the other one as a duvet. As I snuggle in beside Heather, I give her a big hug.

H-Bomb appears suddenly.

"You smell like wood smoke...wood smoke, Daniel. I don't like you smelling like wood smoke! I like you smelling like you, Daniel," I am informed.

"H-Bomb, we both smell like wood smoke. We were sitting around the fire," I respond in a matter-of-fact tone.

Heather is silent for a moment. Next thing I know, I'm violently rolled over onto my back, and H-Bomb is now lying on top of me. Tonight, the sky is clear, and it's almost a full moon. I see her giving me an angry look.

"Are you saying I smell? I don't smell, Daniel. I don't smell!"

Heather rolls off me and faces her back toward me while she begins to pout.

*Great,* I think to myself, *I should learn to keep my mouth shut.*

We both drift off to sleep, and halfway through the night, I'm violently woken up by Heather.

"What the fuck is that noise?" I'm asked.

I listen intently. I don't hear anything.

"Likely just the wind, Heather, it's nothing to worry about," I sleepily respond.

"Daniel, I heard something fucking big moving. Big like a big hungry bear who is coming to eat us!" she hisses loudly.

I once again listen intently. I then hear it. There's an animal, or animals, in our campsite. I hear them rustling around.

I'm now silently alarmed. I know I put the garbage away and stored our food in the cooler in the cab of my truck.

The animals begin to fight—there are howls and screams of pain.

Heather is gripping me tightly and shaking violently—she's a city girl, after all—and I realize how terrified she is.

The howling and fighting continues for

another thirty seconds, and then, there's dead silence.

I whisper to Heather, "I have to go outside and see what's going on. Get dressed and be prepared to run to the truck. Here are the keys."

We both dress quickly.

"Get ready, Heather. I'm going out first with the flashlight to see what's going on. If I tell you to run, run! Okay?"

There's no response from her other than her hand tightly gripping my elbow, and I feel it shaking.

I unzip the tent, turn on the flashlight, and shine into the darkness.

I see eight gleaming sets of eyes staring back at me from the top of the picnic table. Racoons!

I notice they're eating something, I move toward them, and they scamper back into the night. I move closer to the picnic table and see they were eating nuts.

Odd. I'm pretty sure I put the bag of nuts

back in the cooler, which is now in my truck.

Heather grabs me by my elbow—her hand is still shaking slightly.

I look at her. She holds both of my hands and starts staring at her shoes. Well, this is an odd turn of events, she's never done this before.

"Danny Boy, don't be mad at me. I didn't want Chipper to be hungry tonight, so I hid nuts on the picnic table for him…"

Mystery solved!

I firmly grip her hand and push her chin up with my other hand and stare into her beautiful green eyes for a few moments. I then kiss her nose.

"No worries, Heather. Go back to bed, and I'll just clean up the remaining nuts. You can give them to Chipper tomorrow morning," I tell her.

Heather wanders back into the tent, and I clean up the nuts. She must have left half the bag for Chipper!

I get back to the tent, and to my surprise, Heather isn't there. I assume she's walked over to the washroom facility, which is a short walk away. I climb under the sleeping bag and am about to drift off to sleep when I'm suddenly attacked by a wild animal.

I am attempting to fight off the animal when I hear these words whispered huskily into my ear, "Stop it, Danny Boy. You need to be rewarded for my stupidity, and you resisting me is so turning me on..."

Heather had been sitting silently in the corner of the tent, waiting for me to drift off to sleep so she could ambush me.

The next morning, I examine my body. I look at the claw and bite marks Heather has inflicted on me, and damn, they hurt! I look like I've been attacked by a small bear!

We spend the next few days exploring the park and just generally enjoying the beautiful autumn. Chipper keeps us company whenever we're at the campsite. Heather now even brings water to Chipper when she feeds him.

Chipper seems to be fattening up nicely just over the last few days.

It's our fourth day camping, and we need to make a quick run to the nearest town to pick up a few odds and ends.

This town is about a half-hour drive south of our campsite, and we arrive at around 9:00 am. We park at the grocery store and pick up our supplies.

This morning is beautiful, it's about ten degrees Celsius. We decide to walk around the downtown core and have a look at a few of the quaint little stores they have there.

We hold hands as we enjoy a quiet morning stroll throughout the small downtown core while sipping our coffees.

A police car drives by slowly, and the driver takes a long hard look at us. It takes a left at the stoplight, but it makes its way around and drives by us again. This time, the officer really slows down and directly stares at us.

"Hey, Heather, that officer is taking an interest in us," I tell her.

"Danny Boy, I think he's taking an interest in me because of how hot I am," she grins at me.

The police car pulls into a parking spot ahead of us. The officer gets out of his cruiser and starts walking toward us. He has a big grin on his face. Heather is oblivious to all of this.

The officer is now within thirty feet of us. Heather is staring into the window of a store that sells pets and pet supplies. She's looking at puppies and is wondering aloud if it's time to get Tank a brother or sister.

"Heather Ramos! I haven't seen you since police college! How are you doing, H-Bomb?" the officer says.

Heather cranks her head around to see who's called her name, and her face immediately lights up.

"David Brown, oh my God! I haven't seen you in years! How are you doing?" Heather screams out and rushes to embrace the police officer.

Hugs are exchanged, and they banter for a few minutes. I'm kept out of the conversation for almost five minutes.

"Oh my God, I'm so rude! Dave, please meet Dan. He's my boyfriend! We've been dating for about a year and a half!" Heather says to Dave.

I hold out my hand to shake, and all I receive is a glare. No extended hand.

*Fuck,* I think to myself. *Why do I think this is going to end up in a misunderstanding?*

Heather turns to Dave. "David, Daniel is the love of my life. All of my boys have accepted him with only minor issues. Franklin introduced us— you remember Franklin, right? He was in our graduating class. So, you better treat Daniel well, or else!"

"Love of your life, and Frank introduced you guys?" Dave answers with a weird look on his face.

"Yes, David, the love of my life!" Heather responds back.

"Damn, H-bomb, really? That's amazing!"

David then gives me a huge bear hug.

David then tells us that he's very happy for the both of us. He also whispers into my ear that Heather is very special and that I need to be on my best behaviour with her at all times.

I ignore that quasi threat. I know there are several of my own friends who would hurt me immediately if I wasn't good to her.

The list of people who would hurt me just keeps getting longer!

We return to the park after speaking with Dave for about two hours.

This morning is our final day at the park. We take a one last long walk around the park before we need to pack up.

I've packed up most of our camping gear for our return to the city. Heather is sitting at the picnic table deeply engrossed in a conversation with Chipper. I catch the tail end of it.

"Chipper, you need to be safe. There are wild animals around here that want to eat you, and there are humans who aren't as friendly as Danny Boy and me. I need you to be safe, Chipper! Daniel tells me it wouldn't be fair to you if we took you home with us as you likely have a chipmunk family that needs you. Chipper, please be safe!"

Chipper stares at Heather for about ten

seconds and then scampers off.

Heather looks at me, and she's almost in tears.

"I don't like to cry. Only you and chipmunks make me cry… so stop it!"

Heather then walks over to my truck and sits in the passenger seat, and I see her using a few tissues to wipe the tears away.

I grin at her. Clearly my country boy lifestyle is rubbing off on her.

# 18 MOVING IN TOGETHER

It's getting close to Christmas—one of my most favourite times of the year. I always install lots of Christmas lights inside and outside my house. If you fly over my house in a plane, it is likely it would stand out.

My job requires me to regularly travel for work. In any given year, I take about twenty-five trips a year. It's early December, and I must fly out to the West Coast to look at a few buildings.

Heather stays at my house when I travel now. It's far easier on Tank. While he does love doggy day care, he's not a huge fan of staying overnight.

It's about 5:00 am, and I'm waiting for my cab to pick me up. Heather is awake, and she's having a coffee with me as I wait.

She asks me a random question, "Danny Boy, I would like to drive your truck when you're gone. Is that okay?"

"Of course it is, Heather, you never have to ask. I know how much you like driving it," I respond.

Her face lights up. I honestly know how much she likes driving it. It also makes our lives easier to haul Tank around. He just walks into the truck and doesn't have to be lifted in. Not that we are weak, but lifting a ninety pound squirming dog into a vehicle is always interesting at the best of times.

My business trip goes well, and I'm gone for five days. I have the opportunity to take an earlier return flight, so I take it.

I was originally scheduled to be home by 7:00 pm, but the earlier flight gets me back to Toronto around 2:00 pm. I create a plan to make

Heather my prime rib dinner. She loves it. I should be able to have it ready for her when she gets to my house after work.

I get home close to 3:00 pm and walk into the house. Something is different. I can't put my finger on it. My house feels different. It's slightly cleaner and tidier, but it never was that messy to begin with.

I walk into the living room and I realize that my couch is gone. A couch that looks familiar is now residing where my couch used to be.

Then I realize that while everything feels familiar, a lot of my furniture has been replaced with furniture from Heather's house.

*Odd*, I think.

I take Heather's car to the grocery store and buy all the ingredients for a meatatarian dinner.

I get everything ready, the food is cooking, and it's close to 5:30 pm. One of the wonderful things I love about Heather is that she is super punctual. Her schedule for the most part is set at the beginning of the year. I know she will be here around 5:30 pm.

At 5:00, I jump into the shower. After the shower, I walk into the master bedroom and wander into my en-suite closet.

I grab a t-shirt, but it doesn't fit. It's almost five sizes too small. I look around—the entire closet is filled with Heather's clothing! I'm pretty sure that when I left, her clothing wasn't here, with the exception of a few items.

*Interesting*, I think.

I find my clothing in the spare bedroom closet.

What the hell? Heather is a bit of a clothing fanatic. She has over a hundred pairs of shoes. Perhaps she's running out of room in her condo.

Ten minutes later, a very happy Tank and Heather walk into the house. Both of them are glad to see me. Tank spins in circles, getting his back scratched by the both of us.

Heather looks a little tentative. She smiles at me, "It smells delicious in here, what are you making, Danny Boy?"

"Prime rib, garlic smashed potatoes, asparagus wrapped in bacon, and a Caesar salad," I respond.

She gives me her awesome grin, "Why are you home early?" she asks.

I grab her, give her a big hug, pick her up off her feet and spin her around, "Because I wanted to see my two most favourite people in the world sooner than later! I missed you guys."

I let her down and kiss her on her nose.

She grabs my hand, and the three of us walk into the kitchen.

Earlier, I had opened a nice bottle of red wine to let it breathe. Heather takes it and pours two glasses while I attend to Tank. He wants a dog biscuit or three.

Dinner is almost ready. Heather walks up to me and hands me a glass of wine and has a super serious look on her face. I'm taken away by her expression since we've just reunited.

"Danny Boy... I hope you aren't mad, but when you were away, I kind of moved in with you."

"Well, Heather, I kind of figured that when I realized I lost my closet!" I respond. I turn to the oven and start checking on the potatoes.

"You aren't mad, are you, Danny Boy?" she says. I look at her, and she still looks super tentative. It always amazes me that beautiful women sometimes can be so nervous and unsure of themselves. Men would be lining up to live with Heather.

I just laugh, "Let's see… a beautiful girl who is much younger than I am wants to sleep with me every night. Hmm… I have no problem with that!"

Heather grabs both of my hands and spins me around. I'm now facing her. Her green eyes are staring at me, into my soul.

My blue eyes gaze back at her. We stare at each other for a few minutes in silence until we're both satisfied with this change in our relationship status.

Tanky suddenly makes an appearance—he jumps up on his back feet and puts his front paws on our hands. He turns his head and looks at the both of us a few times. His brown eyes now stare at both of us. It's like he approves of this decision somehow.

Heather and I both break out into laughter. God, I love her laugh. It makes me so happy.

I always find the Christmas season a blur. It sprints by quickly. Heather has to work the afternoon shift on Christmas Day. It starts at 3:00 pm and ends at midnight. She's off for the next two weeks. My Christmas present to her is a trip to the Florida Keys for two weeks.

I give it to her when we exchange gifts on Christmas morning. She's super excited, but she has one more shift to go before we head to the airport on the 26th of December.

Two weeks prior, we had agreed that I would serve Christmas dinner to her platoon at our home. We buy a big turkey and all the trimmings. Two of her colleagues are vegetarians, so we create special Christmas vegetarian meals for them.

Dinner goes well. Everybody is as cheerful

as they can be, given that they are away from their families at Christmas. It's the least we can do. Working on Christmas Day must be tough on their respective families. I know I can't do it.

Halfway through dinner, my doorbell rings. Tank goes crazy. He's a big, goofy dog, but when the doorbell rings, he becomes furious. When I first got Tank, he never barked. Then, one day, at the dog park, he barked at another dog who he thought was roughhousing. He has a big dog bark, and when the doorbell rings, it's loud, as if he barked into a microphone!

I go to the door and see it's my nosey neighbour. I don't dislike very many people, but I hate this guy. Years ago, when I was cutting the grass in the backyard, I had left the garage door open. I later found him in my garage looking at my tools.

I knew right then that he was odd. Over the years, his behaviour has become increasingly erratic. I've asked the man several times to not enter my property, but he just doesn't get it. Ironically enough, he's a real estate agent, so I'd assume he would know a thing or two about private property. I've never seen any of his signs up—I really don't know how he makes a living.

He wants to know if everything is okay given the number of police cars in my driveway and on the road in front of my house. I tell him everything is fine without wanting to explain too much, and request him to go home.

Half an hour later, he's back again at the front door of my house. I just shake my head—I can't even be bothered to answer the door. He keeps on ringing the doorbell and Tank keeps on barking.

Frank takes charge. He's an imposing figure when he's in uniform. He's six feet, two, along with all of his police gear and his bulletproof vest on, he looks like he's at least two hundred and forty pounds. I hear him speaking with my neighbour for a few minutes.

Frank comes back to the dining room with a stupid grin on his face.

"Don't worry, Dan, he won't be bothering

you again," Frank states before he breaks into laughter.

I just shake my head, I know Frank has laid it on thick to my neighbour.

I later learn that he told my neighbour that I was being busted for having the city's largest opium den and that some of the other neighbours were also involved. Frank wanted to know if my nosey neighbour was involved. My neighbour never bothered me again.

Our trip to Florida is amazing. Lots of sunshine and margaritas. We don't really do too much except walk around and eat food and drink. It's the most relaxing vacation I've been on in years. We laugh a lot, mostly at each other. Both our faces hurt from laughing so much.

I love holding Heather's hand when we walk. We walk a lot and hold hands wherever we go. The vacation is wonderful.

When we return home, we spend January getting used to living together. So far, it's working out for the both of us.

My birthday is in mid-February. I have this tradition on my birthday—I like to take my friends out for dinner, and I pick up the tab.

This year, I have something special planned. I've had a great year business-wise, and I really want to celebrate. I invite the gang out to the most expensive steakhouse in the city. There are ten of us, and dinner is going to be about $5,000, but I don't care. What's better than celebrating a year of success with my favourite people? I arrange for a limo bus, and off we go downtown.

Dinner is amazing with great company, great food, and great wine. The night is going well. Jokes are being told, stories are shared, and everybody is having an awesome time.

However, Heather is looking rather tentative. She really isn't engaging in conversations with our friends like she normally does.

George asks her what's wrong. She just smiles and really doesn't say anything. That's totally unlike her. Maybe she's coming down with something.

George pulls me aside and wants to know what's up. "I have no idea," I tell him.

After dinner, as dessert is being served, I start opening my presents. I hate it when my friends do this. I really don't have any wants in my life—I'm incredibly blessed. I get a few gag gifts, but the last present is the best.

It's from Heather. It's in a lingerie bag.

Frank, George, and Brian start catcalling, and they give Heather a hard time. They all support her in her lingerie purchase, but I most certainly support her in her lingerie purchase. I'm super excited!

Heather has an odd and nervous look on her face—extremely uncertain, super tentative.

In the bag, there is a small gift wrapped quite nicely and a birthday card. I open the card. It is a normal birthday card, but written in her neat, precise handwriting is the following:

Danny Boy!

I love you! The last 18 months have been

the best time of my life.

You make me a better person, and I am thankful every day for having met you.

I can't imagine living life anymore without you and Tankfordian being around.

I know it hasn't been easy for you, but I love your positive attitude. I have never heard you complain once, even when you had every right to complain.

My friends and family all love you.

Danny Boy, I love you!

I am also concerned that you are so old, Grandpa, that you might forget about me! ☺

I hope you don't mind, but I took the initiative… open the present…

I reach into the bag. Frank, George, Brian, and I all think I'm going to be pulling out a saucy pair of panties. They all grin at me.

I pull out a small, carefully wrapped little box.

The women at the table immediately know

what it is. I most certainly don't. I'm holding the present below the table as I unwrap it. I open the box and see what it is.

I look at Heather. She has tears running down her face, and she's shaking. Apparently, I'm the only person in her life who brings tears to her eyes. I have never seen her like this before.

The boys are looking at me, and they look over to see Heather in tears.

Everybody is stunned or confused.

I look at Heather and ask her, "Really?"

She bursts into tears and nods her head. Her shaking intensifies.

I get up from the table and kneel down on one leg beside her chair.

I take the engagement ring from the box and look at her, "Heather, will you marry me?" I ask.

She says yes.

There's silence at the table.

Everybody is trying to digest what just happened.

Frank has the best line. "Nooo... that so didn't

just happen, did it?" He looks like he's in shock.

The ring of course fits perfectly. She designed it and had it customized for us. It likely is the most interesting engagement ring ever. Heather's family crest has dragons in it. My family crest has snakes in it. Heather found a designer who somehow merged dragons and snakes into her engagement ring, with several gorgeous diamonds. I never find out how much it costs, but it fits her small finger like a glove.

I get up and give Heather a big kiss. I whisper into her ear, "I will never forget who you are. I love you!"

She grins at me and wipes her tears away.

The table erupts—everybody congratulates us. Hugs and handshakes are being given around.

I look at Heather, and she has this look about her. A sense of relief and excitement, I think. I feel incredibly emotional, and I actually start to cry. Heather grabs a napkin and wipes my tears away for me.

The owner of the restaurant hears from his

staff about what has just happened. He joins us and brings a bottle of their most expensive champagne.

Everybody is celebrating. This likely is the best night out with friends ever.

Everything is a bit of a blur. I sit down on a chair. Heather sits down on my lap, and her arm is around my neck. She kisses my cheek. Brian, at that precise moment, takes a picture of us. That picture is one of my favourites of all time.

We both look so happy in it.

# 19 TO BE FAIR, WE DIDN'T HAVE PARENTAL SUPERVISON

Heather and I decide to have an engagement party. It's now July, and the weather is beautiful. When I bought my house, one of the main features that attracted me to it was the inground pool. It truly is a backyard oasis. There is also a cabana bar and three BBQs. Generally, it's just a fun place to be on a hot day.

Heather has to work the day shift on the day of our party. We have invited the usual suspects. George, Brian, and Frank are coming over early to swim, drink, help set up, and eat food around 2:00 pm.

In the morning I make a potato salad, Caesar salad, and my famous watermelon salad. Of all the salads I have made over the years, my watermelon salad gets rave reviews. I had it once in a restaurant, so I created my own version of it.

It's super easy to make—I cube up some watermelon in bite-size chunks and mix in some feta cheese, pine nuts, and a few thinly sliced cucumber slices. The dressing is also easy—a bit of olive oil, balsamic vinegar, and the zest and juice of two limes. I know it sounds like a weird combo, but it's delicious, and everyone loves it.

The boys show up around two. I have draft beer available in my cabana house. It's ice-cold, and on a hot humid day in July, it goes down far too well.

I also have a margarita maker in the bar. The bar is stocked with rum and tequila.

After numerous drinks and lots of swimming, we all sit in the shade. The temperature is almost forty-two degrees Celsius with the humidity. It's too hot even for Tank. He jumps into the pool a few times and then wants to be let back into the house to nap with the air conditioning on.

George looks at me, "Dan, I just noticed your pool doesn't have a diving board."

I respond "I know. I looked at having one installed, but it's a lot more work than you think. They have to dig up the old concrete and pour new concrete, and it was going to cost almost $5,000. I just took a pass on it."

Frank chimes in, "Still, it would be great to be able to jump into the water."

I smirk at Frank, "Well, Franklin, I have a little secret. But you guys have to promise me you won't tell Heather."

The three of them perk up. They all like secrets. Especially ones that Heather doesn't know about and would likely get me into all types of trouble with her.

Brian looks at me, "Do tell, Dan."

I tell them to wait a few minutes, and I go into the house then into the garage and grab the big ladder that I use to install Christmas lights and bring it into the backyard. This ladder is almost thirty-five feet long.

The boys watch me prop the ladder up against the back of the house. Their gazes follow me as I climb up to the top of the second floor of the house and walk up to the peak in the roof. I have measured this once—it's almost forty feet up in the air. I take a small jump and land in the deep end of the pool with a big splash.

The boys grin at me. The four of us do this for the next hour and a half. Between tending to the BBQ, drinking cold beverages, and jumping off the roof into the pool, we have a wonderful afternoon.

I remind everybody that by 4:30 we need to put the ladder back in the garage because Heather would have a melt down if she saw us jumping off the roof and falling forty feet through the air into the pool.

Brian points out that it is now 4:45, and I better put the ladder back. I decide that I'll make one final jump into the pool. However, I'm going to make it an epic jump—the kind that will go down in history books.

I climb up the ladder and then onto the peak of the roof. I turn around and prep myself for a backflip off of the roof.

The boys holler at me, "Don't do it, Dan. Don't do it!"

*I got this*, I think.

I jump up and out and start rotating my body. I actually pull it off. There's only one problem—on the way down into the water, I see the most beautiful girl in the world, and she looks pissed... super pissed. As in—I'm-going-to-be-vaporized-in-front-of-my-friends-as-I-hit-the-water kind of pissed.

I actually think if I hold my breath long enough, she might be less angry. I hold it for as long as I can, then quietly surface and look up.

Frank, George, and Brian are standing in a row staring at their shoes. H-Bomb is going to town on them, and I catch the tail end of the conversation.

"Let me get this straight. You guys have been jumping off the roof all afternoon, and you didn't stop Daniel from doing this?! I thought you guys would be safe, and, you know, not be stupid. But I just saw my soon-to-be husband do a backflip off the roof and fall almost fifty feet into the water. This is my soon-to-be husband who is accident-prone to the extreme. He only hasn't been in the emergency room for the last two months, and nobody thought to stop him?"

Dead silence.

The silence lasts for thirty seconds before Frank puts his head up and says, "Heather, you have to understand that we are men. And to be fair, we didn't have any parental supervision."

Heather just glares at Frank. Without turning to look at the pool, the H-Bomb says "Daniel, I see you. Get out of the pool. We need to talk in the house, now!" Sigh, I know I am so getting it. I'm likely going to be vaporized. But it was worth it. I had so much fun today.

Heather and I go into the house. She glares at me, "Daniel, words can't begin to describe how angry I am at you. That looked incredibly dangerous. You have to be kidding me… a fucking backflip off the roof? Daniel, that was not safe. You're so ridiculous!"

I look down at my feet. "Sorry, Heather, I won't do it again."

She rolls her eyes as she walks away. "In my car are the groceries for tonight. Go get them, and we will talk about this later. I'm going to join the boys in the backyard."

I walk out of the house and start bringing the groceries in. It takes a few trips.

All of a sudden, I hear lots of yelling and catcalls from the backyard and a big splash. *I can't believe the boys would even contemplate jumping off the roof after H-Bomb's chat with them,* I think to myself.

In about thirty seconds, I hear Heather's voice, "Franklin, you better give me back my fucking bikini top or I will hurt you in ways you can't imagine!"

I wonder what's going on. I take the last grocery bags in and organize them on the counter.

Heather's screams at Frank continue. *What the hell is going on out there?!*

I go outside, and I see Heather at the shallow end of the pool, topless. She has both hands over her chest. Frank has the bug catcher out, and in it is Heather's bikini top. He's taunting her with it.

"Just reach out and grab your bikini, Heather," he tells her.

Heather tries several times, but between trying to cover herself up and Frank moving the bug catcher away from her, she just can't grab her top.

I just shake my head. I grab a towel and stand beside the stairs coming out of the pool.

The boys are at the other end of the pool. When Heather walks toward me and up the stairs, she drops her arms, so I can see everything. I just shake my head, and she smirks at me.

"Danny Boy, I can see why you guys were jumping off the roof—it's so much fun!" she grins her amazing toothy grin at me.

Heather has been training hard at the gym so she'll look so hot in her wedding dress. I guess between the force of her hitting the water and her losing a few pounds, her bikini top came off because it didn't fit properly.

I wrap her in the towel and kiss her nose and shake my head at her.

She goes into the house to change. I look at the boys and grin at them. They grin back at me.

Sadly, what was funny when you were ten years old still remains hysterical when you are over thirty-five.

I take the ladder back to the garage so that everyone can be safe.

Over the next five hours, everybody eats great food and tells funny stories about the group. The amount of laughter is unbelievable. Everybody laughs so hard. What an amazing night!

By 2:00 am, people who aren't staying over for the night have left. The people staying over are safely in their beds.

Heather and I are sitting outside by ourselves drinking beers, the music is turned down low. Cheesy 70s songs are being sung quietly in the background.

We don't say anything for a bit.

Heather stares at me—she has a concerned look on her face.

"Danny Boy, that backflip off the roof was so dangerous. It scared me,"

"Heather, to be honest, you're right. I won't do it again, I promise you," I tell her.

Heather looks at me, "You're useless to me if you're dead, Daniel."

I don't say anything. I suddenly realize that because we're getting married, I need to act more like an adult than a teenager. I now have responsibilities and obligations involving the love of my life.

## 20 DAYCARE TAKEDOWN

I'm working from home one day, and I get a text from Heather, *Hey can you make a batch of caramel corn?*

*Sure, I can. What's up?* I reply.

*I need about ten bags of your caramel corn. Long story... will explain when I see you. Need it ASAP at the station.*

One of the things you learn when you're engaged to a girl who has the nickname H-Bomb is that you listen intently to her words, as in, *Roger that, H-Bomb. Caramel corn will be forthcoming!*

To most people's surprise, caramel corn is super easy to make. It only takes about fifteen minutes. Once I've finished making it, I let it cool, and it looks good. People love my caramel corn.

About forty-five minutes later, I show up at the station. I walk in and see Heather being used as a piece of playground equipment by eight children. She has a child attached to each leg and arm and her bulletproof vest, front and back. She's walking around, laughing at all the attention she's receiving.

She looks at me with this most amazing grin.

I burst into laughter and shake my head, then start passing around caramel corn to the kids. They're screaming with delight.

I don't know who's having more fun, the kids or Officer Ramos.

Heather fills me in with the details of what's going on. They raided an illegal daycare today, and they have to wait until the parents pick up the kids. She was put in charge of the kids, and they're running wild in the reception area of the station under her supervision.

I hang around for a few hours, primarily

watching Heather interact with the kids. I've never seen her like this before. She looks awesome. She never fails to smile at the kids while entertaining them.

As I'm watching Heather, Robert, the grief counsellor, walks over to me. We both watch Heather and the kids for about ten minutes. Robert turns to me and says, "I really think Heather would make a great parent."

I respond, "I agree. I think I am getting a little too old to have children at this stage, unfortunately. I don't think I have enough patience, and I'm far too selfish."

Robert gives me a long look, "I don't know, Dan. You whipped up a bunch of caramel corn on demand and have been here for a couple hours. It looks to me like you have all the right qualities to be a good father."

I don't say anything in response. I do a lot of thinking about it though.

One little fellow—his name is Nathan— takes a liking to me. When I'm introduced as Dan, he thinks my name is Dad. I correct him a few times, but I give up. I've been called worse names. Nathan is about three or four years old, I would guess, and has a horrible cold. He's all congested and doesn't have the energy to play.

He asks me to read him a book. I don't have a book, but I do tell him a story about Tank, the wonder dog. He's asleep in about five minutes. He's wrapped one hand around my shirt sleeve and he's sucking his thumb on the other hand. He's drooling snot all over me.

Heather comes over and wants a picture of Dan and his new friend! Eventually, the parents are arriving in bunches. Heather also has to do a short interview with each parent about what was going on in the daycare. They also need to confirm that each child is being taken home by the right person.

There were a few officers doing the interviewing, but they have now left because there's only one child's parent left to be interviewed.

Heather tells me that Nathan is the last kid, and under no circumstances is his parent to take him home without first being interviewed.

"Roger that, H-Bomb. Nathan is not to leave without his parents first speaking with you," I respond. Nathan is a good kid, and I'm sure his parents are wonderful.

Heather turns to the desk sergeant and says, "Hey M.F., you got my boy's six, right?"

M.F. grunts something, and Heather walks off to interview the second-to-last set of parents.

I should tell you something about M.F. Like any organization, the police consist of ninety-five percent capable good people and five percent of the people who shouldn't be in their chosen profession. Mike Farley is part of the five percent. His option for using weapons of force was taken away from him for some reason, and he weighs about 300 pounds and is five foot six.

Everybody calls him M.F. for Mainly Fat. He thinks they're calling his initials.

Nathan is snoring up a storm. He's stretched out, and his head is on my lap. I've put my jacket over him as a blanket.

Robert walks by, smiles at me, and shakes his head. He then tells me, "I told you so."

Today, I was supposed to be working. I'm now responding to a few emails through my phone when I hear a disturbance.

A lady is screaming, "Where is my baby? Where is my Nathan?" I see a larger lady run by me to the front desk where M.F. is sitting, picking his nose. I mean, he's caught red-handed, one knuckle deep. *This guy is unbelievable*, I think to myself.

M.F., being the kind, caring person he is, just points at me, and the lady runs over to me. She snatches Nathan, and my jacket goes up with him.

"Nathan, you need to learn to stay away from the police, especially white ones. They will kill you," she informs Nathan.

Nathan is sound asleep, and I hope he didn't hear that.

One thing I have left out at the beginning of the story is that Nathan, who calls me Dad, has a different skin colour than me. I have this theory about life and friendships. I don't care who you are—you're my friend until you prove yourself unworthy of my friendship. I have a crazy group of friends from all around the world, and I'm a better person because of their friendship. They would also say the same thing about me, I would hope.

I'm a little offended by what this lady said, but I also understand it must be kind of scary to be told your son is at a police station and you need to come and pick him up.

Nathan's mom starts heading toward the door to leave the station, and I run to get between her and the entranceway to the building.

I tell her politely that she needs to be interviewed to make sure Nathan is going home with the right person and that there are a few questions that need to be asked about the daycare. I can tell she is frustrated and impatient, I politely tell her it should only take about five minutes.

"Listen, white boy, I know my constitutional rights. Unless I'm being arrested, you can't hold me. So, get out of my way or I will make you move out of the way."

This lady is about my height and outweighs me by at least a hundred pounds. I have no doubt she will attempt to get by me.

I look at M.F. I catch him again with his finger up his nose.

I wave at him, as in, I need some help over here, M.F.

I explain the situation to her again and point out that Nathan has my jacket wrapped around him as a blanket and tell her that I would like it back.

Out of the corner of my eye, I see an officer walking in through the front door. I can tell by the three stripes on his jacket sleeve that he is a sergeant.

All of a sudden... wham! Nathan's mom slaps me. It was not a gentle slap, it was an open-handed combat slap. I see stars for a few seconds, and my teeth feel loose on the left side of my mouth. Up until ten seconds ago, I had my hands at my side and was not threatening at all.

But right then, I assume a combat stance with my hands up, fingers together to protect myself. Fool me once, shame on you. Fool me twice, shame on me.

I once again look at M.F. and say loudly, "Hey, M.F., some assistance over here would be greatly appreciated."

I then say to Nathan's Mom in a firm voice, "You need to sit down, madam. I am under strict orders by the investigating officer that under no circumstance will Nathan be allowed to leave without you speaking to her first. Do you understand what I am saying? Please sit down."

The sergeant who is standing beside me doesn't say anything. He's just there.

I guess M.F. finally got off his fat ass and pressed the distress button. Plain clothes and uniform officers rush out of the woodwork.

Heather sprints over just in time to see me about to get slapped a second time. At least this time I get my hand up and block the slap.

This is the first time I hear Heather speak in cop voice, "Madam, you need to put the child down and come with me. You're under arrest."

Nathan's mom continues to scream about her constitutional rights and that she is going to sue the police force for harassment. She then looks at me, and it looks like she is going to slap me again.

Heather pulls out her stun gun and screams out, "I'm less than lethal."

Smith arrives. He pulls out his service pistol and points it to the ground and screams back at Heather, "I'm lethal!"

Several other officers pull out pepper spray and their collapsible batons.

Heather screams an order at me, "Hayes, under no circumstances is she allowed out the door. Knee strikes to her upper thigh if required."

I have been given an order by the H-Bomb. I am not allowed to let this lady leave the building. I have also been told what to do if she tries to leave.

I scream back at her, "Roger that, Ramos!"

Heather begins speaking in slow measured tones to Nathan's mom.

"You will not be allowed to leave the police station, ma'am. You just assaulted Hayes twice.

Secondly, I have no idea if you are really Nathan's mother. Listen to me when I say this. If I have to, I will zap you with 50,000 volts—I promise you I will. It's incredibly painful. The downside to me zapping you is that Nathan will also will feel it because you are holding him. If you are truly his mother, you don't want him hurt. I know I don't want to hurt him. Put Nathan down or give him to any police officer. Then, turn around and walk backward toward the sound of my voice."

Nathan gets passed to the sergeant standing beside me, and he hustles him away from what's going to happen next. No child should ever see a parent put into handcuffs by the police. Sadly, we all know that it happens every day.

Heather handcuffs Nathan's mom and takes her away. The police officers involved put their weapons away and nonchalantly walk back to whatever they were doing last.

Smith walks over to me and smiles. I guess over the last little while, he has accepted that I will be in Heather's life.

"Dude, we need to go to the gym together. You need to stop eating punches. We can practise this type of stuff. I won't even swing at you that hard or fast!" He jokingly informs me.

I look at him and smile, "I might have to take you up on that." He gives me a light punch on the shoulder and tells me to take care of myself.

The sergeant who took Nathan comes back with him, and the three of us sit down in the lobby. I hear murmurs from the interrogation room every once in awhile where Heather took Nathan's mom. Heather doesn't sound pleased.

Nathan wakes up and says to me, "Dad, I is thirsty." I give him the bottle of water that I have, and he sucks it down and promptly falls back to sleep.

The sergeant looks at me and says, "You're his father...?"

I laugh, "No, my name is Dan, and he has problems saying that. It comes out as Dad."

The sergeant holds out his hand, "Nice to meet you Dan, my name is Robert Alexander. I'm the auxiliary police sergeant. I haven't seen you around before. Are you new to this division?" he asks.

I burst out laughing. "Me, a police officer? Don't make me laugh, Robert! I could never do what you guys do. I don't have the patience to deal with stupid people. I'm engaged to Heather, she asked me to bring up some caramel popcorn for the kids today. I stuck around to help look after the kids because you guys were short-staffed today."

Robert looks at me and says, "Heather, Heather…" I forgot police officers either refer to each other by last name or nickname.

I help him out, "You know, Ramos or H-Bomb."

Robert just stares at me with a look of awe, "I would have thought you would have been much bigger than you are. At least the size of Smith." He then reaches out to shake my hand.

"We really enjoy working with H-Bomb—she's one of a kind. I always feel better when we're working with her, knowing she's with us.

Congratulations on your engagement. I always wondered what type of person she would end up marrying. You seem to have a big personality and are pretty laid back. Just what I would imagine she would need in her life," Robert tells me.

I shake his hand back and we both laugh.

Robert then gives me his sales pitch, "Listen, Dan, we're always looking for auxiliary police officers who have a full-time career and just want to volunteer with the community. The police force spends a great deal of money and time on training people, and the turnover rate is quite high. We lose about seventy-five percent of our volunteers each year because they have been accepted to another police force. I honestly thought you were a plain clothes officer, that's why I didn't interject when you were engaging with the lady. What you did was textbook. You contained the situation and made sure she couldn't run off. You waited for backup to arrive, and you calmly took everything in its stride."

He pauses for a moment and then continues.

"If you're engaged to H-Bomb, I know you've been code blacked, so you're eligible to be an auxiliary officer. Let me get you the forms, and we can fill them out together."

I look at him, "I guess... I think I should check with Heather first," I respond back.

Robert grins at me.

"That's probably a good idea. All kidding aside, Dan, I think you would be a wonderful addition to our group. I also think our team would be keen to hang around with the person who is going to be married to Ramos. You must be one interesting person! Hey, listen, let me go get the forms for you and a bag of ice for your jaw. That lady tagged you pretty good—it's turning a lovely shade of blue."

Robert walks off.

I continue to sit in the lobby. I hear a voice. There's a new duty sergeant at the front desk. I don't know him.

"Hey—you, sitting in the lobby. Can I help you?" he asks.

"No, I'm waiting for Ramos," I respond.

"Does she know you're here?" he asks.

"Yes, sir, she does know I'm here. Thanks for asking," I answer.

Robert reappears with an ice bag, which I put against my now tender jaw. *Wow*, I think, that lady really tagged me. Robert also brings me an envelope full of forms.

He looks me in the eye and says, "I spoke with Smith. I asked him if he would work with you if you were auxiliary. Smith hates auxiliary officers. He told me he would work with you any day of the week. The position is yours if you want it. Just fill out the forms after you speak with Ramos."

Nathan is sound asleep, oblivious to all the drama that has gone on. Poor little guy, he's suffering from such a bad cold and a parent with poor decision-making abilities.

Heather appears out of the interrogation room. She looks at me and says, "I can't talk to you right now, Danny Boy. Somebody has to interview you other than me." She flashes me her amazing toothy grin. She comes by and takes Nathan from me. Nathan and his mom are reunited in an interrogation room. The mom isn't cuffed, but Heather keeps a close watch on her.

The duty sergeant, whose name I later learn is Bruce Henderson, takes me into an interrogation room.

"Mr. Hayes, you are currently being video- and audio-recorded. Do you consent to this?" he asks me.

"I do," I respond.

"Mr. Hayes, based on my review of the video and audio, you were clearly assaulted today. Your attacker has also admitted to assaulting you. In my opinion, if this went to court, your attacker would likely be found guilty of a misdemeanor and would not serve any jail time other than the time served. However, because there is nobody to look after her son, he would be put into the system," he states.

I am not familiar with the term "the system." I ask him what that is.

He responds, "Her son would become a ward of the state, and he would go into the children's aid system."

I am now fully attentive. I have heard horror stories from Heather, Frank, and assorted police friends about what this means.

*I don't want to be involved with being responsible for a child being entered into that system,* I think to myself.

The sergeant says to me, "I think you need to think about this for a few minutes, Mr. Hayes. Why don't you step out into the parking lot and think about what I've just said?"

Heather has told me about this. While the audio works in the station, only the video works outside. I go outside, and about two minutes later, Sergeant Henderson appears by my side.

"Mr. Hayes…" he starts.

I tell him to stop it. I know what he's all about, and I'm pretty sure he knows what I'm all about.

I tell him to cut to the chase.

"While she has some issues with authority and a few mental health reports, she's a good mom and just needs to learn to control herself," he tells me.

Apparently, Heather has also put the fear of God into her. Heather has told her that because of her poor decision-making ability, it's possible for her child to go into the system and that she is the only person to blame.

"I most certainly don't want my actions to put a child into the system," I tell Bruce. "I'm not hurt, and I have an attachment to Nathan."

We go back inside, and I'm put on video again saying I don't want to have Nathan's mom charged.

This poor lady actually takes the time to apologize to me and tells me she knows Nathan liked me because he is very particular about people.

Nathan waves goodbye to me, "Bye, Dad," he says.

I have restaurant coupons in my wallet. When I'm downtown, I often give homeless people restaurant coupons to get a good meal, as opposed to giving them money.

I have a few restaurant coupons catered to kids, and Nathan's eyes light up as I slip him a few. I tell him, "Nathan, take your mom out for dinner tonight. She's had a hard day."

He responds back, "Yes, Dad."

I smile at him. What a cute kid.

A few minutes later, Heather appears out of nowhere. She looks at me, "You, my Rockstar, deserve multiple beers after today's shit show." She stands on her toes and kisses my nose.

In half an hour, we get to the pub, and the regular cast of characters are there—George, Brian, Frank, and an assortment of other people.

Heather regales them with the story of the day.

I'm silent. I have a lot on my mind.

I'm just starting my second beer, and I get a tap on the shoulder. Sergeants Bruce and Robert are at the pub in uniform on the pretense of a walk-through. Some of the regulars get a little nervous.

They both lay down ten dollars on the bar and tell the bartender the next two beers for me are on them.

I thank both of them, but I inform them that their generosity isn't required, although I am grateful. Robert pulls Heather aside and has a chat with her. She looks at him and then at me a few times. She smiles and nods her head. We chat later about what he has said.

# 21 OFF TO BOOT CAMP

Heather and I have a serious conversation about me becoming an auxiliary police officer.

She claps her small hands and gives me her toothy grin, "I would never date a cop, but you in a uniform, I would find that really hot! You might give me Blue flu!" Blue flu usually inflicts women—it's when women find cops incredibly attractive.

Then our conversation gets serious. She informs me that until I prove myself, I won't be treated as an equal but much like an idiot brother. I have a bit of pedigree, so she thinks I should be okay.

H-Bomb also has some advice. "Daniel, it's highly probable you are going to see something that you will never be able to unsee again. There are situations that likely will make you ill. I know you—it's going to make you cry."

I fill out the forms, and not shockingly, I'm told to report to the August indoctrination. It lasts two weeks—fourteen days including graduation. During the two weeks, in theory, the instructors cram enough information into you that you will know your role in the police profession, the legal ramifications of your actions, self defense, and use of force options.

I, being the seasoned veteran I am, know that there is no way you can learn all of that information in two weeks. It's a bit of a joke, but I get it.

I report to the police academy, as detailed in my contract. I arrive an hour early. It's just myself and the training cadre. All the training staff are younger than me. I immediately earn a nickname. "Father Time" is now my new name. *If the shoe fits, wear it*, I think.

Our reporting time is Saturday at 3:00 pm. It's now 3:00 pm, and none of the cadets are there other than me.

Precisely at 3:00 pm, my indoctrination from civilian to law enforcement begins. I am alone, as no other cadets have appeared yet.

I am being screamed at, "Father Time, drop down and give me ten push-ups!" I do as I am told. I don't even think twice about ten push-ups. I'm screamed at to do ten sit-ups. I'm beginning to think this is a joke. For the next hour, I am screamed at to do minimal exercises.

During the hour, other cadets start to appear. They are all late by at least twenty minutes. I can't believe that out of a hundred cadets, I'm the only person who showed up early or on time. I just shake my head. I'm at least fifteen years older than them. The training staff turn their attention to the other volunteers. I'm left in the corner of the gym with a bottle of water. I really haven't even broken a sweat.

I watch the other people. They're having a hard time doing even ten push-ups.

At 5:00 pm, they call us together. There are about eighty-five of us now—fifteen people have already dropped out of the course in the first two hours. I once again shake my head—*what were they expecting?* I wonder.

The cadres scream, "Father Time will be the troop sergeant. Does anybody disagree?"

A young man in his late twenties objects. The training staff eats this stuff up. We are both summoned to the front of the room.

I am asked, "Father Time, how badly do you want to be troop sergeant?"

I honestly don't care, but I say "Sure, I want to be troop sergeant."

The training staff confer briefly. It's announced that the winner of the most push-ups will be the troop sergeant. With one exception, I have to do double the number of push-ups than the kid challenging me.

The kid is told to go first, he gets to thirty-five push-ups. I can do double thirty-five push-ups in my sleep.

When I start my push-ups, one of the training staff puts his foot on my shoulders. My arms burn.

I'm at sixty-five push-ups and another staff member puts his foot on me. It's clear they want me to fail. I try my best, but I can't beat seventy push-ups with all of the weight that is being pushed down on me.

I get it. I am meant to fail.

I am screamed at for failing and told that I must remain behind after everybody has left for dinner. The other cadets all run out of the room to the cafeteria. I'm left alone with the training staff and told to get down and do a hundred crunches. I'm halfway through my crunches and I get a gentle love tap from a combat boot on my head.

"Stop, Father Time," I'm told.

I jump up to attention, waiting for the next direction.

I'm told, "Relax, Father Time," by the most senior training staff member.

I'm then given a can of beer, and I have a chat with the staff sergeant who is in charge of the training program.

"Listen, Dan, we have two weeks to weed out the people who shouldn't be here. It's a short time.

We know all about you. You're considered one of us already. We just need your help to weed out the people who aren't safe to be in law enforcement at the auxiliary level, for themselves, our officers, and especially the public."

I nod my head. I get it.

At reverie, which is 6:00 am, bells go off. I've been up since 4:30, which is my normal time to get up. I've already showered, shaved, and I am in my PT (physical training) gear. I've stretched myself out, made my bed, and got my locker in order.

Just like the movies, the training staff are flipping over beds, screaming about stuff not being in its proper spot. The newly minted troop sergeant can't even be bothered to get out of his bed. He's getting screamed at—they rip his locker and bed apart.

They get to my bed and locker and it is promptly destroyed. Everything is wrong.

The training staff has decided a new troop sergeant is required.

All in favour of Father Time being in charge,

they ask. Some other young person says they want to challenge me.

One of the members of the training staff says something into their radio, and a female instructor appears in the male dorm.

"Cadet Hayes, assume the push-up position," I am told. The female training member, who is about 120 pounds, sits on me. Heather and I do this exercise all the time. It's a crazy full body workout.

The kid who spoke up starts doing his push ups, and I match him push-up for push-up until we get to forty-seven. My arms start shaking. The girl sitting on my shoulders wraps her leg around my right arm and forces my arm up off the ground. I am now expected to do one arm push-ups with her on my back. I can't. I collapse on the ground.

The training staff scream at me to get up. The female training staff member, whose name I later learn to be Annie Anderson whispers into my ear, "Well done, Father Time, you tied the record!" She then takes a step back at me and screams at me, "Father Time, your cot and locker are a fucking disaster, get it organized now!"

I quickly fix everything, it takes about thirty minutes. A few of the guys are weeping. I'm eating this stuff up!

We have a 1.6 kilometer run at 7:00 am. It's a timed run, meaning you must do it in under twelve minutes. A twelve-minute mile run is a light jog for me. We're put in groups. I'm put in a group of ten men and ten women. A training member leads our group. I know how fast a twelve-minute mile run is, and I realize we are nowhere close to that speed. I could almost walk at the same speed we are running at. They are setting this group up to fail this portion of the physical testing. We were told that we could run at any pace we wanted, and that the training member was just there to keep everybody honest. For a short distance like this, my comfortable running speed is about seven minutes. I accelerate past our group and run to the finish line.

The staff sergeant makes a note on his clipboard and tells me, "Looking strong, Father Time."

Everybody in my group fail this test. While they aren't immediately dropped from the course, they are put on corrective detail. During breakfast, they run wind sprints until they are literally sick.

After breakfast, we shower and get dressed in uniform. We have to wear all of the gear. Cap, bulletproof vest, utility belt, handcuffs, collapsible baton, pepper spray can, and assorted odds and ends. The last thing I do is I give my boots a quick little polish. I look in the mirror and see Father Time grinning back at me. *I actually look pretty good*, I think to myself. Heather would be proud.

We are taught to stand at attention while the training staff inspect us. They make slight adjustments and corrections to people until they get to the troop sergeant. They pay attention to every single detail, big or small. So-and-so's boots aren't polished, or someone's shirt is only partially tucked in.

The training staff begin to have a meltdown, they're supposed to lead by example but their example is shit.

A training staff member screams at us, "Father Time, front and centre." I run up to him and stand at attention.

The staff sergeant screams out, "Father Time is now troop sergeant. Does anybody want to fucking disagree with me?"

Dead silence.

"Congratulations, Father Time, you are now troop sergeant. Now drop down and give me ten push-ups to celebrate your new role, Father Time."

The training staff pull me aside at break and give me the lowdown on what they want me to do. Some of the people there don't know how to make their bed, polish their boots, fold clothing, or how to be an adult in general. I won't be able to save everybody, but I can polish a few diamonds in the rough, I am told.

I begin to help those who want help, and those who don't want help flounder and are told that perhaps being an auxiliary police officer isn't something they are best suited for.

We are halfway into the training now. I'm

really enjoying it. From 6:00 am to 10:00 pm, our day is scheduled for us. I really don't have to think about it too much. It's awesome. In my normal day-to-day business life, I have to make all the decisions and set the agenda, which I have been doing since I was twenty-four.

On the paging system, I hear my name, I'm being summoned to the training cadre's office, it's 9:00 pm. I knock on the door and am ushered in.

"Sit down, Dan," the training sergeant tells me.

The entire training team is present, and I get handed a beer.

"We have a bit of a problem. We have identified two people who need to leave, but we have tried almost everything, and they are still hanging in. How do you feel about milling?"

"I'm not sure what that is," I respond.

Milling is then explained to me. "It's one minute of all-out aggression. You wear boxing gloves, a mouth guard, and light protective headgear. You can't block or avoid punches. You must punch all the time and eat the punches the other person is throwing at you. You get graded on your aggression and non-avoidance of being hit."

"Sounds like my type of fun. Sign me up!" I respond.

To demonstrate for the rest of the class, we decide that I will be the first person milling tomorrow mid-afternoon. I wonder which one of the two guys it will be. Sadly, I learn it won't be a fellow cadet— it will be Mitchell. Mitchell is the use of force and self defense instructor. He's about my height and weight, but his knuckles have calluses. He's incredibly fit—he's a gifted instructor, and rumour has it that he has fought Smith and won.

*Why does this shit happen to me all the time*, I wonder for about the millionth time in my life? *In for a penny, in for a pound*, I think.

After a use of force class, the training sergeant stands up in front of the class.

"Ladies and Gentlemen, because of how outstanding all of you are doing, or at least some of you are doing, we are going to have a special event over the next few days. It's called milling. The rules are simple—you punch your opponent as hard as you can for one minute. You can't avoid the punches, you will lose a point for each punch you avoid. You can only punch, no kicking, elbowing, or anything else—just punching. Ladies and gentlemen, this is a pass or fail event. If you pass, you may continue, if you fail, you are out of the course. No exceptions."

There is literally stunned silence from everybody.

"Troop Sergeant Hayes, you are up first. You will be milling with Mitchell. Troop Sergeant Hayes was briefed on this yesterday, so he fully understands the rules."

I put on my headgear, mouth guard, and gloves.

The cadets sit around the mats in the centre of the gym. I'm getting hopped up, and my adrenaline is starting to flow. *This is just going to be like a bar fight*, I think.

Anderson, or, as I like to call her, push-up girl, is the referee. She blows her whistle, and

Mitchell and I go at it. Most people don't realize—punching non-stop for one minute is exhausting. When I train with Kru Achilles, we do this drill all the time on a heavy bag. It's slightly different today, because somebody is punching back at me.

I remember to breathe. I'm punching Mitchell, and I am eating punches. This goes on for one minute. When Anderson blows her whistle at the end, we are both bloodied and bruised. I know I have a pretty good black eye, and so does Mitchell. We both grin at each other.

The training sergeant jumps up. "Outstanding, gentlemen, outstanding!" as he claps his hands. "Fucking outstanding!"

He then turns to the cadets. "I will post your respective milling matches later today. Milling will commence tonight after dinner. You have a free half hour to practice or grab some grub!"

Mitchell and I get sent to see the duty nurse. She laughs at us as she patches us up, "The two of you are grinning like little schoolboys who got into a fight at the playground! Please grow up, you're making me laugh!"

After we get patched up, we both agree we have to hang out after boot camp and drink pints together. Mitchell and I become friends after the milling.

I take a quick shower and go to the board where our agenda is listed. I look at the milling list, and, apparently, I'm up first against another cadet. This person, in my opinion, is one of the weaker potential candidates. He's fixated on guns to the point that that's all he talks about.

I'm trying to learn more about communication and helping people. I suspect we were matched for a reason.

I'm exhausted—there's no gas in my body. *I have no idea how I can even be expected to fight tonight*, I wonder to myself.

I rest for a few hours on my bed, tossing and turning.

Tonight, the gods are on my side. My opponent, who is larger than I am, lacks the intestinal fortitude to fight me. He gets bounced.

One down, and one more to go.

## 22 FIRST TIME OUT

After I graduate from the Auxiliary Training Program, I spend three nights a week for the next month training with the other Auxiliary Officers at the division before I get cleared to be on the road.

Obviously, I can't go out on the road with Heather. She volunteers Frank to take me out, and I quote, "So, my cherry can be popped."

It's a beautiful Saturday morning in August. I'm not sure who's more nervous, Heather or me. It's like the first day of school all over again. She gives me a few pointers, including how best to wear all of the gear and how not to get too hot given it's going to be a scorcher today.

I stand on a scale to weigh myself. I have everything on—my boots, body armour, forage cap, and belt. Attached to my belt are my pepper spray, a collapsible baton, and two sets of handcuffs. I had weighed about 162 pounds in my underwear this morning. As I look down at the scale, it tells me I am now 197 pounds. I have almost thirty pounds of gear on.

"Danny Boy, take a few steps back so I can see the overall effect," Heather directs me.

I do as I'm told and take a few steps backward. She stares at me intently for a minute.

It's getting a little uncomfortable, and I ask her, "What's wrong?"

"Nothing. I just think that women will be throwing themselves at you, and I'm trying to figure out how best to prevent that!"

H-Bomb also makes an appearance.

"Daniel, two things you need to know today. You are mine, so don't go around falling for some other woman who loves the uniform. More importantly, if you get hurt today, you better be dead. As a matter of fact, both you and Frank better be dead. I will personally kill you both if you get hurt."

"Roger that, H-Bomb!" I respond.

Frank tells me he's doing me a favour by taking me out on the road for my first shift. Usually, Auxiliary Officers are kept at the division doing filing for the first little while. He also informs me I better make him a great lunch for taking me out. I make us my old school Italian sandwiches, which I put on top of a half a dozen bottles of water in a cooler with an ice pack. Cool water and sandwiches will be needed today given how hot it's going to be.

I have to be at the station at 6:00 am when the morning shift officers meet and get briefed by their sergeant about the previous night shift and what to expect for the day. After the briefing, we go out on the road.

I show up about ten minutes early to settle in and be prepared. The duty sergeant happens to be M.F. He looks at me and doesn't say anything. I don't have a swipe card, so I can't get back into the secure area. I text Frank.

*Hey, brother, I'm in the lobby, where do I go?*

He responds back, *Hang on, I'll come out and get you.*

Frank comes out and gets me. We walk back to the parade room, and half the people are there already. Frank takes me around and introduces me to the people there, then we sit near the back of the room. This isn't Frank's normal platoon, but they're apparently short-staffed today so they scheduled him in. The platoon sergeant or supervisor is a familiar face. It's Bruce Henderson.

Sergeant Henderson does roll call, and my name is last.

He then starts on his overview for the day.

"First off, I would like to welcome Auxiliary Officer Dan Hayes. He will be riding shotgun with Frank. Hayes, or 'Father Time' as he is called, is engaged to Ramos from 'A' Platoon."

People who don't know me turn around and stare. Apparently, the H-Bomb is well known, and they want to have a look at the person she is engaged to. Also, the stories of my early exploits with her are well known around the division.

*Hopefully in a positive way*, I think.

Sergeant Henderson then informs everybody that he has a note from Ramos, which he reads aloud to the platoon. To be more precise, it's from the H-Bomb, "If Daniel gets hurt today, I am holding everybody accountable."

Uncomfortable looks are exchanged around the room, and they are generally directed at me. Nobody wants to feel the wrath of the H-Bomb.

Sergeant Henderson continues, "There are no special events planned for our division's coverage area. It's going to be a hot one today, people. Make sure you drink lots of water and keep yourselves hydrated. I expect that this will be a quiet Saturday with nothing out of the ordinary happening."

Little do we know, Mr. Murphy will be making multiple appearances today. Mr. Murphy is excited about my new volunteer activities, and he wants to make my life interesting.

Frank and I head out to the parking lot and go to our scout car. A scout car is just a normal police car, I have no idea why they are called scout cars. We check to make sure all the lights are in working order.

We're about to head out on the road, and Frank looks at me, "Where's lunch?" he asks.

I almost forgot the cooler that's in the back of my truck. I go grab it and take two bottles of water out of the cooler then toss the cooler into our trunk.

I hand a bottle of ice-cold water to Frank, who grins back at me, "This might be one of my best shifts yet. Cold water, good food, and I get chauffeured around town!"

Frank jumps into the passenger side of the car.

I guess I'm driving.

Heather texts me, *How goes it?*

I respond back, *okay, so far.*

She also texts Frank. *Franklin, if Daniel gets hurt, you better hope you are hurt worse than him.*

Frank shows me his phone and just shakes his head, so do I.

We drive around for about two hours. It's about 9:00 am. A radio dispatcher is advising that a dog is locked in a van with the windows up and it looks non-responsive due to the heat.

Frank picks up the radio mic and responds, "Bravo-12 will respond."

I look at Frank, "Should I put on the lights and sirens?" I ask.

"No, man, it's all good. Just drive fast," he responds.

We get to the parking lot of a grocery store. It's extremely hot today, it has to be almost thirty-eight degrees Celsius with the humidity. There's a crowd of people around a van that likely has seen too many miles. The windows are tinted very dark.

Frank and I both peer into the rear windows. We see a dog lying on its side, and it isn't moving. We pound on the windows and rock the van to see if it moves. The dog doesn't move. I'm a dog person, I know this isn't good. How can anybody lock an animal in a vehicle on a hot summer day?

Frank jots down the license plate number in his notebook and walks into the grocery store, and they page the owner of the van. Nobody responds.

There are about eight people begging me to break a window and rescue the dog. However, there is a protocol for this because it happens far too frequently. A supervisor has to be called, and they break the window.

Today, Sergeant Henderson is busy on a domestic abuse case. He tells Frank that it's his call. Frank looks at me, "What do you think, Hayes?" I look once again in the back of the van. I turn to Frank, "The dog doesn't look good, let's break the window."

Frank gestures at me that I need to break the window. I pull out my baton and hit the window with it. The window doesn't break. I look at Frank.

"Hayes, you really need to use a lot of force to break a window. Deploy your baton and hit the window as hard as you can," he informs me.

Roger that.

I deploy my baton and then hit the passenger side window as hard as I can. It breaks cleanly, and Frank unlocks the door and opens the sliding door. He goes into the van and is in there for about ten seconds. He walks out of the van with a weird look on his face.

He turns to me, "The dog didn't make it."

Fuck, it looks like a beautiful golden retriever. I enter the van and wonder if perhaps we could do CPR on it or pour water down the dog's throat.

I touch the dog and then realize it's a life-size stuffed animal replica of a golden retriever. I start to giggle.

*Heather is going to love this story*, I think to myself.

Of course, the owner of the van magically appears then. He was with his ten-year-old daughter at another store in the plaza.

Frank explains what happened. The guy peers into the back window and turns to us. "Okay, I can see how that could happen. But who is going to pay for my broken window?" he asks.

Frank points at me and says, "The guy who broke it!"

I ask the guy how much he thinks the window is worth. He says $500, I go to a nearby bank machine and get him his $500.

Frank spends ten minutes typing up a report in the cruiser and he submits it from the computer.

The text messages begin to pour in. We're being mocked by our colleagues, and they're calling us "Turner and Hooch" in reference to an old movie.

Frank looks pissed. He mutters, "I knew I shouldn't have got up today. It's going to be one of those days, I just feel it."

I start driving the scout car down the street. Lesson one of thousands more that I will learn. Before breaking a window, make sure the animal in distress is actually an animal.

Frank receives a text, and he tells me to drive to an industrial park. I see a Supervisor's SUV, and Frank tells me to pull up close to it. It's

Sergeant Henderson.

He's barking at us. "Woof, woof, do I look like a dog? Please don't break my window, Hayes. I don't want you to be out another $500!" He's killing himself laughing.

I start to laugh, and so does Frank. What a weird situation! Anybody could have mistaken the toy dog for a real one.

Sergeant Henderson tries to reassure me, "Hayes, don't worry—this story is going to be passed around the division for years. It's great! The first round of beers after the shift are on me. I want you guys to run traffic down at Albert and Locust Streets. Our regular traffic guy is off sick."

Frank is irritated. Most police officers hate doing traffic. You have to write a book of tickets on your shift, which means you have to ticket twenty people who likely had a momentary brain cramp. It's never a great experience for any of the parties involved.

I drive us down to the requested area and park back from the intersection.

Frank gets out of the scout car and opens the trunk. He grabs two cold bottles of water and two sandwiches and climbs back into the passenger seat.

"I fucking hate traffic duty," he informs me. He's now sulking. His phone continues to beep— he's getting tons of emails and texts teasing him about saving a stuffed animal. He isn't pleased with me.

He starts eating his sandwich. He looks slightly happier after a few bites.

I tell him I have a plan to make it up to him. I'm going to stop the next vehicle that looks suspicious.

He mutters something about how if I couldn't tell the difference between a real dog and a stuffed animal, I likely wouldn't be able to see a suspicious vehicle if it had the word "suspicious" painted on it.

He may have a point.

Frank is halfway through his sandwich, and I see a suspicious vehicle. This car is a German car. It has various models. I'm a car guy. This is a high-end model of this manufacturer. It's worth about $180,000 and has a limited production run. There is a two-year waiting list for this car.

It looks like it has about a thousand pounds of something in the trunk. *Nobody who would own this car would do something like that*, I think.

I turn on the lights and the sirens and follow the car. It immediately signals and pulls over. Between taking bites of his sandwich, Frank types in the licence plate number into the computer system. As if the heat and stuffed dog wasn't enough for today, the computer is being slow, and it takes a long time to receive the information.

Frank tells me to go get the driver's license, insurance, and registration. He thinks this is a waste of time.

As I walk up to the car, I see the female passenger trying to hide something. It's a big, clear plastic bag and it's full of some green stuff, it kind of looks like lawn clippings. I pretend I don't see it. I politely ask the driver for the required documents and casually stroll back to the cruiser. I give Frank the documents. The computer is still running slow.

"Franky, they have a big plastic bag full of green stuff. The passenger has it hidden against the door and her seat. I saw her put it there." I tell him.

Frank looks bored, "How big a bag?" he asks.

I grab the bag that has the sandwiches in it. "Like this big," I tell him.

Frank perks up. "Really?" he says. "Let's go out and see what it is."

We both exit the cruiser. I walk up to the driver's side, and Frank walks up to the passenger side.

I ask the driver if he could shut the car off. The driver complies.

Frank asks both of them to step out of the car. They both comply. There is no bag in sight. Nothing falls out of the passenger door.

Frank asks the couple to sit down for a minute on the curb. He walks over to me and asks me quietly, "How sure are you?"

"Positive," I respond back.

Frank explains to the couple that I think I saw a plastic bag, and he wants to know where it is. The couple begin to look really nervous—they look like startled deer who are about to run.

Frank now buys into what I'm selling. We handcuff them and put them in the back of the cruiser. We search the car and find the bag. It contains about two pounds of weed.

Frank is grinning. "This is a good score," he tells me. We then open the trunk of the car. It's loaded with vacuum sealed pouches of drugs. All types of drugs. It looks like a pharmacy.

Frank takes a step back. "Whoa!" he says.

He looks at me and tells me to call it in.

I have no idea how to call it in.

I look at Frank, "What do I say?" I ask him.

Frank grins at me and tells me how to call it in.

This is my first police radio transmission, and thanks to Frank, it made me sound like a seasoned veteran on the radio.

Our call sign today is Bravo-12. This is what

was said:

"Bravo-12 to Dispatch. Priority Traffic."

"Go ahead, Bravo-12."

"We have a heavy 10-200 requesting a Supervisor and DS at our 20. We have two in custody and are Code 4."

There was a 30-second pause.

"DS is requesting how heavy the 10-200 is."

I look at Frank. I don't know how to respond. He rolls his eyes. He's grinning, "Tell them record breaking."

"Advise DS, it's likely record breaking."

"Roger that, Bravo-12; super heavy 10-200 requesting a Supervisor and DS at your 20. Take care."

The civilian version of what I said is as follows:

"Hi Dispatch, it's Dan and Frank. We have an urgent message."

"Tell me whatever information you want."

"We have a large drug bust, requesting a Supervisor and the drug squad to come to us. We have arrested two people, and everything is fine."

"The drug squad wants to know how large the quantity of drugs you have found is."

"Lots."

"A supervisor and the drug squad are headed to your location."

Frank is staring into the trunk. He's taking a few photos with his phone. He's grinning at me.

"Dan, you have just made up for this morning, my friend. I now owe you at least a dozen beers!" he says, as he high fives me.

It takes an hour and half for us to clear the scene. Sergeant Henderson and the drug squad guys are ecstatic. Lots of pats on the backs and goofy grins. People are shaking my hand. I guess we did well today.

Heather sends me a text, *Go Starsky and Hutch. :)*

Over the next few days, the drug squad executes a few search warrants related to our traffic stop and uncover almost ten times the number of drugs we found.

A few days later, the white shirts, as they are called, make an appearance. They're the staff inspectors who appear on TV, speaking about the drug bust.

However, today, Sergeant Henderson sends us on our way. "Gents, well done, you have done great work today!"

I drive a few blocks down the road and park the scout car in the shade.

Frank is busy texting people, sharing the story and the photos. He's so excited. "Dan, you have no idea how good this is. It's awesome for our careers!"

I just shake my head. It's my first day, and I'm not anticipating a full-time career in law enforcement as I am only volunteering.

I'm still driving the scout car and watching for another "suspicious vehicle."

Frank is super animated—his phone is ringing off the hook, and he's getting congratulatory texts.

He's oblivious to what I am doing. I'm

stalking, I'm waiting for the right vehicle.

Mr. Murphy is also assisting me. He's up to his regular tricks. He has a special plan for me today. He has decided I need to go for a run.

I then see what I'm looking for. A beat-up pickup truck with a motorcycle in the back. My gut tells me something is wrong. I pull out and go after the truck.

Frank perks up, and he looks at me. "What's going on, Dan?" he asks.

"Just my gut." I tell him.

The pickup isn't stopping, despite the sirens and the flashing lights.

Frank runs the plates. The computer is now running properly—the plates don't match the vehicle.

Frank grins at me, "Book 'em, Danno!"

The truck finally stops. I pull in right behind it. The driver bolts out of the pickup, and so does the passenger.

Frank and I both jump out and chase our respective people.

I'm chasing the driver, and Frank is chasing the passenger.

I have my radio earpiece in, and I hear Frank on the radio.

"Dispatch—Bravo-12, we have multiple 10-80s."

Dispatch responds back, "Bravo-12, I confirm multiple 10-80's. All Units Code 33 on this channel. Bravo-12 has priority. Bravo-12, define."

I have no idea what's being said. I'm focusing on chasing my guy. I know I could have easily outrun him if I had no gear on. Now, I am literally four steps behind him—I just can't quite catch him.

Frank is back on the radio. "3314 is Bravo-12A, Bravo-12B is Aux Hayes." Because I haven't taken the radio course, I don't have a personal radio call sign.

We then get assigned two different dispatchers. Frank quickly detains his suspect and goes off the radio.

The person I'm chasing is proving to be

elusive. I've been chasing him for almost seven minutes now.

I hear this through my earpiece, "Bravo-12B, what is your 20?"

I honestly have no idea where I am. I'm currently running up a paved bike trail, so, I don't respond.

The dispatcher is getting concerned.

"Bravo-12B, what is your code?" I'm asked.

I have no idea how to respond.

I then hear Frank. "Dispatch, we have a newbie Aux. Baby steps, first shift."

"Bravo-12B, are you okay?" I'm asked.

I respond, "10-4, chasing suspect on the paved trail."

On the radio, I hear a few people cheering me on. I hear the words, "Go, Father Time!" a few times.

The Dispatcher announces, "Bravo-12B has priority on this channel, everybody."

I'm just a few steps behind the guy, but I can't quite catch him. *If I didn't have the full gear and boots on, I could have easily caught him,* I think again.

I hear a familiar voice on the radio. It's Smith's. "Bravo-12B, I'm at the top of the path you're on. Just chase him up to me."

The guy I'm chasing then drops something. As I run by the object, the situation just got more serious. Seriously scary. The guy dropped a pistol.

I now have to get on the radio and warn everybody how dangerous the situation is. I can't remember all of the radio codes, so I blurt out what I hope accurately conveys how serious the situation has become.

"Bravo-12B to dispatch. Priority traffic." I say into the radio.

"Go ahead, Bravo-12B," I hear in response.

"Code 2, this guy is 10-32," I say into the radio. I even got the code right. Code 2 means the situation is urgent and that I need help, and 10-32 means the guy has a gun.

The radio dispatcher is trained to be cool, calm, and collected during stressful times. My dispatcher's voice, while sounding professional, has now become cold and calculating. Her job is to warn everybody that the situation is dangerous, and the guy has a gun.

I then hear on the radio. "Bravo-12B, I confirm your code 2 and that the suspect is 10-32." A short pause, and she continues, "All units, Bravo-12B is now code 2, and the suspect is 10-32. If you are responding to Bravo-12B, please acknowledge the 10-32."

I suddenly hear sirens in the distance. Many sirens.

On the radio, I hear Frank. He sounds serious.

"Bravo 12A, I confirm the 10-32."

I then hear Smith "Bravo 2, roger the 10-32."

Over the radio, I hear at least five more acknowledgements of the 10-32.

A funny thing happens—the guy is dropping stuff as though they're going out of style. I suspect he's dropping bags of drugs.

I suddenly get pissed off. This guy is dangerous to the public, and my friends who are on their way to help me.

I speed up and get close to him—I give him a push and he falls over. Today, Mr. Murphy is on my side. The pavement on which I'm chasing this guy is horrible. Luckily, I trip over a broken piece of pavement and land on the suspect's back, knocking the wind out of him. I grab my handcuffs and cuff him in about two seconds.

Heather has this theory. The most dangerous time for both the officer and the suspect is the ten seconds before the suspect is handcuffed. Ever since I signed up to be an Auxiliary Officer, we practise handcuffing every night for ten minutes before we go to bed. My practise pays off. The suspect is handcuffed in about two seconds.

I say into the radio, "Bravo-12B, I have one in custody, and I am code 4."

The dispatcher responds back, "Bravo-12B, I confirm you are code 4. All units responding to Bravo-12-B, please acknowledge that Bravo-12B is now code 4."

I hear multiple times on the radio, "Confirmed; Bravo-12B is code 4."

I'm still sitting on the suspect, I'm waiting for somebody to help me. I really don't know what to do next. Smith and Frank appear almost at the same time. They're both grinning, I get off of the suspect, and Smith begins to pat him down.

Frank is grinning at me, "That might be the longest foot chase this year. How far did you run do you think?"

I shrug my shoulders. "I don't know, I lost track of time. Maybe three kilometres?" I respond.

We then hear Smith, "Looky, looky, I found a cookie!" He holds up a pistol that the guy had on him. Smith unloads the pistol. It had fourteen rounds in the magazine and one in the pipe, as they say. This guy was one trigger pull away from making my first day my last day.

Frank takes the guy and escorts him back to Smith's cruiser. Smith and I collect everything he's dropped. Smith whistles, "This guy was up to no good!"

We find the other gun that he dropped. We find out that one's also fully loaded. Smith looks at me. "You are so lucky, man."

"No, we're all lucky. If I had been shot, H-Bomb would not have been happy with any of us," I respond back.

Smith looks at me with a grin. "True," he says.

We walk back up to the cruisers, and I see Frank. He's grinning. "Oh my God, this is huge!" he informs us.

It turns out that both of the guys are wanted suspects, both here in Canada and down in the States. They're going away for a long time. The guy I was chasing was apparently on the most wanted lists in several law enforcement agencies down in the States.

Sergeant Henderson shows up. "Gentlemen, outstanding! You guys are having a great day! You're off traffic duty. Drive around, cool down, and enjoy the day."

Frank takes the wheel this time. I down two bottles of water. I'm thirsty from my little run.

I look at Frank and tell him, "Man, I have no idea how you guys do this. We're halfway through our shift, and I'm exhausted. I never knew that this was you, every day."

Frank looks at me, "Dan, are you kidding me? Today is abnormal. I've never had two busts like we just had back to back in a single day. This day is huge!" he grins at me. "Dan, I owe you beers for at least the next month. This is awesome. I'm going to put my papers in to be transferred to the D-Squad!"

The D-Squad is the detective squad.

H-Bomb also gets into the act, and I receive the following text. *Daniel, while I am proud of you, the guy had two loaded guns on him. You could have been dead.*

Before I get a chance to respond, H-Bomb floods my screen with a few more texts.

*You are useless to me if you are dead, Daniel.*

*Useless!*

*Daniel, do you understand what I am saying?*

*Daniel, you are not permitted to be dead unless I tell you to be dead.*

*Do you understand what I am saying, Daniel?*

*Roger that, H-Bomb. I am not permitted to be hurt or dead without your expressed permission. I am useless to you if I am dead*, is my text back to her.

I receive a happy face in response.

Mr. Murphy has one more special thing planned for me today. A family BBQ.

A person on a street flags us down. He tells us he has smelt smoke for the last little while, he explains that he has finally figured out that it is coming from his neighbour's house and that he isn't sure if it is a BBQ or something more serious.

Frank and I see the smoke, and we make our way to investigate. We walk behind the house in question and see the air conditioner—it's on fire.

Frank calls it in.

We walk up to the front of the house and pound on the door, and an elderly lady answers. We explain to her that her air conditioner is on fire and that she needs to leave her house immediately.

Suddenly, there is a small explosion. The air conditioner has gone from smouldering to a full-on fire.

The lady starts screaming about her babies; she tells us they are upstairs in a cage. Frank and I confusingly look at each other. English is most certainly not this lady's first language and perhaps she misspoke. A crib perhaps?

I look at Frank, "I guess we're going in."

Frank's responds. "Roger that, Father Time."

We sprint into the house—the smoke and the heat is unbelievable. We race upstairs to the second floor where the babies are. We hear squeals of fear and we run toward the sound. We manage to make our way through the smoke and fog to the bedroom. Sure enough, the babies are in a cage. There are six puppies and a female dog in a crate. I grab one end of the crate, and Frank gets hold of the other end. We race back out of the house with the dogs.

The fire department is now here. The fire captain goes off on us—we could have died rescuing animals.

I explain the babies thing, and the fire captain kind of gets it, I hope. I look at Frank, his uniform is still smoking and has burn marks on it.

He looks like he's medium rare. Based on my BBQ experience, I'm sure I am as well.

We're both hacking and coughing. The paramedics offer us some oxygen that we gladly accept.

We hear on our radios, "Bravo-12, this is Sierra Actual—Whiskey Tango Foxtrot, Gentlemen!"

I look at Frank. He starts to laugh. It's the staff sergeant, and he apparently thinks we are killing it today. "Whiskey Tango Foxtrot" is the phonetic spelling of WTF.

We both have grins on our faces. Frank

looks at me and says, "Dan, I'm changing your nickname. It is no longer Father Time. It's Dangerous Dan. I have never been on as fucked up of a shift as the one today. You are the root cause of it."

Dangerous Dan as my nickname sticks even to this day.

If you're looking for action or if you're on your sergeant's shit list, you invite Dangerous Dan for a ride-along. It is guaranteed something big is going to happen if Dangerous Dan is riding shotgun with you.

# 23 JUST A REGULAR TUESDAY

After I finish all of my training and became certified, on top of my excellent performance, I am proven to be road worthy. I've decided that I will volunteer for the day shift every Tuesday. I get to the station at 6:30 am for the morning roll call and briefing and volunteer until 5:00 pm.

Today, Heather is working the afternoon shift. So, our paths should cross at some point, I would assume.

During the briefing, I'm assigned my first radio call sign: Alpha 12. Alpha stands for Auxiliary Officer, and I am the 12th Auxiliary Officer at this division.

Today, I'm with the D Platoon. I haven't worked with them before, and so I don't know their sergeant. I learn that his name is Sergeant Taylor. He pulls me aside and tells me I will be riding with Larry J.

I also get this friendly heads-up from Sergeant Taylor. "DD (Dangerous Dan is sometimes too long for people to say), Larry J is two months from retiring due to his age. He's getting sloppy and careless—I need you to be extra careful out there with him."

I am essentially babysitting a fifty-nine-year-old fully grown man. I don't say this out loud, but I'm not thrilled about this.

I get a text from Heather. *Danny Boy, who are you riding shotgun with today?*

I respond back, *Larry J.*

She texts back, *Eyeroll! Good luck!*

For the first few hours, nothing too exciting occurs. Larry J and I speak about sports mostly. He's a huge Yankees and Cowboys fan. He also isn't a fan of the "new" police with their fancy computers and technology. Larry J points at the computer in the scout car, "I barely ever read that thing."

Larry J tells me about his upcoming retirement plans. He plans to spend six months in Florida and six months back here. He's always been a bachelor, and he plans to spend most of his retirement fishing and golfing.

We drive around in the zone we're covering, and we see a car being driven somewhat erratically—Larry J turns on the lights to pull the driver over. The car pulls over, and he runs the plates.

Most people don't realize this, but all police cars have interior and exterior high-definition cameras with high quality sound. It's there to protect the police and the public. The microphones are so good they can actually pick up what police officers are saying to people up to fifty feet away.

Larry J takes a casual look at the computer and doesn't say anything to me. He gets out of the car and starts speaking to the driver.

As I'm watching him, my job requires me to also watch the passenger side of the car in case somebody jumps out or something gets tossed out the window.

I'm watching Larry J, and he's doing everything wrong. He's not standing back behind the car door—instead, he's standing beside the door, square to it. If you stand behind the car door, it's far less likely for you to get shot if the person has a gun in their hand. The person would have to aim backward to shoot you.

I'm watching Larry J, and something is wrong, it's like everything is going in slow motion. I see Larry J. slowly drop his hand down to his pistol. I hear him screaming, "keep your hands where I can see them!"

The driver we pulled over is revving his motor wildly.

Larry J is now in front of the vehicle with his pistol out—I am now potentially in his field of fire. I need to move fast.

As I am a civilian, I can't look at the computer unless the officer I am with allows me to. Larry J hasn't offered me the opportunity to, and he should have. Regardless, I take a quick look at the screen. The notation on the computer system is this: The owner of the plate is armed and dangerous and has a hatred for the police. It also states that this person should not be approached alone.

Fuck, Larry J. Fuck!

I have trained for this, though I never really thought I would have to do it. I press the distress button on my radio. Immediately, dispatch knows we are in big shit. The radio channel I am on now is clear only for me. My GPS coordinates are also sent to dispatch. I already hear sirens—they are likely to arrive in a few minutes.

I hear this on the radio from dispatch: "Alpha-12, what is your code?"

I click the mic once. This means I am Code 1—I can't talk and need immediate assistance.

I then unlock the fully loaded C-7 that is mounted between the two front seats and shove two additional magazines into the front of my vest.

Each magazine has thirty rounds in it. I have ninety rounds on me.

A C-7 is the Canadian equivalent of an American M-16. It's slightly shorter in length—technically, it's considered a carbine. It's a machine gun that shoots 5.56 calibre bullets up to 900 rounds a minute.

Its sole function is to kill people, which it can do with incredible efficiency.

I exit the scout car with the C-7 in less than four seconds after seeing Larry J pull his pistol out.

I turn the safety of the C-7 to semi-automatic mode and not automatic—while I did qualify as expert in the use of C-7, there is going to be no need to hose the car down with bullets. Sadly, this is going to be up close and personal.

For some reason, Larry J is still standing in front of the car. The driver of the car is still wildly revving the motor of the car. Larry J is still pointing his pistol at the driver of the car. I have no idea what Larry J is thinking—pistol rounds have a hard time breaking through thick safety glass such as front windshields.

I remember from my training to never run

between the scout car and the suspect's car. It would be easy for him then to back up and pin me between the two cars.

I run behind the scout car and out into the road, I'm about five meters from the suspect's car.

Larry J looks at me and unbelievably aims his pistol at the ground. *What is he thinking?* I wonder. Accordingly, we are in a "textbook perfect" L-shape. It's physically impossible to shoot each other within this range.

I have the C-7 pointed downward toward the suspect. I check to see and estimate where my bullets will go when I unleash my first three shots. It looks like they will travel into a ditch onto the side of the road, which is good. These bullets will still have enough kinetic energy to kill somebody else even after they go through the suspect.

Luckily for everybody involved, I can see that the car is in park. The suspect is still wildly revving the motor of the car. He has both hands on the steering wheel.

As we were trained, I must decide how far I

am going to let him go before I shoot him. I have decided that if the suspect takes his right hand off of the steering wheel and moves it toward the gear shift, my first three round burst will be at his head and not his centre mass. The angle that I am at means that to hit him centre mass, I would likely have to shoot through the door. Bullets do ricochet.

I have now decided. This all takes a split second. I start screaming at the driver, "Stop revving the motor, stop revving the motor!" I can't tell him to turn the car off, because he will use his right hand to shut off the motor, and my no-shoot/shoot involves his right hand moving.

I hear sirens. Everything seems to be moving in slow motion.

The suspect is laughing wildly at Larry J.

On hearing my voice, he turns and looks at me. He does not like what he sees.

He sees me looking down at him with a machine gun in my hands. It's pointed at his head. Today, I am his angel of death, and he is within my gun sight.

My finger has taken up all the slack in the trigger. I'm a millisecond away from committing the ultimate human sin.

Killing another human being.

Today, the chances that I will be judge, jury, and executioner are good.

While I am screaming at the suspect to not move and stop revving his motor, I am internally pleading him with "please don't make me kill you, I really don't want to. Please."

I sense somebody beside me. It's Sergeant Taylor, and suddenly on my other side, there is another police officer who I don't know. Both of them have their pistols out.

Though we have practised different takedown scenarios, this is one that hasn't occurred before. An auxiliary officer with a C-7 that's ready to go, a suspect in a car, another officer in front of the car—who would likely be run over by the suspect, and two other officers with their pistols out.

At this precise moment, if anybody—the suspect or a police officer—makes a wrong move, the result would be disastrous. At this range, none of us would miss.

The driver, we later learn, wet himself—was that terrified.

Eventually, he meekly puts his head down and stops revving the motor.

"DD—keep your eye on him," I'm told by Sergeant Taylor.

One of the other officers yanks the guy out of the car, he handcuffs the suspect and pats him down.

I point the rifle up into the air, take a step back and several huge, deep breaths. According to our training, you need to walk away from the situation once it is over. I walk back to the cruiser and stow the C-7, making sure that the safety is on and taking the extra magazines out of my vest and securing them properly. I grab my water bottle and take a sip of it. My hands are now shaking.

Sergeant Taylor approaches me, and he is pissed. Pissed isn't a strong enough word. He's fucking beside himself.

"What the fuck were you and Larry J

doing?!" he screams at me.

I look at him, and he emphatically states, "I have a senior patrol officer not doing what he should be doing. I have an auxiliary officer doing something he was never told to do but was the right fucking thing to be doing. I now have to open a shit investigation, and it isn't going to end well for you, Dan!"

*Fuck!* I think to myself. *How do I get myself into these situations?*

There is one major problem with what I did. I'm not to touch a firearm unless directed to do so by a police officer. Larry J clearly has communicated this already to Sergeant Taylor.

I'm told I can't speak to Larry J until we both give our written statements. I ride back to the station with Sergeant Taylor in silence.

I sit at a computer and type my statement up—it's as detailed as I can possibly make it.

As I am sitting there at the desk typing away, Heather walks up to me and gives me her amazing grin. She runs her fingers through my hair and whispers into my ear, "Trust me, you don't have anything to worry about. There are rules and then there are rules. Danny Boy, the rule stating that an auxiliary officer can't pull out a weapon on his own without permission from the other officer is a stupid rule. Everybody knows it. Try not to worry."

I give her a weird smile and continue to type.

After handing in my report, I'm told that until a final ruling has been made, I am no longer eligible to participate as an auxiliary officer. I'm also informed that I need to turn my uniform and gear in by no later than noon tomorrow.

Before I leave the station, I have to have a mandatory half-hour interview with Robert the grief counsellor. I head to his office, which is called "The Confessional." It is the only room in the station, with the exception of the washrooms, that have no cameras or microphones.

Robert's door is always open, unless he's speaking with somebody. I poke my head into his office, and he glances up at me and points at a chair. I sit down, and he closes his office door.

"Hi, Dan, how are you feeling after what happened?" I'm asked.

"Not bad. My hands are still a little shaky, but I think I'll survive," I respond back.

Robert stares intently at me for a few moments. "Dan, just so you know, I reviewed the video and audio of what went down. You know I'm not the final arbiter of this, but I honestly don't think you did anything wrong. I think your gut instincts were correct, and Larry J put you in a position where you had to act."

Robert and I chat for another twenty minutes. I'm told that if I start having nightmares about what happened, that's normal. If it starts impacting my personal life, that isn't good, and I need to come back and talk to him about what happened.

As odd as this sounds, I don't dream about the situation, even though I have always been a vivid dreamer.

However, for the next four weeks, I keep contemplating what I should have done or shouldn't have done. In the final analysis, it really doesn't matter. The situation actually unfolded in less than four minutes from start to finish, and nobody was killed or hurt.

I get a phone call from Sergeant Alexander, who is in charge of the Auxiliary Unit.

He wants to meet to have an off-the-record conversation.

We meet at a local coffee shop, and we both grab a coffee and sit down at a table.

I make direct eye contact with Sergeant Alexander, hoping I get an indication of where this conversation is going.

He then begins, "Dan, Professional Standards has had two investigators review what happened last month. Never has an auxiliary officer, in the history of this police force, armed themselves with a C-7 and got fully prepared to apply deadly force with it, if it was required. Dan, you violated the holy of the holy of auxiliary rules—Thou shall not pick up a firearm unless otherwise directed to so by an officer of the Law. You are a civilian with specialized training, and that is it. That itself is immediate grounds for dismissal and a federal criminal charge."

*Ah fuck, I am done now*, I think to myself.

Robert continues.

"Dan, you have no idea how bad Professional Standards wants to do you, me, or any of the other auxiliaries, just to prove a point. They fucking hate us. They think we're doing the jobs of paid officers, which most of the time we aren't, but sometimes we do."

Sergeant Alexander pauses and takes a sip of his coffee and looks up at me with a sly grin.

"But Professional Standards has a big fucking problem. What you did was so textbook and so well documented with audio and video, they were only able to find one fault." He takes another sip of coffee. "If you had been told to deploy the C-7, you likely would be up for a valour medal. But you weren't. If you were a regular officer and you did what you did, you would be fine. Sadly, you aren't a regular officer. Dan, you went rogue. You didn't follow the god damn rules!"

My stomach is slowly sinking. I now wonder if Sergeant Alexander wanted to meet here so that when I am arrested, Heather and the neighbours won't see it.

*I'm big boy, I can take it*, I think to myself. I mentally prepare myself to be taken away to jail. I just stare at my coffee.

Sergeant Alexander looks at me, and I'm informed "Auxiliary Officer Hayes, at 09:00 am tomorrow, you will make yourself available for a formal board of inquiry at the station. Do you understand, Auxiliary Officer Hayes?"

I confirm I do.

I walk out of the coffee shop, jump into my truck, and drive aimlessly for a little while. What am I going to do? I guess we will have to cancel the wedding. I'll need that money for my criminal lawyer.

I break the news to Heather, "Heather, I had a coffee with Sergeant Alexander today. I have a formal hearing tomorrow morning at 09:00 at the station. I think there is a good chance I'm going to jail."

Heather looks at me, "Danny Boy, just relax. You aren't going to jail."

Sadly, I don't share her optimism. I toss and turn all night. Heather has to be at the station by 07:00 am. I'm left alone with my thoughts. I polish my shoes and put on my best suit with a conservative tie and shirt, which totally isn't like me.

I get to the station and report to the Duty Sergeant. "I'm here for the inquiry," I tell her. I sit down on the really uncomfortable hard-plastic chairs in the waiting room.

I wait for about five minutes until a Staff Inspector, who I don't know, comes out and brings me to the back. I'm then put into a large meeting room full of white shirts. I really don't know anybody there.

I am so fucked.

The presiding Staff Inspector brings the hearing to order.

"Auxiliary Officer Hayes, do you still agree

with your prepared statement?" I'm asked.

"I do." I respond.

I'm then asked a series of questions, but the last one is one I've thought about at great length.

"Auxiliary Officer Hayes, are you familiar with Auxiliary Police Regulation 132-4? A copy of it is in front of you."

Familiar with it? I can recite it off the top of my head.

I begin, "Panel members, Regulation 132-4 states No Auxiliary Officer of the Police Service shall deploy a use of force weapon without first obtaining consent from at least one serving member of the Police Force."

Complete silence from the panel.

I stare at them, and they stare back at me. My stomach is jumping around.

"Auxiliary Officer Hayes, the Auxiliary Police Regulations have to be a living, breathing document. It is based on many practical lessons learned in the field. What occurred a month ago is a reason why this document needs to be changed from time to time," I am told.

I am then presented with a revised Auxiliary Police Regulation 132-4. It now reads, "No Auxiliary Officer of the Police Service shall deploy a use of force weapon without first obtaining consent from at least one serving member of the Police Force. However, if in the opinion of the Auxiliary Officer, members of the Public or another officer are in imminent danger and there is insufficient time to be given consent, then the Auxiliary Officer is authorised to deploy any use of force option   necessary to end the situation."

I look at it. It sounds about right. I look up at the panel members, I'm still waiting for the axe to fall.

The panel chair looks at me and smiles, "Let me guess. Sergeant Alexander didn't say that you weren't in any trouble?"

"No, he failed to mention that. I was actually prepared to go to jail today," I respond.

The panel members all start to chuckle.

As they get up to leave, one staff inspector

walks over to me and slaps me on the back. "Son, what you did that day was brave and was the right thing to do. I watched the video almost a hundred times and listened to the audio. I also reviewed your notes. I'm in charge of the Professional Standards Bureau. You were put in a no-win situation. The Regulations can't cover all situations. But just don't be thinking you can now go around breaking Regulations at will."

It feels like the weight of the world has been lifted off my shoulders. At the pub tonight, drinks are on me. There're about five of us at the corner of the bar we like.

I regale Frank, Heather, Brian, George, and Karla about the "hearing." Only Frank and Heather knew what has been going on for the last few weeks.

George puts it best, "And you actively volunteer for this shit, Dan?"

## 24 WORLD'S BEST DOG

It's about two months to our wedding. Heather and I take Tank to the park. I let him off his leash and start throwing his ball for him to fetch. This is Tank's favourite time, he's so happy that he keeps running circles around us. When he wants his ball thrown again, he'll either drop it at our feet or put it in our hand.

We play this game every day. I'm not sure who has more fun—Tank, Heather, or me. We also play dog tag sometimes. Tank will chase us and bonk his nose against the person he's chasing, and then he goes off to chase the other person.

Today is another special day. Mr. Murphy

has decided that I haven't been injured enough recently. To my surprise, I don't see him hiding behind a tree laughing at me when we get to the park today.

The three of us are at the park for about half an hour before Mr. Murphy gets me. Tank is running around like the ninety-pound, big, goofy dog that he is. He has his ball in his mouth, and he's running at me. He normally veers away from me at the last possible moment. Today, however, he decides he's not going to veer away from me, and his body collides with my right knee.

There's a loud pop. Immediately, my knee doesn't feel right.

I hear Mr. Murphy chuckling in the distance.

Heather runs over to me, "Danny Boy, are you okay? That didn't sound so good. How bad is it?"

I take a deep breath. My knee really doesn't feel so good. I try to take a few small steps. Something isn't right, but I can't put my finger on it.

"I don't know, Heather. Something doesn't feel right. It's probably a good time to walk home now," I respond. My stomach tells me something is seriously wrong.

Heather is always super cautious with me when I get hurt. My high pain threshold sometimes hides serious injuries. The three of us slowly walk the four kilometers back to our house. I mostly limp. My knee is twinging, and every once in a while, it hurts. A sort of mind-numbing pain.

Tank is oblivious to what he's done. When he's on leash and decides he wants to go in a different direction than we are currently traveling in, he's strong enough pull me over.

On the way home, he decides to go in a different direction than we are walking. My knee buckles, and I grunt with the pain.

"Danny Boy, what's going on?" Heather asks.

I don't say anything to her. I hand her Tank's leash.

Tanky is in his element, just smelling around

and being a big goofy dog.

Heather just stares at me, and she has a look of concern on her face.

We get back home with no other incidents.

Heather is working night shifts this week, and she needs to get a few hours sleep before she goes to work. It's about 5:00 pm, and she needs to be at the station around 11:30 pm. We climb into bed. Heather has this amazing skill—she can fall asleep literally anywhere, at anytime. Within two minutes, Tank and Heather are sound asleep.

My knee is throbbing. Deep down, I know something is wrong. I don't want to say anything to make Heather worry.

Heather wakes up around 10:45 pm and takes a shower. I lie in bed, my knee is still throbbing. Tanky is snoring up a storm beside me in the bed. He's now lying where Heather was sleeping. I guess the blankets are warm.

Heather looks at me concernedly. "Danny Boy, if you are broken, you are useless to me. What's going on?"

"I'm sure I will feel better with a good night's sleep, don't worry," I respond.

Heather's shift ends around 6:30 am, and she's usually is back home around seven. I have a hard time sleeping the entire night. My knee is throbbing. Every once in awhile, Tanky places a leg or his head on my bad knee, and it is agonizing. I have to sleep on my left side. If I sleep on my right side with my left leg on my right leg, the pain is immense.

I get up around four, and I sit at my desk and try to relax. It isn't helping. At five, I take Tank for our normal five kilometer walk. A few times during our walk, the pain in my knee feels absolutely mind-numbing. I can't think. I know something is really wrong.

I prep breakfast for Heather. This morning, it's homemade sausage patties, two baked eggs on an English muffin, and a bowl of fresh fruit. Easy to make, healthy, and above all, it does not need me to stand up for very long.

Heather walks in looking exhausted. This is

her first night shift since coming off the day shift. The first shift is always tough. I could never work shifts. She's a Rockstar.

She sits down at the breakfast table and takes a sip of the coffee that I already have waiting for her.

"What a shitshow last night! We were on call non-stop, the entire night! How's the knee, Grandpa?" she asks.

"It feels slightly better than yesterday," I respond. I know I am lying to her, but she's tired, and I don't want her to worry.

We finish breakfast, and she heads off to bed. The world's best dog snuggles up to her and begins to snore. Heather is quickly asleep.

It's now about nine, and my knee is aching. I can't even think about work. I text my cousins who are paramedics and describe my symptoms to them. Their response isn't very optimistic—*go to the emergency room now.*

I sneak out of the house and call a cab. I get to the emergency room. The triage nurse takes one look at my knee and puts me on the green room regime. I get to see an ER nurse within twenty minutes of my arrival. I'm then sent to the x-ray area. Within the first thirty-five minutes, I'm x-rayed ten different times.

One of things I do on my many frequent visits to emergency room is joking with the people who work there. My favourite line is, "I'm the healthiest sick person you will see today." It usually gets a lot of laughs and often accelerates the treatment process.

I've witnessed people hurl horrible insults at nurses and doctors just because they don't get to have their way. It boggles my mind why people do this.

I, on the other hand, just go with the flow. There really is no sense in getting upset. I have a book and my phone to keep me entertained.

It takes about an hour and half for the ER doctor to see me. I'm sitting in a chair and not the bed, because in my mind, I'm not severely hurt. The doctor introduces herself as Nicole and asks me to lie on the bed.

She examines my left knee and says that it's super tight. Given my sporting and accident history, she is a little surprised by how tight it is.

She then examines my right knee. This knee isn't so tight—the lateral movement on this knee is significantly more than my left knee, which is an indicator of an MCL tear and meniscus damage. I am given an appointment with an orthopedic surgeon at the fracture clinic for the following week. I'm told that I won't really know what's wrong until the orthopedic surgeon reviews the x-rays and takes a look at my knee.

Tanky strikes again! The world's best dog.

I take a cab back home and get dropped off a block away. I don't want Tank waking Heather up. I stop at the grocery store and pick up a few items for Heather's lunch. I also need plausible deniability in case I get caught by Heather.

Sure enough, when I get back home, Heather is downstairs getting something to eat.

"Danny Boy, where were you?" she asks.

"Out for a bit of a walk and grocery shopping," I say as I show her the grocery bags.

Heather looks at me for a few seconds, and H-Bomb appears, "Daniel, if you were out for just a walk, why do you have a hospital bracelet on?"

I had completely forgotten about the hospital bracelet. I should have cut it off before I walked into the house. You probably would think that, by now, I would have learnt not to hide the truth from Heather. She's all-seeing and all-knowing.

"I went to the hospital to have my knee checked," I respond.

Heather just stares at me. The vein on her forehead is beginning to pulsate. She's about to go off on me, and it looks like a 50-kiloton explosion.

"Why didn't you mention to me that you felt it was necessary to go to the hospital? You told me your knee is fine. Daniel. I know you, you only go to the hospital if you are really hurt. What did the doctor tell you?" she asks.

Being the idiot that I am, I decide to lie to Heather.

I give her the reader's digest version of what I was told. I also leave out the portion about the torn MCL and meniscus.

"Daniel, what you are telling me is that you basically went to the hospital because you aren't injured. Is that statement correct, Daniel?"

"That is correct, Heather," I respond.

Her beautiful green eyes just stare at me. Sadly, I know what's coming next.

"Daniel, if you are lying to me, you know I will find out. I always do."

"Yes Heather, I am aware of that," I respond.

*I'm so fucked now*, I think to myself.

I gallantly hobble around the kitchen making Heather her lunch. I am in agony—I can feel my kneecap partially dislocate whenever I make a movement. I try to ignore the pain, but it is mind-numbing.

Heather is watching me like a hawk. She knows that my knee is hurting, and so, she tests my honesty. She asks me to go to her car and retrieve her gym bag. I comply. I go down the stairs toward the driveway, but I have to stop to catch my breath. I take several deep breaths as I get her gym bag from her car.

Heather is unusually quiet during lunch. I whip up my old school Italian sandwich recipe. They are so good, people beg me for the recipe. Heather loves them.

Today, we eat in silence. Heather just stares at me, she looks angry and hurt at the same time.

"Daniel, I think your knee is hurt, and you're trying to hide it from me. Why?"

"Heather, I tweaked my knee, nothing to worry about. It's all good," I respond.

I am your typical middle-aged man— someone full of bravado and injury proof who thinks only weak people get hurt.

I spend the rest of the day in my office working on appraisal reports. My knee keeps on getting dislocated, and the pain is all-encompassing. I don't complain about anything—that's not my style.

Heather is sleeping. Tank usually sleeps beside her when she sleeps during the day. Today, however, he decides to come and pay me a visit. He sniffs my knee. He looks at me with his beautiful brown eyes, and he starts to cry. He knows that I am injured and can't help me.

It's now 5:00 pm. I can't get any more work done, the pain is that intense. I climb into our bed and lie down beside Heather. Tank jumps up onto the bed and lies on his back between Heather and me, his long dog legs sticking up toward the ceiling.

Despite Tanky playing defense between the two of us, Heather somehow makes her way over and snuggles up to me. She sleepily whispers into my ear, "Danny Boy, I love you. Don't be broken, you're useless to me if you are broken."

I run my fingers through her hair. I love this girl. I kiss her nose and tell her that I'm tougher than the average person and that she doesn't need to worry. I can pretend to be invincible all I want, but sadly, reality is going to catch up with me.

The alarm goes off around 10:00 pm.

Heather and I get up. Tank does not have anything to do with this. He stays in bed and curls himself up into a ball at the spot where I was sleeping. Heather jumps into the shower, and I head down to the kitchen to get a meal and prepare her lunch for work.

My knee is pulsating, and my leg is turning an ugly green colour. I struggle to make bacon and eggs and something else for her lunch. When I hear Heather coming down the stairs, I sit down at the breakfast table and hide my knee.

Heather cleans off her plate and starts eyeing mine. "Danny Boy, aren't you hungry?" She asks as she steals a slice of bacon off my plate.

"No, I am feeling a bit under the weather. Go ahead," I offer her my plate. She gobbles down my breakfast. I have no idea where Heather puts all of the food she eats. Whenever we go out, she often eats the leftovers on my plate.

"How's the knee, Grandpa?" she asks.

"No worries," I respond.

Heather cleans off my plate and puts the

dishes in the dishwasher and heads off to work.

I go back to bed and lie down. I twist and turn. I can't sleep because of the pain. I call for a taxi and head back to the hospital. It's the same triage nurse as before, so I immediately go to the green room.

A doctor sees to me, and I explain that my knee has dislocated seven or eight times. The doctor then tries to set my knee, but it keeps on popping back out.

The doctor then asks for the emergency room orthopedic surgeon, who is supposed to be on call. He arrives in half an hour and explains to everybody, including two of the attending resident doctors, that resetting a knee takes a lot of manipulation and that a loud pop will occur when it resets.

I'm then given a drug that will numb the pain that I am about to feel. In half an hour, I don't feel any pain. I'm telling jokes and singing Jimmy Buffett songs to the medical staff. The orthopedic surgeon has problems getting my knee to reset. Part of the problem is because my jokes are that funny. At one point, he gives me another shot of whatever he gave me earlier to make me be quiet.

I can't talk anymore. It's like I'm having an out-of-body experience. I look down at the doctor as he struggles to reset my knee. A nurse is literally kneeling on my hips trying to keep me still—it's wild to think that the doctor has to use that much force to reset my knee.

Then, it happens. I see the most beautiful girl in the world, and she looks pissed. Unbeknownst to me, an ER nurse has kindly contacted Heather, because she is the emergency contact that has to drive me home due to the drugs I was given.

Heather comes to my bed, she looks gorgeous in her uniform. I ask myself, what exactly does this beautiful woman see in me? I try to convey my love to her, words escape me. I tell her, "Ih lob you, babhtyrh!"

Precisely at that moment, there is a loud pop, and my knee resets. Heather turns green, and it looks like she might faint. A nurse, seeing this, grabs a hold of her and gets her to sit down on a chair and brings her a fruit juice.

The orthopedic surgeon tells us that I am one tough guy. Most people would be screaming and yelling after what I went through. My knee was the toughest knee he has ever had to reset. Likely due to how muscular my legs are.

As I still can't coherently string two words together, Heather asks the doctor why I am here. I struggle to say something, but I can't. I know I'm in deep shit now.

"Mr. Hayes' knee was hurt on Sunday, and since that time, it has dislocated eight or nine times. We had to reset it to prevent any further damage to the ligaments and the meniscus," the doctor explains.

Heather cocks her head and looks at me, "Tell me doctor, what is wrong with his ligaments and meniscus?"

The doctor explains to Heather that I have likely had a partial tear of my MCL and meniscus and will have to wear a special knee brace for the next two to four months before finding out if I need surgery or not. The knee brace will help protect my knee from any further damage. The one thing we will have to be careful about is that there is a forty percent chance that I will damage my other knee, as my body is now off-kilter.

Heather just nods her head and turns and looks at me. "Daniel will explain it to me in greater detail when we get home. Won't you, Daniel?" The vein on her forehead is pulsating. I am totally in trouble! But I really don't care at this point, because I don't feel any pain.

I'm cleared to go home. When Heather got the call from the ER, she was out on patrol and had immediately drove to the hospital in her cruiser. I'm wheeled out of the ER in a wheelchair by a nurse and I see Heather waiting for me outside. She does not look happy. She unceremoniously tosses me into the back of the cruiser. She mentions that I'm lucky that I didn't get handcuffed for the scare I gave her when the hospital called her.

I doze off, the car stops, and I wake up. I'm not at home, I am now in the sally port of the police station. I'm so confused. *It has to be the drugs*, I think to myself, I must be imagining things. Heather disappears, and I doze off once again.

I feel myself being shaken, not politely either. I hear an authoritative voice, "Wake up, broken knee boy." A few gentle slaps on my cheeks. I open my eyes and I see Frank's smiling face.

"Hey, brother, how are you doing?" he asks.

I try to tell him about how much trouble I'm in with Heather and that I need his help.

All I can get out is "ADFad gafd afdjk adeig!"

"Oh my God, Heather was right. You are so high right now!" he exclaims. "This is going to be one of the best nights of my life!"

Heather and Frank gently haul me out of the back seat of the cruiser and escort me into an interrogation room.

Smith appears with a plastic bag from an all-night pharmacy. In it is a bunch of cosmetic products. Lipstick, eye liner, nail polish—you name it, it's there.

He's almost giggling, he's enjoying himself that much.

"Daniel, close your eyes. We're going to make you pretty. Sit still," Heather commands. When I close my eyes, I fall asleep again.

I have no idea how long I'm out of it. I feel like I'm being carried, I hear Tank barking, and then darkness once again.

I wake up in my bed. Heather and Tank are both sleeping beside me. I have to pee, so I quietly get up and limp to the washroom. After I'm done, I look at the mirror in the washroom. The view isn't typical of me—I look like a man with far too much makeup on my face.

I look so cute!

At that precise moment, I decide that Frank won't be in my will.

I take a shower—the makeup removal program isn't going well. Water apparently doesn't remove makeup or nail polish. My knee aches. I go back to bed.

Heather is off for the next four days, and she wakes up first and gets up. I lie in bed sulking.

"Danny Boy, are you coming down for breakfast?" she calls from downstairs.

I don't answer. Both my body and pride are injured.

Heather appears in the bedroom and sits down on my side of the bed. She grabs my hand and stares at me.

"Danny Boy, why did you hide how hurt you were? Remember, we are getting married soon. I want to know everything about you—the good and the bad. I love you!"

I stare back at Heather for about thirty seconds, and she suddenly bursts into laughter. "Oh my God, Danny Boy, get out of bed and I will help you get the makeup off. Your mascara is running!"

I burst into laughter, and we both walk to the washroom. Heather helps me remove the makeup.

And with that, we are good again.

## 25 THE WEDDING

Our wedding plans are coming together. I've been to so many wedding parties that I literally could plan an entire e wedding on the back of a cocktail napkin and execute it without any issue in just a few days.

Heather, on the other hand, is worrying about everything. I remind her, in all the weddings she has been to, the food, speeches, and music have been the most important things. Everybody remembers the food, speeches, and music.

I let her worry about the details, but I take charge of the food and music.

I was raised a Catholic, and Heather was

raised a Buddhist. Given my age and life experience, I am now more Buddhist than anything else. Heather wants to make sure my parents' wishes are taken care of. I, as well, want to fulfill her parents' wishes. The middle ground is easy to find.

Our wedding party is likely the most ethnically diverse wedding party ever, I suspect. The members of the wedding party are from all around the world. For a farm boy growing up in a homogenous society, I suspect most people would be shocked at the cultural diversity of our wedding party.

The wedding is fairly small, with only about 175 people attending. We rented a hall where the ceremony can be held and dinner can be served. Heather agrees with me about having great food and fantastic music, she's pleased with my selection.

We are likely about three minutes from the start of the wedding. I'm standing at the front of the room when Frank taps my shoulder and nods his head toward the back of the room.

My mom and dad are standing at the entrance. I walk back to them and give my arm to my Mom and escort her to the front row. My parents are rock stars. They both have huge smiles on their faces. They love Heather.

I resume my position at the front of the room. Once again, Frank taps my shoulder. Heather's mom is at the entrance. I walk back and offer my arm to Heather's mom and escort her to her seat in the front row.

Heather's mom waves her hand at my parents and gives me a kiss on the cheek. She grabs my hand and looks me in the eye. We don't say anything, she knows what I'm all about. She gives my hand a squeeze and smiles at me. Oddly, for the first time, I find out where Heather's beautiful goofy grin comes from.

I am near tears.

I return to the front of the room.

Heather makes me laugh. Her wedding entrance song is Pachelbel's Canon. I think she did it on purpose. She knows I am a sucky baby. It's very dramatic.

When I hear the opening notes, tears begin to well up in my eyes.

Her father starts escorting her down the aisle.

I try to take a deep breath. I start crying harder when I see her.

Heather is slowly walking down the aisle—she looks so beautiful, almost angel-like. Her dad is smiling at me. I'm not sure how I got so lucky to have met this girl.

*She can do so much better than me*, I think. *So much better*.

George puts his hand on my shoulder. My tears continue to fall.

Heather and her father get to the altar. He offers me her arm. I shake his hand and hug him. *I'm so lucky to have met this girl and her wonderful family*, I think.

I smile at Heather and accept her arm from her Father. I'm shaking. Heather smiles at me. She looks stunning. Her beauty takes my breath away.

I'm a mess. Tears are pouring down my face.

The minister begins to speak. I don't hear a word he's saying. I'm just staring into Heather's beautiful green eyes. She's staring back at me, smiling at my tears of joy.

Time seems to be standing still. We just stare at each other.

We have worked on our own vows separately. All of a sudden, Heather begins to speak.

"I, Heather Ramos, take you, Daniel John Hayes, to be my husband. Despite you being frequently injured and tragically clumsy." The guests begin to laugh. "I will nurse you through the injuries inflicted on you by my colleagues and animals," she continues.

I start grinning like a madman at her. She's on a roll, but her speech now starts sounding super serious.

Heather grabs my right hand, starts squeezing it tightly, and stares deeply into my eyes.

"Daniel, every day I am with you, I am a better person because of you. You never have an unkind word for anybody. You are always happy. When I see you at the end of work, you always make me smile, even if it has been a rough day."

Heather takes a deep breath, tears slowly start coming from her soft eyes. This causes me to start crying again. Her little hand is starting to crush my frequently broken right hand. I don't care about the pain.

"Daniel, I will always be by your side. I know I can be difficult to deal with at times because of my temper. You are the only person I know who can withstand the H-Bomb, because you're the strongest person I know."

We stare at each other for twenty seconds.

She continues, "Daniel John Hayes, I love you, you make me a better person."

The both of us are now crying. Technically, Heather only has a few tears running down her face. I'm openly sobbing. If you average it out, we're both crying.

The minister turns to me, "The groom will now say his vows."

Between sobs, I manage to get out my vows.

"I, Daniel John Hayes, take you, Heather Ramos, to be my wife. I promise to stand by your side no matter what happens or whatever injuries I may have." I pause and take a deep breath. "Heather, the day I met you, you took my breath away. Your beauty and intelligence amaze me every day. I can't imagine not spending the rest of my life with you."

I look at Heather's beautiful green eyes. My chest feels tight, and my heart is racing.

"I believe that we were destined to meet. We are going to be on an amazing adventure for the rest of our lives together. I know there will be moments of doubt, moments of sadness. The one thing I am confident in is this: I love you."

I look at Heather, and she actually starts to cry.

The rest of the ceremony is a blur. We're signing this and signing that, having pictures taken and shaking hands with people. An hour and half is gone in the blink of an eye. After all the wedding pictures are taken, Heather and I have twenty minutes to sit down before dinner. We are by ourselves in her dressing room. I have somehow managed to grab a bottle of beer in the midst of the hustle and bustle in the dining hall. Heather is sitting down on a chair in front of a mirror. The makeup person has just finished touching up her makeup and has left us alone.

I pull up a folding chair and sit down beside her. She grabs the bottle of beer out of my hand, takes a big chug of it, and lets out a belch.

We both grin at each other.

"I know, so ladylike! I'm thirsty and hungry," Heather says with her amazing goofy grin.

I just smile at her. I love this girl so much. Tears start coming from my eyes.

H-Bomb magically appears, and she isn't happy with me.

"Daniel, you have cried far too much today. It's now embarrassing for you and me. You need to stop it. No more tears, or I am going to get mad. You don't want me to get mad on our wedding day. It will make the wedding night very boring for you."

I most certainly do not want the wedding night to be boring.

I regain my composure. No more tears. Roger that, H-Bomb.

Dinner goes off without a hitch. There are ten courses, and they alternate between our cultural backgrounds. I hear people raving about the food. I'm super pleased. Happy bellies mean happy guests!

We are now into the speeches. Sadly, most weddings have boring speeches because most people hate public speaking. In my mind, speeches should be entertaining. We are selective on who we ask to speak.

George and Frank regale everybody with the story of how we first met and several of our early dates. George tells my side of the story, and Frank tells Heather's side of the story. It's really humorous. Everybody is laughing out loud. How did we ever manage to get married given all of my missteps and injuries? Their speech sets the tone for the evening.

Frank brings up my Muskrat Love sticky note and Heather's response to it. People are giggling out loud.

The final slide of their speech gets the most laughs. It's a picture of Heather, Smith, Frank, and me. The three of them look very respectable in their police uniforms. I, on the other hand, look very pretty with my knee in a brace and lots of cosmetic products on my face. I should have known that somebody would have taken at least one picture of me all dolled up after my most recent hospital visit!

Luckily for me, Frank is kind enough to explain exactly what happened and that I am not some sort of weird, injured crossdresser.

Heather and I had originally decided that we will say our speech together. She will start, and I will finish our speech. However, tonight, Heather has other plans.

The both of us get up and approach the microphone. Heather starts speaking.

"Dan and I would like to thank everybody for coming here tonight." She then looks at me, she has a super smirky grin on her face. She asks our guests, "Who here thinks Daniel has cried far too much today? Who wants to see him cry some more?"

My nieces and nephew are screaming their encouragement out loud. They love Aunt Heather. It's fun to see Uncle Dan cry. The head table starts chiming in their approval. My cousins start yelling their encouragement. Based on my general observations, everybody wants to see me cry some more. *Awesome*! I think.

Heather, as always, has other plans.

From somewhere out of her dress, Heather pulls out a pair of handcuffs. Not the cute fluffy ones, but real handcuffs. As in the type you wear when you are going to jail.

To this day, I have no idea where she hid the handcuffs. Like most of her clothing, her wedding dress is form fitting to show off her athletic figure.

I am unceremoniously handcuffed behind my back and escorted back to my chair.

The crowd is laughing.

H-Bomb appears.

"Daniel has cried enough tonight. It's embarrassing for everybody. I'm going to say our speeches now to circumvent him from crying."

Heather then starts her speech.

"I would like to thank everyone who is here tonight. It's an honour to have all of you here for our wedding. In particular, a special thank you to the wedding party. From beginning to end, all of you are rocks for being there when Dan and I vigorously discussed menu options! Who knew there were so many food choices!

"To everybody who has traveled a distance to be here today—thank you for travelling to spend your night with us. Dan, Tank, and I love you!

"To both our moms and dads—we wouldn't be the people we are today without your love and guidance. We love you!"

Heather looks at me with a smile, and I see the hint of a tear in her eyes. She stares at me when she continues to speak.

"Daniel, I knew we were destined to be when I first met you. You made me laugh like I have never laughed before. I never knew how amazing a relationship could be until I met you."

She pulls out a notebook full of sticky notes and waves it at our guests. The sticky notes look familiar to me.

"Perhaps some of you know how cheesy Dan can be, but only I truly know how cheesy he is. When he makes me a meal for work, he always attaches a sticky note with lyrics from a cheesy song. I always search for the songs on the Internet and listen to them. For the most part, they always make me smile. One song, as you know, made me cry. However, I really don't want to discuss muskrats in love."

Heather pauses again. A few more tears are falling down her face.

"This notebook contains every single sticky

note on which Dan has written song lyrics to me. I have never felt the need to save anything from a man before. I put the first sticky note I received from him with song lyrics in this book. My colleagues teased me horribly. Deep down, I knew he was the one. However, I denied it for a while."

Heather's beautiful green eyes are staring into my soul. My heart races. I can feel my eyes watering up and my vision blurs.

I know I can't cry because I have been told not to.

"Daniel, I am a better person because of you. The world is a far kinder place because of you. Thank you for being you."

There's dead silence other than me crying.

Heather looks at me and actually bursts into tears.

Our guests start to laugh. What a wonderful heartfelt speech—I have goosebumps!

Heather regains her composure and then speaks into the microphone and waves a piece of paper in the air. "I wrote this speech for Daniel to

432

say tonight, and I will leave it on the podium for him. This is the non-crying speech he needs!"

Heather walks behind me to unhandcuff me. After thirty seconds of her standing behind me, I hear her whisper in my ear, "Shit, where is that key?"

I turn to her and say, "Really?"

Heather races to the podium and speaks into the microphone, "Please tell me somebody here has their handcuff key on them right now."

Laughter rings out across the room.

Somebody from the back of the room slowly strolls up to the front and provides Heather with a handcuff key.

People are laughing, snickering, and just generally finding the situation of having a handcuffed groom hilarious! This would only happen to us, and I'm so grateful for that.

After I'm released, I walk toward the podium.

I'm somewhat tentative to look at the speech that Heather has prepared for me. I'm sure it's not what I would normally say.

I look down at the paper, and it's completely blank. Well played, Heather.

I look out at our guests and then turn to look at our wedding party.

"Ladies and Gentlemen, I am going to stray from my script tonight!"

I grab the blank piece of paper, crumble it up and toss it over my shoulder.

There's a gasp from the guests. How much trouble has Dan gotten himself into by tossing his specially prepared speech over his shoulder?

I look at the head service person at the banquet hall and nod my head.

In turn, he signals the servers, and they run to each table and deliver two shots of Wild Turkey to each person.

I begin my "impromptu" speech.

"Some of you are aware of how Heather and I met. If it wasn't for Robert and Frank, I suspect we never would have met."

I look at Frank. He nods his head.

434

"Robert and Frank, I met first. Sadly, Robert passed away suddenly, and through that, I met Heather. I won't bore everybody with the entire story, but every once in a while, some of us drink Wild Turkey to remember Robert."

I grab a shot glass that was placed in front of me, and I raise it to the ceiling. "To Robert!" I pronounce.

Everybody raises their glasses and in unison say, "To Robert!" and drink their shots of Wild Turkey.

"Heather left an important person out of her speech. I suspect she wanted to save the best for last," I state to our guests.

I walk over to Heather, take her hand, and escort her back to the podium.

I look at Heather. She's all smiles. She lobbed the ball at me, and I knock it right out of the park.

"There is a person here tonight who is very modest about his role in bringing me and Heather together. If it weren't for him, there is no doubt that none of us would be here tonight."

Heather and I both start grinning at Frank.

Frank looks back at us. He appears to be caught somewhat flat footed in his response, which is totally out of character for him.

Heather calls him up, "Franklin, please join us at the podium!"

Frank sheepishly joins us. Heather and I decide he should be between us.

"If it hadn't been for Frank introducing us, we wouldn't be here tonight," I state.

I grab my second shot of Wild Turkey and raise it to the roof. "To Frank! Thank you for introducing us!"

All our guests respond back with, "To Frank!"

Everybody drinks up.

I look at Frank, he certainly wasn't expecting this by the look on his face.

Frank gives both Heather and I a big hug each and returns to his seat.

I grab Heather's hand and look into her

green eyes.

I stare at her for a few seconds and then say.

"Heather, I love you. The last two years have been amazing, and I can't wait for the next forty!"

Heather gives me a big kiss, and everybody applauds.

The rest of the night is a bit of a blur, with the exception of our first dance.

For some reason, the first dance is important to both of us. Heather has taken dance classes since the age of five.

I, on the other hand, am self-taught. My signature moves are the grocery cart or the lawn sprinkler, which really aren't first wedding dance moves.

Before Tank the Wonder Dog took out my knee, we had a hip-hop and 70s cheesy mix that Heather somehow got me to be able to dance to. I looked really good, in my opinion. However, I'm most likely overstating my ability to dance.

Tonight, for our first dance, we are slow

dancing to a song that Heather and I had worked on for the last few weeks. It looks elegant and actually is quite easy for somebody with two left feet and a bad knee. We do a simplified waltz. We dance to Linda Ronstadt and Aaron Neville singing "Don't Know Much." It is a remake of an older song from 1980—slightly outside the 70s cheesy music we all enjoy.

People gather around the dance floor and watch us dance. It's perfect for us.

We're both staring at each other. We don't say anything. We're in a magical moment.

Time seems to slow down—my mind is racing. I ponder once again why I'm so lucky that this amazing person loves me unconditionally for all of my warts and issues.

I whisper the words of the song into her ear.

My tears then slowly start.

Heather moves in closer to me and whispers into my ear. But it isn't Heather, it's the H-Bomb. She's not super happy with my tears, but she understands.

"Daniel, I love it that you love me, and I know you know that I love you. You can't be crying the entire time at our wedding. It's an awesome night, and I'm concerned that you aren't having fun. Daniel, I want you to have fun. You are amazing, and I love you! You better smile at me or you are in trouble."

That comment makes me grin. The tears stop, and I kiss the most beautiful girl in the world on her nose.

We finish our first dance without any further tears from me. Go, Dan!

I'm normally not an attention seeker and prefer to be lowkey. Today has been all about us. While I enjoyed every minute of it, I'm exhausted.

Several hours later, Heather and I say goodbye to the last of our guests and take a limo to our hotel. At last, we arrive at the entrance of our hotel room where we can wind down and cherish the last moments of our wedding day together—just the two of us. I grab the closest chair to the door and hold it open. Then I turn to Heather and pick her up off her feet. She's screaming at me about being careful with my knee and me not being safe.

I hear her say something along the lines of if my knee gets hurt because of this and we can't go on the honeymoon, she wants a divorce. Heather is so animated and dramatic sometimes, but that's one of my favourite quirks about her.

I walk over to the bed and drop her onto it from about four feet above. We're both laughing. I open the fridge and take out a bottle of champagne. The both of us have big plans for the remainder of the night.

Sadly, we both take a few sips of the champagne and fall asleep fully clothed on the bed.

The next morning, we wake up feeling refreshed and excited, despite all the running around and celebrations. Our flight doesn't leave until mid afternoon, and we're going for three weeks. Tank is being looked after by one of the girls at the kennel. We know he's in good hands.

We sleep in until 7:30 am. Generally, the both of us are early risers, so 7:30 is late for us.

Then again, we didn't get back to the hotel until 3:30 am. Four hours of sleep—aren't we lucky!

Once we're both up and ready, we race back to the house to put away our wedding gifts and finalize our packing for our tropical vacation. We both pack light.

We take a limo to the airport. I organized our honeymoon, so we're flying business class, and the flight journey is about four hours.

When the flight attendants find out we're on our honeymoon, they bring us little bottles of champagne. They think we're a cute couple.

The plane gets up to its flying altitude.

I grab Heather's hand and kiss her nose. The both of us then fall asleep for the rest of the flight. We didn't even eat a meal or partake in business class benefits, but we sure are cozy and happy. We wake up when the plane lands.

# 26 THE HONEYMOON

My agent is not happy with me.

I have thirty versions of this chapter residing on my computer, all of varying lengths and details.

Apparently, a chapter needs to be 3,000 words long. I frankly don't give a shit. This has been the hardest chapter for me to write.

Fuck.

The three weeks of our honeymoon we spent together were amazing.

Heather and I spent a lot of time mapping out our future.

We discuss at great length about perhaps having children and getting Tank a new brother or sister.

I'm sorry—I can't give you anything more, it's too hard...

# 27 THE END OF THE BEGINNING

It is a beautiful early October day, one of those gorgeous Indian summer days. No humidity and low 20s during the day. It's a bit of a tease—everybody knows that it will get cold within the next three to four months.

I don't care. Fall is my favorite season.

Fall has the best of all seasons—warm, cool, and a chance of beautiful snow.

Best of all, it makes great hiking weather. Heather, Tank, and I have a big hike planned for this Saturday on the Bruce Trail.

I make Heather her lunch for her first shift after the honeymoon.

Heather gained two pounds on our honeymoon, and she's concerned about her weight. She asks for a special diet lunch. The night before, I made a bean salad, which is one of her favourites. I pack the bean salad, a pork chop, and veggies and dip in her lunch bag.

As I have done a hundred times before, I grab a sticky note and write the lyrics from a cheesy 70s song on it.

This time, I pick a beauty, a song from Firefall. I look down at the sticky note, and scrawled on it in my horrible handwriting is the title, "Just Remember I Love You and it Will Be Alright." I draw a smiley face on the bottom of the sticky note for added emphasis.

I finish packing her lunch, and she runs downstairs and gives me a kiss and grabs her lunch bag. "See you later, Danny Boy!" she says as she always does with her signature grin.

And that's that.

That's the last time I see Heather.

That's the last time I see the most beautiful

girl in the world.

I should have stopped her from going to work. I should have handcuffed her to the staircase or acted like I was injured. Anything but let her go to work that day.

Fuck.

As I'm waiting for the 8:30 am train, I get a call from Heather. "You are such a dork! 'Just Remember I love you and it Will Be Alright.' That has to be the cheesiest one yet!"

She's clearly found the note. I respond back with "Guilty as charged!"

I hear the police radio in the background burbling, and Heather says, "Hang on for a minute, Danny Boy."

I hear her say something into the police radio.

"Okay, Danny Boy, I have to run. We have a call that doesn't sound so good. I need to apprehend an evil villain," she jokes.

"Be safe," I respond.

And that's that.

That's the last time I speak to Heather.

The last words I say to her are "be safe."

That's the last time I speak to the most beautiful girl in the world.

I wish I could have expressed to her how much I loved her.

How much I cared for her...

How much she meant to me...

How she made me a better person...

How the world was a better place because of her...

"Be safe" is what I said instead.

She isn't safe.

The most beautiful girl in the world

IS

NOT

FUCKING

SAFE.

Fuck.

I'm at our downtown office on a Tuesday, and it's about 9:30 am. Our office is located in the financial district.

My cell phone rings, and it shows an unknown number. All police officers have their cell phones set this way. This way, nobody they contact can call them back.

I know it's her.

I answer the phone with, "Hello, Gorgeous, I can't wait to see you!"

Dead silence on the other end.

I then hear, "Dan, it's Frank. Where are you?"

I have never heard Frank this way, and it puzzles me. He's speaking to me in his "cop voice."

"Frankie, what the fuck is your problem, man? Give a brother a little respect."

"Dan, Heather has been hurt. Where are you?"

I take a deep breath. This has happened before—she's a tough cookie. She survived a beating from a John. She likely has a bad paper cut, and this is a joke they're working on to cause me a few more gray hairs.

"Frankie, I'm in our downtown office."

is somebody there to pick you up."

I look around and I don't see any police vehicles. Those are fairly distinct—it's hard to miss a car with flashing, shiny lights on the roof.

"Frank, I don't see any police cars."

Frank is literally screaming at me, "Listen, you dumb fuck! Can't you see a scout car in front of you?"

"Frank, there are no cruisers in front of me." Frank and I are good buddies. I am not sure why he's so agitated, but I have never heard him like this, let alone heard him speak this way to me. I'm starting to feel a pit at the bottom of my stomach.

I then notice three gray SUVs parked on the curb, which I hadn't noticed before. They're all lit up and ready to go with their lights and sirens going off. All the pedestrians step back—it's an impressive display of sound and lights.

"Okay, Frank, I see them now. What should I do?"

"Just get into the vehicle, and they will take you up to the top of the highway. I will meet you

451

there. Don't listen to the news. See you in a few minutes, brother." And with that, Frank disappears from the line.

I start walking toward the SUVs, and the passenger in the middle SUV shouts at me, "Are you Dan Hayes?"

At that moment, I receive my second look of pity. God, how I have learned to hate that look!

I nod my head, and he indicates to me to get in the back seat.

We accelerate quickly in the midst of mid morning traffic. The driver of the SUV tells me to put my seat belt on. He glances in the rear-view mirror at me, and I see him giving me a look of pity. I look down and focus on my water bottle, I notice my hands are trembling slightly.

*There's nothing to worry about until there is something to worry about*, I think to myself.

Deep down, I know something has happened—the speed that we are driving at in the city streets is likely three times the posted limited. At every intersection, one of the other two SUVs have it blocked and what normally takes ten minutes to drive takes two minutes now.

I think about texting or calling Frank, but I don't want to bother him if he's driving.

The police radio comes to life, and I hear a woman's voice: "An update on the officer who was shot this morning." The passenger in the front seat quickly turns down the radio, and both he and his partner put their earpieces in for their portable radios.

The driver looks at me again in the rear-view mirror, the look of pity is still there. I look back at him, we both pretend I didn't hear what I just heard.

So, she's been shot, likely got hit on her bulletproof vest. Maybe a few broken ribs. Maybe a flesh wound. Nothing super serious, I lie to myself.

We're now on the highway, travelling at least at 200 km/hour. Cars are pulling over to let us pass. I wonder what these drivers think is going on. I look down at my water bottle—it feels safe and comfortable. My trembling hands are much more noticeable.

The trip up the highway takes only about five minutes, and we arrive at the spot just south of Hwy 2 where police often set up radar traps.

Frank isn't there. The police officers tell me there is a call they have to get to and fast. I later learn that I was riding with the members of the tactical unit.

I get out of the SUV, and they're gone, lots of dust and sirens. Just like in the movies.

This is so odd. I'm literally standing in the middle of nowhere, between the northbound and southbound lanes of a busy highway. Traffic is going by quickly, and I'm standing still.

All of these people are going places, and here I am, alone in the middle of a highway median not moving.

Standing still, alone.

I feel like I'm watching this scene from a thousand miles away. I take a sip of water—my hand tremors are becoming more violent. *I need to get this under control,* I think to myself.

*Nothing to worry about until there is something to worry about*, I think again.

I hear a siren in the distance and see flashing lights. I wonder for a moment if this is all a big joke and Heather will be picking me up for an afternoon of passion. I'm going to tell her that all this was far too elaborate and all she needs to do is ask.

The cruiser pulls into the median, and I see Frank behind the wheel. I climb into the passenger seat and put on my seatbelt. And off we go, traveling faster than I have ever traveled in a car, sirens wailing and lights flashing. I remain silent.

Frank looks grim. He's clenching his jaw. I've never seen him like this before. He looks like he's aged a decade since I last saw him.

Sadly, I saw him last night at the pub.

Fuck.

I wait for a few minutes before I say anything.

I ask him, "How bad?"

"Bad," he chokes up. Tears are streaming down his face.

455

Funny how one small three letter word can sound so ominous. I look down at my water bottle—my hands are now shaking out of control. I take a deep breath.

I look at Frank, he's trying to drive the cruiser and keep his shit together. I decide to remain silent. If it's bad, I will find out how bad shortly.

Frank's cell phone rings. He answers and listens to the other person. He lets out a deep sad sigh and says into the phone, "Roger that. We will be there in a bit."

Frank turns off the siren and lights and starts slowing the cruiser down to the speed limit.

He's looking straight ahead and ignoring me.

This goes on for several minutes.

He clenches his jaw again. I wonder how much stress he's under. A few moments later, he says, "Dan, Heather is dead."

A part of me hopes this is some kind of sick police initiation right. Deep down, I know it isn't.

We both sit in silence for the rest of the trip

with tears silently running down both our faces.

As we get close to the hospital, Frank picks up the police radio and manages to choke out, "3214 – 30 seconds out."

I notice TV broadcast trucks parked out in front of the hospital, and crowds of people have gathered to watch.

Frank pulls into the rear loading dock area of the hospital. Waiting for us are six officers who have formed an impromptu honour guard and are standing at attention. The Chief of Police, the Police Chaplain, and Robert the Police Grief Counselor are there waiting for us.

Chief Smith opens my door, salutes me, and gives me a hug.

Chief Smith was at our wedding, Heather at one point in her career has worked in her office, and they had become friends.

"Dan, I wish we could see each other under different circumstances." Tears stream down her face.

I really don't know what to say. I just look

at her like a deer in the headlights. I look down at my hands—the water bottle looks like it is on a roller coaster, my hands are shaking that violently.

The impromptu honour guards are from Heather's platoon. None of them make eye contact with me.

Tears are streaming down their faces.

Out of nowhere, Smith appears. He's besides himself. He embraces me in a huge hug, nearly breaking my spine and taking my breath away.

"Fucking Ramos took my bullet. It was square on me, centre mass. It would have hit my vest, I'm sure of it. She jumped in front of it. Dan, it was my fault. She took my bullet. It was my god damn bullet, and she took it."

Smith lets go of me.

I look at him, he's covered in blood. The blood on him is now on my shirt. I later realize it's Heather's blood.

I ask him, "Smith, are you okay? Are you hit? You're covered in blood."

He drops to his knees and mutters, "That was my bullet, she wasn't supposed to take it."

Robert the Grief Counselor springs into action and starts quietly speaking to Chris.

The Police Chaplain is also looking at me, ready to spring into action if required.

I hear Heather's voice in my head. "Daniel, you need to get control of this gong show before it becomes a total fucking disaster. Take charge."

Roger that, H-Bomb.

I kneel beside Chris and hold his hand. I can't imagine how he's feeling.

"Chris, I know if the roles were reversed, you would have done the same thing. You guys loved each other. Nobody blames you for what happened. The only person to be blamed is the person who pulled the trigger. Remember, we're all on the same team."

I give him a big hug and whisper to him, "We got this. We need to be strong for everybody else. Chris, I have your back. I need you to have mine."

Chris looks at me with a 1,000-yard stare and quietly says, "Thank you. I have your six."

I stand up and take a deep breath.

Frank is beside me, "Hey, man, you need to change your shirt. I got you this t-shirt."

I look down, my shirt is covered in blood. I know that it's Heather's.

I know I need to act like a big boy. But all I really want to do is to just curl up in the fetal position and cry. I don't, though. The H-Bomb is watching, and she wouldn't approve.

I put the t-shirt on. I later learn that the shirt that Frank had taken from me was put in an evidence bag.

I look down at my water bottle. Shockingly, the shaking has stopped.

I then speak to each member of the honour guard—they were all at our wedding. I address them by their first name and shake their hands. They all try to avoid eye contact with me, but when they do, I give them a big hug.

Everybody gets a hug.

Many tears are shed. Most of them mine.

I'm escorted into a private area. The Chief of Police, the Police Chaplain, Robert the Grief Counsellor, and a doctor are waiting for me. We are going to have the conversation.

## 28 THE CONVERSATION

I look at my watch. It isn't even noon yet. So much has happened since this morning.

We all sit down at a table. We're waiting for the police media person to arrive. Frank is hovering in the background—he's standing behind me. It's almost like he wasn't invited to the adult table.

I'm now channeling the H-Bomb. I get up and pull out a chair and tell him to sit down. We're still waiting for the police media person, who I'm sure is running around like a mad person, given what a shitty day it is.

I take charge.

"Okay, what is the protocol during such

situations?" I ask.

Chief Smith speaks first, "Dan, this is an active criminal investigation. We need to maintain strict control of all communication. Therefore, nobody can speak to the media about what has happened other than the press release from our own media person. Dan, this is very important. We need you to comply with this, without exception."

I respond with a "Roger that, Chief."

Everybody is silent for a few moments.

I then state, "I would like to see her."

Then the conversation gets real.

Real shitty.

Real quick.

Uncomfortable looks are exchanged by everybody at the table.

The doctor breaks the silence, "I am not sure if that is a good idea, Dan." He then explains to me that while we have to wait for the coroner to confirm the official cause of death, he thinks a bullet likely entered her chest through an opening in her bullet proof vest and caused significant trauma to her heart and torso.

"Significant trauma to her heart and torso" resonates in my head.

*If I go see her, it likely isn't going to be overly pleasant*, I think to myself.

"Significant trauma to her heart and torso" echoes in my head again.

I get up and go stand in the corner of the room and stare at the ceiling, pondering about what to do.

I really want to see her and hold her small hand one last time.

Say goodbye, one last time, to the most beautiful girl in the world.

Kiss the nose of the most beautiful girl in the world goodbye, one last time.

Fuck.

I now have tears streaming down my face.

I am standing in the corner like a little kid on a timeout. I'm there for a while just staring at the ceiling.

I sense somebody behind me, it's Frank. I

look him directly in the eye.

"Should I go see her? I ask.

"Dan, it's not good, man. It's grim. Don't go," Frank states categorically. I know he's seen her. It pisses me off that he gets to see her, but they don't want me to see her. She's my H-Bomb, dammit.

My heart is literally breaking, piece by piece.

More tears.

I take a deep breath, turn around, and stare at the ceiling for a little while longer.

I don't know what to do.

I then hear her voice: "Danny Boy, I love that you want to see me, and I want to see you too... but don't go. Nothing good can come out of you seeing me now. I'm not here anymore, Danny Boy. I promise you, we will see each other again someday. Not today though. Just remember I love you."

The H-Bomb has spoken.

It's odd. I hear her voice numerous times

over the next little while. In certain moments, I truly think I'm going crazy. My newly deceased wife is providing me guidance. However, her advice is always sound and gets me through many difficult obstacles. I try not worry too much about hearing her voice, but I am concerned. Maybe I'm losing it.

I wipe away my tears and return to the table.

We must now notify Heather's parents. We agree that I will break the news to them. The Police Chaplain and Robert will accompany me.

My day is going from really fucking bad to really fucking heartbreakingly bad.

Heather's parents live close by. They are both retired.

The fucking most difficult thing I have ever done in my fucking life is walk up to her fucking parents' house and knock on their fucking front door.

Fuck.

Her mom answers. She sees the Police Chaplain and Robert with me. She sees my tears. She immediately knows what has happened.

Her mom had heard on the news that a female police officer has been killed in the line of duty. She had called Heather's phone a dozen times to try and reach her. Heather never answered her phone because she couldn't.

She wasn't safe.

Fuck.

I break the news to her mom and dad. My heart is breaking. They are both hysterically in tears. No parent should ever see their child pass away before them. I know it happens all the time, but this is truly a shitshow.

Many tears are shed. At one point, I have to get up and walk out of the house because I'm about to lose my shit. I mean, really lose my shit. As in the kind where I'm going to have to lie on the ground and sob in a fetal position.

I am now standing outside Heather's parents' house, looking at the sky, with tears streaming down my face.

Once again, I hear her wonderful voice and her great laugh, "Danny Boy, I'm fine, please don't worry about me. You know I'm fine. Please be strong for my mom and dad. They need you. Everybody needs you. You're a rock. I know it's difficult, but you got this. Be strong."

Then H-Bomb appears out of nowhere with additional guidance.

"Daniel. You need to get your shit together. The next little while is going to be difficult for everybody. Your crying isn't going to make it easier for anybody. Everybody is going to take your lead. Don't fuck this up."

A thousand questions are running through my mind. The primary one being *why do I have to be the adult in this situation?* My heart is broken. Doesn't she understand what I'm going through? Why is she yelling at me? Why is this happening to us?

H-Bomb reappears, "Daniel, don't question me. I'm the H-Bomb. I'm all-seeing and all-knowing."

I stare at the sky some more. I now hear Heather, "Danny Boy, I love you. You know that.

But you are the person everybody is going to be looking at for guidance. You need to lead by example. Take ownership of this is all I am asking. It will make it easier for everybody if you do, especially for yourself. You know I'm right. Promise me."

At that moment, I realize that the most beautiful girl in the world is right. She always is. I make a conscious decision to keep it together as best as I can. It's going to be difficult, but she's right.

Roger that, H-Bomb. I promise you, I will own this.

Robert comes out of the house. "How are you doing?" he asks.

"I feel weird. I hear her voice. She's giving me directions, telling me what to do, what to say, that I need to be strong for everybody else and that I need to put my big-boy pants on."

Robert stares at me for a few seconds.

"As long as she isn't telling you to load a sniper rifle and sit in a clock tower, what you are experiencing is normal. It's nothing to be worried about."

We both burst into laughter. I need to laugh. It feels like it has been years since I last laughed.

The police service is amazing when it comes to the situation we are facing now. No request goes unanswered. People are available for everything.

I go back inside to speak with Heather's parents. I'm strong. I smile. I'm there for them. Lots of hugs. I don't cry. I own the situation. I will not let Heather down, because I have promised her that I won't.

With all things considered, everybody is doing their best to keep it together. Robert is going to stay for a while with her parents to walk them through all of the next steps.

The Police Chaplain drives me back to the station.

The flags are already at half staff, I notice.

Before we part, the Chaplain offers me some advice. "Dan, I can't imagine what you are feeling or going through. Everything you feel or think is normal. I am always available to chat. Here's my card. My cell phone is always on."

I thank him and walk into the station. The duty officer sees me and puts me into the only available room. It happens to be the children's room. It makes me smile. Somehow, it's appropriate.

Chief Smith comes in and sits down. She looks at me. "Tough day, kid. How are her parents?"

"They're devastated, but they're solid people." *What else can I really say*, I think.

There's a knock on the door, and the media person enters. Her name is Tina. I don't know her, but she seems nice. She looks stressed.

She asks Chief Smith for a private one-on-one.

Chief Smith declines. "Tina, we are all family here. No secrets. What's up?"

"The press is all over this. They've found pictures from Officer Ramos' wedding online. Those pictures are circulating. They want a statement from you or the family," Tina informs us.

Chief Smith looks pissed. "They do know this is an active homicide investigation, don't they?"

"Very aware, Chief. Um, how do I say this… Officer Ramos was very attractive, and this has garnered additional interest." Long pause. "What do you want me to say to them?"

"We will issue our standard statement and her official picture. That's it until the case is closed," the Chief firmly states.

This is the official statement given by the police:

Police Constable, Heather Ramos, has died at the age of thirty-four. She was killed in the line of duty while protecting a fellow officer. Officer Ramos was a ten-year veteran of the Force and leaves behind her husband and her parents. Officer Ramos has three bravery awards in her name and was the 2010 Officer of the Year. She will be missed by her many friends, colleagues, and family.

She will be honoured with a full regimental

funeral on Wednesday, October 20th. Further details about her memorial service will be provided as they become available.

The public is invited to sign a book of condolences available at any police station in the city.

As her death is an active homicide investigation, no further comments related to her death will be forthcoming.

# 29 LONG WALK OUT OF THE CITY

It's early. Still dark outside. Tank is quietly snoring on our bed. Yesterday morning, the three of us were sleeping in the same bed. That won't ever happen again.

I feel sick.

I'm heart broken.

Heather drove my truck to work yesterday, as her car is in the shop. She had my keys on her when she was killed. I can't get them back as they are now "evidence." I had left my spare keys in my briefcase, and that is in our downtown office because I hadn't thought to bring them with me.

I get up at my regular time, 4:30 am.

I always do the majority of the cooking in the house. It's something I like to do. I plan every single meal out the previous week. I make sure that I have the ingredients beforehand. According to my chart, we are supposed to have mango bacon syrup with homemade whole wheat pancakes containing lime zest, today. It sounds complicated, but it is super easy to make.

It is one Heather's favourite breakfasts.

I feel sick—I start dry heaving in the washroom. Nothing comes out. I haven't eaten in almost twenty-four hours.

I make some toast and eat it dry. I'm not hungry.

I take Tank for his morning walk. Tank senses something is wrong, but he's always game for a walk. We do our normal morning five kilometer loop.

I know I just have to ask for somebody to take me downtown. I don't.

I really just want to be left alone for awhile.

I walk Tank down to the kennel that he stays

at when I travel for business. It's about four kilometers from my house. The girls at the kennel love Tank.

Funny story. When I first got Tank, his name was Spike. I had a list of dog names fifty deep. He only responded to two: Tank and Princess Foo Foo.

So then, Tank it was. You can't have a ninety pound black lab, border collie, greyhound cross named Princess Foo Foo, even though he answers to it. The girls at the kennel often refer to him as Princess Foo Foo. It always makes me laugh. When people hear this, they think I'm picking up a very small dog. And then, out comes this crazy, huge, zany dog.

The girl running the counter checks him in. I tell her that he will be spending the night as well. I upgrade him to the "Presidential Suite," as it is called. I feel guilty and want him to be pampered. I know they will give him lots of hugs and treats.

The girl who is checking Tank in hasn't put two and two together. She knows Heather. I guess she hasn't listened to the news. I don't blame her, I don't want to listen to the news either. I don't say anything.

It's going to be another beautiful day. I'm wearing a t-shirt, shorts, and hiking sandals.

I wait for the 7:25 am train into the city. People are dressed in their business attire. They look at me with envy. They want to be the guy in the shorts and t-shirt. I most certainly can't tell them they don't want to be me.

On the train, I overhear several women discussing Heather.

"It was so sad to hear about that police officer. She was beautiful. How could somebody do something so horrible to her? Her family must be devastated."

I concur with this woman wholeheartedly. I want to say something, but I don't. I put my earbuds in for my phone and block out the world. I want to listen to a sad song. I look at my playlist, and I find the perfect one.

"Blue Eyes Crying in The Rain" by UB40.

When it's halfway through the song, I listen to the words intently.

My blue eyes are crying. People sitting around me are becoming uncomfortable, they're staring at me. I don't give a shit. I replay the song. The opening verse gets me more wound up. Even more tears.

And it happens again—H-Bomb's disapproving voice.

"Daniel, this isn't helping. You promised me. I know you're hurting but stop it. Put your big-boy pants on."

I choose to ignore her and hit replay again.

I'm openly weeping. People are actually moving away from me. My blue eyes are crying. I'm sure people are wondering what my major malfunction is, and rightly so. I'm having a one-man pity party, and I am the star in it.

H-Bomb reappears. "Daniel, this isn't good. Crying isn't going to help anything. It won't bring me back." The H-Bomb isn't stupid either, she offers me a compromise. "Daniel, today, you get a free pass. Mourn me how you see fit. But that's it. And I mean it."

The tears stop. I'm a mess. I am sure people think I am on glue.

For the first time, I feel a bit better. Today is all about me, and I have permission from the H-Bomb to be a mess.

I get off the train and grab a coffee. I get to the office early. Nobody is there yet. I sit at my desk and stare at a blank computer monitor while sipping my coffee. My brain is free from any thoughts. I feel tranquil. People are slowly coming into the office. They avoid me for a bit. I continue to stare at the blank monitor.

Angela, our second in command, had sent this email out last night to the entire company after I had texted her about Heather's death:

"Team:

It's with great sadness and a heavy heart that I am informing you that Dan Hayes' wife, Heather Ramos, was killed yesterday while in the line of duty. We don't have any information about her burial arrangements yet. We will forward the details as they become available.

If you are working on any projects with Dan, please send me the file number. It is likely that Dan won't be available to work on any assignments for the foreseeable future."

Helen, a girl who works in our downtown office, is the first to speak to me. She pulls up a chair and sits down beside me. She's quiet for a few minutes. She holds my hand.

"Dan, what are you doing here?" she asks.

I don't respond.

She grabs my arm and shakes it. "Dan, are you okay?"

"Oh. Hey, Helen, sorry about that. I'm on a different planet. I have to get my spare keys for my truck. They were in my briefcase. Heather had my primary set of keys on her and they've been taken as evidence."

Helen looks at me. "What do you mean taken as evidence?" she asks.

I look at her. "Heather had my truck keys in

her bullet proof vest. Everything she had on her is now evidence."

Helen bursts into tears. "Oh my God, Dan, I'm so sorry. That was a stupid question."

I grab a few tissues and give them to her.

"No worries, Helen. It's all good," I reply.

I stare at my blank monitor. It calms me.

And then it starts. People want to pay their respects and say how sorry they are. From 8 am to 9 am, I see that look of pity far too many times. I am accommodating. After speaking with everybody, I take a brief break. I check my transit schedule that I keep in my wallet. There are no buses or trains northbound until 1:00 pm.

What am I going to do? I need to get out of here. I check online. According to the maps app, it's only twenty-six kilometers to my house from the office.

*Fuck it*, I think. *I'm walking out of the city.*

I grab my spare keys and head out of the office. I say goodbye to a few people—they all hug me.

I get downstairs and buy a bottle of water from the mini-mart.

My phone is buzzing, texts and emails are pouring in. People are offering their condolences. I ignore them.

H-Bomb has said this is my day. I get to do what I want. I get to cry, pout, stomp my feet, and do whatever I need to do.

I have decided walking is what I need. It's a beautiful day. I start heading north. I put in my ear buds. The first song I hear is a Jimmy Buffett cover of "Southern Cross" by Crosby, Stills, Nash, and Young.

The chorus sticks in my mind.

I put it on repeat. It's the soundtrack to my hike out of the city.

I think about how many times I have fallen. Heather was always there to pick me up. She never really fell, not even once. The one time she did, I wasn't there to save her. I feel horrifically guilty for some reason now.

I wonder about how and why we met. Why

would anybody take her away from me? I was raised a Catholic. I'm now more Buddhist than anything else. Karma—why have you done this to me? I live a good life. I don't even kill bugs.

I begin to weep.

People look at me. I keep walking and weeping.

The song keeps repeating.

And I keep walking and weeping.

My phone keeps going off. There are texts, calls, and emails from friends. I notice that George, Brian, and Frank have all called and texted a dozen times. I don't respond.

My phone rings. It's Angela. I always answer her calls.

"Hey," I say.

She asks, "Dan, where are you?" Angela doesn't sound overly happy to be speaking with me at this point.

"Walking home from the office. What's up?" I respond.

"Dan, your friends are concerned. They've

called me a few times. I'm also concerned about you. Somebody would have driven you home. Call a cab and charge it back to the company, or I will pick you up."

"Angela, I'm good. I need to do this. I am clearing my head," I answer.

"Okay, Dan. We're here for you. If you need anything, just ask."

I text Frank, George and Brian. *Hey guys, I'll meet you at the pub around 4:00 for a pint. I'm just out clearing my head.*

H-Bomb appears out of nowhere. "Remember, Daniel, today is the only day you get to do this. However, I would prefer if you stopped the crying right now."

I then start a conversation with her.

"I'm scared and alone. I love you, and you aren't here. I feel like I failed you. I miss you. I want you back."

I then hear her amazing laugh, "Danny Boy, stop it. You haven't done anything wrong. Be strong. Make me proud. Tears aren't going to help."

It's funny to be getting a pep talk from somebody who isn't there. I wonder again if I am losing my marbles.

*I need to get my shit together*, I think for the millionth time since yesterday.

I continue to walk north toward my house. The day is so beautiful. I stop listening to music in the hopes that my tears will stop.

I have a promise to keep, and Heather wouldn't be happy if I broke it.

For the next twenty kilometers, I literally think of nothing. It's like my mind is overwhelmed, and it can't process anything. It's free of any thoughts as it does a hard reset.

I actually begin to feel slightly better.

I'm running a bit ahead of schedule. There are a few pubs in my neighbourhood that I frequent. I'm meeting the gang at the one closest to my house. My bottle of water is empty, and I need to pee. I stop at a pub that's a twenty-minute walk to my house. Before I go in, I check my phone. I am interested in seeing how much I walked today.

My phone informs me that I am approaching 60,000 steps. Almost thirty miles or fifty kilometers.

I enter the back door of the pub and sneak into the washroom. I like everybody here, but I really don't feel like chatting with anybody today.

It's about a fifteen-minute walk to the pub where I'm meeting the gang. I realize I have only had minimal food and liquid today. Given my mood, I suspect when I see the gang there will be copious amounts of alcohol drank. *I better get a little more non-alcohol liquid onboard*, I think.

I walk to the entrance of where the servers come out of the kitchen and try to catch the attention of the bartender. She's one my favourites. She doesn't see me, she's staring at one of the TVs.

I then realize the volume is turned up on the TV and that everybody is listening to the all-news TV channel. Heather's death has now become 24/7 news. Reporters and special guest commentators are speaking about the whys, the whats, and the ifs.

I try to sneak away, but my movement

catches the bartender's eye. She sees me, and she bursts into tears. I get a big hug. Her and Heather always bantered and teased me about how clumsy I am.

She drags me out into the bar area. People want to pay their respects. I shake a lot of hands and receive many hugs. I also turn down numerous drink offers. Perhaps another day, I tell them.

I am strong. I know Heather is watching, and I want her approval.

I also know the gong show that awaits me slightly further north with my little gang of friends.

The bartender refills my water bottle and looks at me. "Dan, you are shrinking. Make sure you get something to eat today, okay?"

I agree that I will eat something.

It's about 3:45 pm. I start the short walk north to the other pub.

I know I'm going to be a sloppy mess, but this is my day to do what I have to do to mourn.

I then hear H-Bomb's voice.

"Daniel, you need to eat something before

you drink. Tonight is going to be a gong show, and it's your gong show, Daniel. You are responsible for everybody tonight, so you need to set the tone and make sure everybody is okay and stays safe. Especially you, Daniel. Safe is what I want you to remember. Daniel, do you understand what I'm saying?"

I respond with a "Yes, H-Bomb. It's my gong show, I am responsible for it, and everybody needs to be safe."

I arrive at the pub. Brian, George, and Frank are there already. Karla, the Bartender, runs over to me and gives me a fierce hug. There are tears in her eyes. After hugging Karla, the boys line up, and I get lots of hugs. The four of us are kind of a mess.

There are lots of tears.

There are a few people at the pub who don't know us. I'm sure they're wondering what's going on with all these men who are crying and hugging.

I remember Heather's advice. I order a cheeseburger and fries.

I eat my food and have a beer. The food is

tasteless to me. Everybody is strangely quiet while I eat. On the TV screens around the pub is a re-run of a baseball game from last night.

Brian turns to me, "Hey, Dan, do you want to bet on this game? I'll take the home team and give you two runs!"

This is our inside joke. I actually took him up on it once, and then I realized it was a replay. Shockingly, I lost that bet.

"Sure," I say.

There's weak laughter from the gang.

I then have a little pep chat with everybody.

My pep chat goes like this:

"Gentlemen, I have promised Heather that this is the only day that I will be a mess. I expect you also to only be a mess today, and we will honour her wishes."

Then it begins.

We start having fun.

I tell totally inappropriate, and quite frankly, offside jokes. People are laughing.

Frank texts his larger work gang. They start

to appear at the pub, either just off their shift or before their shift.

I hear Heather's voice, "Danny Boy, let's make this a wonderful night for everybody. I want to pick up the tab for everybody."

I give Karla my credit card. I tell her Heather is picking up the tab for everybody tonight.

Karla smiles at me through her tears.

We're all standing at the bar. There are almost fifty of us. The owner of the pub asks us if we could move to the back room to make room at the bar for people who are showing up for wing night.

Our numbers swell to almost a hundred. We're telling funny stories about Heather. People are laughing.

I walk around the room and hug everybody and tell them I know that Heather approves.

I get a brainstorm and grab Frank.

We discuss my plan, and he has a grin. We both agree on: Let's do it!

I stand on a chair and scream at my loudest.

"Everybody, shut the fuck up, I have an announcement! We are going to invade the bar because Heather has something special planned for us!"

People get excited. The H-Bomb's plans are always good. The crowd is now likely close to 150 people.

I am sure they wonder what Heather has planned.

A hundred and fifty people move into the bar area. It's already packed, but now it's rammed with us.

I grab the owner of the pub, and I order two shots of Wild Turkey for everybody in the bar. The owner looks at me; that's almost 500 shots. I look at him and tell him to make it happen.

A baseball game is on, it's a playoff game. People are interested in the game, but Heather has other ideas for everybody.

The bartenders pour 500 shots. Everybody is given two shots; people are told it's a special night and that they will learn why. Just don't drink the shots until you find out why.

I grab the TV remote and shut off all the TVs. There's a gang of boos because people can't watch the game. It's the 7$^{th}$ inning stretch; they really aren't missing anything other than a load of commercials.

There's a bell at the bar—it's fairly large and quite loud. It's usually rung to signal last call. Tonight, at 9:30 pm, it is going to signal a different type of last call.

Last roll call.

Frank grabs the bell and gives it a huge ring.

It's so loud, everybody in the bar area stops.

I stand up on a bar stool. My bad knee be damned.

"Tonight, we will have two last roll calls. Please grab your first shot!" I shout out to everybody.

"To 1714!" I scream out and chug down my shot, and so do most people in the bar. 1714 is Robert's badge number. I likely would never have met Heather without him.

I grab my second shot.

Frank rings the bell again.

I take a deep breath.

"To 1569!" I scream out and down my shot. I hear a lot of people scream back "1569!" at me as they down their second shot. 1569 is, or was, Heather's badge number. I'm not sure how to refer to her now.

The baseball game is immediately put back on. However, one of the teams has scored one run. There are several tables who are really unhappy about missing a single run. They start giving the servers a hard time. Several of the tables are being really rude.

I walk over to the tables and apologize and pick up their bills.

However, one table of eight guys are really irate. I offer them additional drinks, but they are pissed.

I explain that we were honouring two friends, one of them who died recently.

They put two and two together.

Their table agrees that a dead cop is a good cop.

I keep my shit together—I turn to the server and tell her I will no longer be picking up this table's tab. I turn to walk away.

My shoulder is grabbed, and I am spun around. One of the bigger guys at the table is in my face. He's at least fifty pounds heavier and six inches taller than me.

He tells me several things in very clear terms. His explanation of the benefit of a dead cop is far from accurate. Sadly, he doesn't realize he is referring to my wife.

*His worldview is somewhat short sighted*, I think.

He threatens me that I will be picking up their tab and buying them very expensive shots or else.

I explain that my wife was killed yesterday and that he is mistaken about his previous statement.

I turn to walk away, but he grabs me again.

He looks me in the eye and opines, "Listen, there is nothing better than a dead cop—but a dead female gook cop, that's fucking awesome."

I am caught flat-footed. Are we stuck in the late 1960s and early 1970s to be using such horrible words? I find what he has said interesting because he is a minority himself. He clearly doesn't get it.

I believe it is now time for an attitude readjustment.

This is exactly where I need to take my frustrations out.

Before I throw my first punch, Frank, George, Brian, and eight other people pounce on the table, and the fight is on.

Smith grabs me and literally carries me out into the parking lot before I have a chance to really engage anybody.

I haven't thrown a single punch, nor have I been hit.

Smith says, "Come on, man, Heather wouldn't approve of this."

I turn to him and say, "H-Bomb would

though."

We both stare at each other for a moment and then burst into laughter.

She would so approve.

We then go back into the bar and try to break up the fight. Smith has more success than me because of his size and his ability to encourage people to stop fighting.

A few scout cars show up. They run background checks on the eight guys at the table. Shockingly, six of them are wanted on warrants. And in a shocking turn of events, the gentleman who was mouthing off to me is wanted in a few countries for drug trafficking. In his car, copious amounts of narcotics are found.

Dangerous Dan strikes again.

It's now closing time, 2:00 am. I ring the bell at the bar, and then I stand up on a chair and announce to everybody, "The party will move to my house!"

En masse, we move to my house. I immediately fire up all of my BBQ's, and because it has been such a nice autumn, my pool is still open.

People swim, I make lots of food. It feels almost normal.

There's one person missing though.

The most beautiful girl in the world.

She isn't here. Nor will she ever be here again. I start to feel sick. I go to the washroom and stare at the toilet.

I wonder how I'm able to deal with my current situation. I lie to myself and pretend that everything is okay on the outside. *There is no right or wrong*, I think. Fake it till you make it, right?

I feel my stomach beginning to twitch. I know what's coming next, and it isn't pretty, but I feel slightly better.

I really haven't eaten much in almost thirty-six hours. Perhaps tomorrow I will feel like eating normal again.

It's about 4:30 am. I'm exhausted. I walked too much today, and I guess that would include yesterday. My bad knee is super swollen, I drank too much, and I'm emotionally drained.

I go to bed with the hope that I wake up and the last two days was just a horrible nightmare.

However, I know that when I wake up, the nightmare will still be there. This is my new reality.

# 30 BEGINNING OF THE END

When I practised the eulogy at my house, it lasted about twenty minutes. I have been speaking for eighteen minutes now, according to my watch.

People have laughed, cried, smiled, and shook their heads in disbelief, but the look of pity hasn't been there for a little while.

I'm two minutes from completing my eulogy. Many tears have been shed. Not one of them were mine.

Now comes the difficult part.

I take a long pause and gaze out at everybody and smile.

"When I heard Heather the other night, she

wanted me to give everybody here a challenge. I didn't know what she wanted. This morning, while I was out walking Tank, it came to me. She would like everybody to have an opportunity to have a relationship like ours.

"I have specific requests for the civilians and the law enforcement professionals who are here today.

"To the civilians who are here, the next time you see a member of the police in uniform, please approach them and smile and introduce yourself to them and say, 'Heather wanted me to say hello.'

"To the members of law enforcement who are here, when somebody approaches you and introduces themselves and tells you that Heather wanted them to say hello, return the hello and engage them in conversation.

"Only good things can come out of this.

"Trust me.

"We are them. And they are us."

My tears begin to start.

I stare at the ceiling and take a deep breath.

I then gaze at the crowd.

I somehow manage to choke out words between sobs, "Because I can tell you, right now, somewhere, someplace, two guys are walking into a bar, and they will meet two other guys. Any of those guys might introduce you to somebody as amazing, as beautiful, and as passionate as my Heather."

I look out at the crowd. Everybody is silent. Then, in fifteen seconds, it starts. Scattered applause. The applause starts to build. People are standing up. I suspect I have received the first standing ovation for a eulogy.

The rest of the day is a blur. The burial service is short. I literally shake a thousand hands. The one thing I notice is that everybody is cheerful. A real positive vibe is being generated, given the circumstances.

A day later, #HeatherWantedMeToSayHello is trending on social media.

I'm asked to be on talk shows on TV. For some reason, I'm asked to give presentations to law enforcement about community-based policing. Frank and I work extremely hard on this presentation.

Currently, there are a lot of police officers who view the world as us (police) versus them (everyone else). This isn't healthy.

On one of the talk shows I'm on, I'm asked an interesting question. Why do I think that police officers and civilians have an us versus them kind of relationship?

I think I have a unique perspective. I'm a civilian, but I also understand what the day-to-day activities of law enforcement are like through Heather and my volunteer work.

The reality of the situation is this: Police officers are often held to the standards of superheroes. People don't realize that police officers are only human. They too are real people with real emotions and feelings. They have to deal with people at their worst, usually when they are in a crisis.

That being said, the police have to realize

that not all people are inherently evil, nor are they adversaries.

A few kind words at the beginning of an interaction with the public can go a long way in resolving whatever situation is occurring.

# EPILOGUE

It's been six years since Heather has been taken
from my life. I don't know how time has passed so
quickly. Tank and I both have many more gray hairs
now. Funny how that happens.

As with the death of any loved one, you tend
to hang on to the other person's belongings for a
little while. I donated all of her clothing to a charity
several years ago. However, I have kept one item.

Her toothbrush still resides in my master
bedroom washroom in the toothbrush holder—I
guess in hopes that she would come back and need
it. I just can't throw it out.

Every time I brush my teeth, I look at her

toothbrush.

Sometimes I smile at her toothbrush and remember her beautiful goofy grin. Other times, my eyes well up, my chest feels tight, and I have a hard time breathing.

As I write this, Tank is snoring up a storm on his dog bed. He's having dog dreams of chasing rabbits. He quietly yelps and barks about whatever hunt he is on.

My dreams are different.

Every night, I dream of Heather. Good dreams, bad dreams, weird dreams, fun dreams, and sad dreams. Heather was only in my life for three short years. She's been dead for almost two times longer than the time I knew her.

I dream about her every night without fail.

About once a week, I have the worst dream. It bothers me so much that I can't sleep for the remainder of the night. When that happens, I just get up, take a shower, and start my day. It happens so frequently that I now know I won't be able to sleep after that dream. If I'm lucky, it happens after

4:00 am. Sadly, it usually happens earlier.

In my dream, I see her in a crowd, and we make eye contact. I know she sees me, but I can never quite catch up to her. The crowd is huge, and she is moving too fast. I don't understand why she won't slow down and wait for me. She keeps looking back at me with her shit-eating grin.

"Please, Heather, wait for me. I want to tell you something!" I yell at her.

I guess she doesn't hear me or want to wait for me.

Fuck.

My heart breaks each time I have this dream.

All I want to do is kiss the nose of the most beautiful girl in the world and tell her how much I love her, one last time.

That's all I want.

It never happens.

I'm never able to catch up to the most beautiful girl in the world for some reason.

It seems to be such a simple thing. I don't

understand why she won't wait for me.

Fuck.

I know I need to move on—Heather would want me to. I have limited success.

I've tried dating, but it's difficult.

I've joined whatever dating app was popular at the moment.

I've met a few women for coffee. I tell them I've written a book about myself. They're intrigued and buy the book. The next time we meet for coffee, I sit down, and when I look at them, I see the look of pity that I so despise.

There never is a third date.

I bury myself in my work and volunteer activities. That feels safe.

As I write this, I gaze at the two pictures of her on my desk.

One picture is of her in her ceremonial police uniform and the other picture is of her with her shit-eating grin taken during our honeymoon.

I look at both pictures and smile.

I hear her voice, "Danny Boy, just remember I love you, and it will be alright."